Voodoo

(Matt Drake #26)

By
David Leadbeater

Copyright © David Leadbeater 2020
ISBN: 9798666724033

All rights reserved.
No part of this publication may be reproduced, distributed, or transmitted in any form or by any means, including photocopying, recording, or other electronic or mechanical methods, without the prior written permission of the publisher/author except in the case of brief quotations embodied in critical reviews and certain other non-commercial uses permitted by copyright law.

All characters in this book are fictitious, and any resemblance to actual persons living or dead is purely coincidental.

Classification: Thriller, adventure, action, mystery, suspense, archaeological, military, historical, assassination, terrorism, assassin, spy.

Other Books by David Leadbeater:

The Matt Drake Series
A constantly evolving, action-packed romp based in the escapist action-adventure genre:

The Bones of Odin (Matt Drake #1)
The Blood King Conspiracy (Matt Drake #2)
The Gates of Hell (Matt Drake 3)
The Tomb of the Gods (Matt Drake #4)
Brothers in Arms (Matt Drake #5)
The Swords of Babylon (Matt Drake #6)
Blood Vengeance (Matt Drake #7)
Last Man Standing (Matt Drake #8)
The Plagues of Pandora (Matt Drake #9)
The Lost Kingdom (Matt Drake #10)
The Ghost Ships of Arizona (Matt Drake #11)
The Last Bazaar (Matt Drake #12)
The Edge of Armageddon (Matt Drake #13)
The Treasures of Saint Germain (Matt Drake #14)
Inca Kings (Matt Drake #15)
The Four Corners of the Earth (Matt Drake #16)
The Seven Seals of Egypt (Matt Drake #17)
Weapons of the Gods (Matt Drake #18)
The Blood King Legacy (Matt Drake #19)
Devil's Island (Matt Drake #20)
The Fabergé Heist (Matt Drake #21)
Four Sacred Treasures (Matt Drake #22)
The Sea Rats (Matt Drake #23)
Blood King Takedown (Matt Drake #24)
Devil's Junction (Matt Drake #25)

The Alicia Myles Series
Aztec Gold (Alicia Myles #1)
Crusader's Gold (Alicia Myles #2)
Caribbean Gold (Alicia Myles #3)
Chasing Gold (Alicia Myles #4)
Galleon's Gold (Alicia Myles #5)

The Torsten Dahl Thriller Series
Stand Your Ground (Dahl Thriller #1)

The Relic Hunters Series
The Relic Hunters (Relic Hunters #1)
The Atlantis Cipher (Relic Hunters #2)
The Amber Secret (Relic Hunters #3)
The Hostage Diamond (Relic Hunters #4)

The Rogue Series
Rogue (Book One)

The Disavowed Series:
The Razor's Edge (Disavowed #1)
In Harm's Way (Disavowed #2)
Threat Level: Red (Disavowed #3)

The Chosen Few Series
Chosen (The Chosen Trilogy #1)
Guardians (The Chosen Trilogy #2)
Heroes (The Chosen Trilogy #3)

Short Stories
Walking with Ghosts (A short story)
A Whispering of Ghosts (A short story)

All genuine comments are very welcome at:

davidleadbeater2011@hotmail.co.uk

Twitter: @dleadbeater2011

Visit David's website for the latest news and information: davidleadbeater.com

Voodoo Soldiers

CHAPTER ONE

Matt Drake turned his head to the window, preferring the view through the grimy, mud-streaked porthole to the drab, listless interior of the bus and the poker faces of his fellow passengers.

It was a cross-country ride. After Washington DC, they'd left everything remotely familiar behind and appeared to be following one featureless highway after another through the great American wilderness.

Stay safe, stay strong, he'd told his team just a few days ago. Looking back now, it felt like six months ago. *Wait for me. Have faith in our bond. Be sensible, and we will meet again.*

It'd been a long time since he'd classed himself as a civilian, even longer since he'd been alone. Self-isolation wasn't a whole hell of a lot of bloody fun. The world had changed for him—and the entire SPEAR team. Where did they belong in this brave new existence?

The split had been contentious. Alicia had exploded with anger; the others had barely concealed theirs. There had been a lot of sadness, more than Drake could handle. So, he'd fled. Gotten out of DC first, to help make the only clear decision he could envisage that might both save their lives and keep them out of jail.

We only killed those who were trying to kill us. Or . . . those that deserved it.

But *deserve* was a gray area for a ghosted Special Forces

military team. When President Coburn was killed by the Blood King the faucets that sustained seven Strike Force teams were abruptly turned off, their operators left out in the cold. No information was forthcoming; not the merest scrap from any government agency, and in particular not from the new president—the old vice-president—John Lacey.

The Strike Force initiative had been Coburn's baby and thus came under the purview of the incoming president. It felt odd then, that one of the first things he'd done was to end the program without warning and with no explanation. Drake and the others were stunned, but found solace in the fact that G—their mission coordinator—soon got in touch and asked to meet at a party being thrown on the twenty-sixth floor of a skyscraper in Los Angeles by Connor Bryant, the owner of a private military firm called Glacier.

Only it turned out that G was long dead, and they'd been lured into a trap by their old nemesis—the Devil. Drake felt comfort in the fact that both the Devil and the Blood King were now dead. The only slight concern was that Team SPEAR—as he now thought of them—had killed them as civilians, which further blurred the already gray landscape that was their future.

We left no real proof behind at that casino . . . we nullified the video feed afterward . . . but there will be suspicion. And sometimes, especially in the eyes of President Lacey it seemed, suspicion was a confirmation of guilt.

The team were effectively lying low. With their worst enemies—and the worst known enemies to mankind—dealt with, they could afford to take a step back and disappear for a few months. The only problem was that they were forced to disappear . . . apart.

Drake focused as another tired town passed by the same grubby window. He'd lost count of towns and hours. The bus rumbled along, same pace, same direction, putting distance between himself and those he loved. Drake could barely bring himself to raise his head.

Nondescript shopfronts and then rows of anonymous homes flickered past the window: a brief, sleepy glimpse into the daily lives of faceless thousands, soon gone. Drake wondered as to the character of the people that lived in the nameless town he'd just passed. Were they good? Astute? Was the community spirit high? Were there serial killers nestled in some of those unidentified homes? He reckoned he'd probably just passed by the entire gamut of human qualities in a few seconds—from domestic violence to indifference and love and death.

Drake turned away from the window to see nothing had changed around him. Across the aisle, an older woman with bleached blond hair and a short skirt swiped away at her cellphone as though her life depended on it, oblivious to the physical world. Beside her, leaning against the opposite window, a long-legged youth sat in some discomfort, wriggling around in his threadbare seat every minute or so. Neither suggested a threat to Drake, but his nature and training continued to evaluate every situation, night and day. In front, a man and boy had their eyes glued to video games, passing the time. Drake couldn't see much beyond that, but on embarkation had given everyone a good once-over. Nothing had raised his hackles.

Another town rolled by. Another few minutes of non-interaction with countless, unidentified lives. Drake returned his gaze to the window and allowed the difficulties of his current situation to roam free inside his head.

How long would self-isolation last? Would their world be a better place after it ended? Would the other members of the team—especially Alicia and Cam—be able to stay under the radar? And how the hell would they find each other again when the time came?

There were no safety nets here. For security, nobody knew where the others were going, and they had no way of contacting each other. The team was, essentially, sundered; broken apart with no way to put the vital pieces back together.

Drake turned to the seat beside him, empty apart from a large backpack. He'd bought the bag before leaving DC and filled it with some essential items for the next few weeks before he established a firm footing. Items like food and water, a toothbrush and paste, toilet roll.

There was a first-aid kit and field dressings, the kind of wrappings and medicines the military used. A lightweight Becker utility knife and a TBS Grizzly survival knife. A ground sheet and a Gore-Tex bivvy bag. A polyester, olive green, one-man tent. It had been a long while since Drake lost himself properly in the rough country, but this seemed as good a time as any.

He carried no technology save for a top-of-the-range Casio G-Shock watch, the next best thing he could find on short notice to a military precision instrument. He carried a small amount of cash, and bank cards for use at an ATM machine—he had no intentions of going completely native. He'd packed a range of clothing, enough for good and bad weather, warm and cold. The only luxuries he'd allowed himself were chewing gum and a pair of wraparound sunglasses to cut out the glare.

Oh, and an Alicia-style baseball cap that read: *No Fear, Bitches*.

He probably wouldn't wear it, but it was a fitting accompaniment if he couldn't have the real thing.

At the very bottom of the backpack, wrapped, was a well-used Glock 43, a 9mm with a six-round capacity.

The bus pulled up after a few more hours, stopping at an unremarkable, windswept bus terminal in the middle of nowhere. Still, three people climbed aboard and two disembarked. Drake amended the passenger number inside his head. The bus driver announced a fifteen-minute break and left the bus, followed by a number of passengers. Drake saw restrooms and a grocery shop outside but nothing else. He stayed put.

More towns and another terminal later, he was feeling drowsy. The constant motion of the bus didn't help. He ate some fruit and took several sips of water. They passed a river that filled a ditch by the side of the road, running parallel for twelve miles. They passed a children's playground that appeared to sit half a dozen miles between towns, rolling hills, and thick stands of trees you couldn't see through, all laid out under an endless canvas of cloudy blue skies.

Many hours into his journey, Drake tried to look forward to the future. Whatever lay ahead he wanted to face it with positivity, and that meant no more dwelling in the past. Even if that past was less than two days old. Even if that past held everything he cherished and needed and had ever dreamed about.

What *did* lie ahead?

Nothing he could easily predict. He was headed through the middle of America on a journey that would take him to the Rockies. Once there, he would lose himself for as long as he thought necessary.

You've already lost yourself. What the hell are you doing?

Alicia's voice.

Where are you now?

Drake shut the past down. The future offered a new kind of solace. New and less dangerous adventures. New meetings. New people and new situations. Starting afresh was as hard as any overseas mission.

Drake sat up as the bus trundled off the highway and entered a two-way blacktop that twisted and turned for several miles. The weather outside was bright and crisp, with blue skies and a keen wind bending the tops of trees as if pulled them by invisible elastic bands. Drake could see acres of trees marching off in all directions and, beyond them, the distant shadow-shapes of high mountains. According to the driver, they were nearing his destination.

Another forty minutes passed. The mountains grew clearer. The blacktop opened out as it approached a new town similar to those Drake had seen during the long journey.

"Now entering the town of Coyote," the driver called. "We'll be stopping for an hour here, folks. Comfort break, stretch your legs. I recommend Verity's Diner for a good meal."

Coyote? Drake thought. This was his stop then.

When he made the booking, it had seemed an auspicious stopping point.

Now, he read the signpost bearing the name as an ill omen.

CHAPTER TWO

Drake rose from the seat when the bus stopped, grabbed his backpack, and hurried down the aisle. He jumped off, boots landing in standing water, and took a slow look around. The terminal was a row of three high curbs with plastic shelters and a well-stocked vending machine. What appeared to be a cramped ticket office stood to the right, door closed, but Drake didn't need that. He walked away from the bus.

He squinted against the bright light. A single wide path led through trees away from the terminal, presumably in the direction of town. The terminal was ringed by more trees. Drake made a quick recce, noting that the only other person to follow him off the bus was a middle-aged man with a side-parting and a nervous twitch. The man wore a suit that might have looked good in the nineties. Drake didn't see anyone else, but the trees were dense enough to hide an army.

Leaving his mobile home of the last few days behind, he started along the path. It ran arrow straight for several hundred yards. Drake drew his coat close as the mountain chill fell over him. It was still winter and even more so up here. Coyote was one of Colorado's highest towns, popular with tourists in the winter for its ski slopes and incredible scenery. It was also one of the higher gateways to the Rockies at large, surrounded by a vast, staggering wilderness.

Drake found himself approaching the backside of the town's major high street. The path led through an alley onto the main sidewalk. Drake stood there for a few minutes, getting his bearings.

Cars bearing snow chains rumbled along a slushy road or were parked along its considerable length. Stores were open to both sides and doing a brisk trade. Drake saw a hardware store, a grocery shop, a place that sold guns, and a bar. There was a gas station at the far end of the street—he could just make out the canopy.

"Can I help you, son?" Drake turned to see an old man with a gray beard sitting outside a nearby convenience store. "You're looking a little lost."

"Just getting the lay of the land," Drake said. "New in town."

"What the hell kind of accent is that? You Australian?"

"No, mate. That's some pure old Yorkshire from the land of fish and chips and scraps."

"All right. Well, you got everything you need right here. You a backpacker?"

"Not really, but I have been on the odd camping mission through hostile territory."

"Well, this country's no place for tenderfoots, son."

"Thanks, mate." Drake nodded at the old guy and made his way across the road. He'd come prepared but there were still several things he needed. First though, a good meal was in order.

Verity's Diner was a big place, warm and friendly with plush red seats. Every table was a booth, so Drake took one by the window and laid his backpack beside him. When the waitress came across, he ordered endless coffee, pancakes, and sausage links. The coffee was complimented by half-and-half, the pancakes by maple syrup. It was a comforting meal, although loaded with fat and sugar that Drake felt he needed to walk off.

Well, there would be plenty of that to come.

Back outside, he found the convenience store and walked through the door, smiling as a bell tinkled. He hadn't heard a sound like that on entering a shop since his youth when he used to visit the local newsagent with 10p every day on his way home from school. Those days were long gone, lost in the deep, rich tapestry of his life. But the memory of innocent and stress-free days still made him smile.

Inside the store he bought a good local, laminated guide map, several meals, more water and a bottle of bourbon. He'd studied maps on the bus and had a good idea of where he wanted to start. On leaving the shop, he stowed his new purchases in the backpack and headed out of town, purposely following the entire length of Main Street to fix in his head exactly what stores and goods he could find there. The town of Coyote, whilst not his firm base for the next weeks and months, was still his only potential lifeline.

Cold, fresh air blasted his face. The mountains rose ahead, framing the borders of the town, distant and rising to craggy heights topped with snow. The further he walked the quieter it became. Drake followed a trail out of town, striding past a parking lot that appeared to act as a last outpost, and then disappearing among thick stands of trees. The smells of plants and trees, of decaying loam and passing animals, reached his nostrils. The sun disappeared beyond a high canopy, glimmering intermittently through treetops. Drake pulled his jacket tighter around him.

An hour later, he left the beaten track.

The going got harder. Drake found himself scrambling down slopes, wading through streams and pulling himself up steep, earthy banks. Despite the cold, he started to sweat. It was good, hard work and he found himself enjoying the honesty of it. He paused in the late afternoon for a drink of water, sitting atop a fallen tree with thick shrubbery all around.

The world shrouded him in deathly silence.

It was so far beyond the norm that, at first, he disliked it. The norm was Alicia, Dahl and Mai and the others, all chatting or fighting alongside him or figuring out new moves. It was constant noise and banter. It was perpetual danger. Out here in Colorado the silence, the peace and safety . . . was ridiculously unnerving.

Drake shrugged it off and continued, using a compass to follow a map in his head. If once he faltered, he would consult the map he'd bought but, for now, all was well.

Darkness descended on his first night out in the wild.

Drake found a clearing and pitched his tent. He didn't plan to use it every night, but since this was his first, he decided at least a little comfort was in order. Once the tent was ready, he built a small fire—he'd already checked and there were no current fire bans in place across Colorado—and sat on a tree stump to eat a cold meal. The shadows grew long, and darkness deepened. Drake held his hands out toward the flickering flames. A branch snapped inside the fire, making him blink.

When he looked around utter darkness had fallen, shadows creeping through the surrounding trees like silent mercenaries, arranged around him like menacing guards. At 10 p.m. he crept into his tent, fixed the flashlight to a hook and turned it on before pulling his backpack across the ground sheet toward him. Inside, he dug around for a phone, his gun, the Grizzly knife, and the bourbon. He took two hits of the alcohol and fell asleep.

The next morning was cold and silent as it dawned over the high peaks of Colorado. Drake woke, feeling tired and alone, wondering for the millionth time if he was doing the right thing. But worrying didn't help. He exited the tent, revived the fire, and dug through his camping supplies before boiling a pot of coffee over the campfire—a home luxury he just couldn't do without.

He sat in the cold dawn, listening to the sounds of trees creaking, branches swaying, and the distant run-off of water from some snowy plateau. He pulled out the map and took a while to fix his bearings. Ideally, he didn't want to have to refer to it again for the rest of the day—a superfluous but necessary test to his soldier's mind. An hour later he was packed and ready to move out.

That day passed much like the previous afternoon. The next day passed the same way. Drake was treated to some incredible views, some stunning vistas. He came out of thick greenery to find himself at the edge of a tiny plateau of rock overlooking a deep rocky canyon or a vast stretch of eastern plains. Great stands of conifer and aspen lined the sides of mountains with great gray peaks jutting above, their higher sides covered sparsely by alpine vegetation. Drake drank it all in, losing himself in the natural splendor.

On the third night he didn't unpack the tent, just lay inside a rocky lee with the ground sheet for a bed. The star-strewn dome above was all he needed to drift away for the night. The fourth day found him circling around to Coyote once more—not to visit the town but to keep it within a couple of days walk in case he needed to return.

Drake enjoyed the freedom. He checked his supplies regularly, and realized they were lasting well. A long time ago, the regiment had taught him how to hunt and survive off the land, but Drake had already decided he wasn't quite that dedicated on this trip. Pre-packed goodness was plenty good for him.

The fifth day presented a change.

In the morning he set off toward Coyote to replenish his supplies. The beauty of not following any track meant he never saw the same thing twice. It also put him more at risk. In the early afternoon he was clambering through a dead fallen tree, staying relatively silent, when a large, black shape drifted across his field of vision.

Drake stopped.

The bear was ambling along, massive paws dragging along the ground as to give it an almost drunken look. Drake knew it was nothing of the sort. Its head swung from side to side, testing the air. Drake already knew he was downwind of the animal and halted, unmoving, with a light sheen of sweat on his forehead and a pounding heart. The last thing he wanted was to hurt any wild animal in its natural habitat, and he would do all he could to keep that from happening. The bear sauntered steadily out of range, vanishing to the far right into a dense clump of trees.

Drake amended his route, aiming more for the eastern edge of town.

By the time he arrived, it was late afternoon, evoking a sense of déjà vu, since he'd been in the same position just five days earlier. He hefted the backpack and visited the grocery store first, picking out a range of relatively healthy meals for the next five days or so and enough drinks to keep him going. He bought snacks too and other things he'd forgotten like a pack of cards, a notebook for errant thoughts, and spare batteries for his various flashlights.

This time, during his indulgent meal at Verity's Diner, after taking his order the friendly waitress recognized him.

"You staying around here?"

Drake shook his head, wary of saying too much to strangers. "Passing by."

"You Australian?"

"Nope. From Yorkshire."

"My friend went to Yorkshire in 2010. Never seen her since."

"It's that kinda place, love."

"Dangerous?" The waitress's face dropped.

"Overwhelming. Beautiful. Awe-inspiring. You'd stay."

"Some say that about Coyote. Me? I've lived here my whole life and am now officially friggin' sick of it. I need me some hot weather all year round, I do."

"I hear the West Coast does that."

"Nah. Too many Californians for me. I was thinking south of France. Maybe Italy. You been there?"

"Once or twice." Drake nodded. "Great places. Expensive, but great."

"Well . . . you come by anytime. This is my place. I'm Verity." The waitress held out her hand.

Drake shook it, smiling. "You serve delicious food, Verity."

The waitress nodded. "You see my counter over there?" She pointed. "Keep a sheet of key contacts and phone numbers. You take one when you leave, y'know, just in case."

Drake thanked her again, touched. She didn't have to point that out. He decided that he would take one even though he couldn't think of anything, out here in this slow, peaceful beauty spot that might possibly be dangerous if treated with respect.

CHAPTER THREE

Through the following days, Drake pressed deeper into the Colorado wilderness.

Moving faster, starting earlier and sleeping later, he covered far more ground. The high-mountain chill didn't affect him. He'd been expecting worse weather, but this part of the Rockies at least appeared to be experiencing early spring-like conditions. More than a week after he arrived in Coyote, Drake found that he was able to relax and spend hours at a time not thinking about his friends or what they were doing.

It was a surprising, bittersweet realization.

After all, where was his family?

Drake trudged through stands of trees and alpine vegetation, crossed mini-ravines and camped by fast-flowing streams. The one problem that weighed on his mind was just that—*family*.

He remained convinced that he'd made the right move. As a team they were—potentially—fugitives and targets. Admittedly, both were a gray area. But the fact that their official status as a US Special Forces team had been torn asunder was not. Enemies would come at them from all angles. And until they had a way of fighting back in the manner they were used to, they simply couldn't take everyone on.

Going off the grid was the right and only answer.

Separating . . . that was the unclear issue. For Alicia and

others that shared her views, it was the wrong move. But Drake thought their opinions were colored by emotion. He didn't blame them. Breaking up the family was the hardest thing he'd ever done—nothing else came close. But it wouldn't be forever.

It won't be forever.

He repeated the mantra as he walked and climbed and leapt between rocks. He felt deeply for his family as he sat overlooking a deadly gorge. On the eighth day he trekked back to Coyote and bought himself a compound bow with a set of carbon arrows. He didn't visit Verity's Diner, not wanting to lay down even minor connections in this town. Getting friendly with the locals wasn't why he was here. He took the new purchase into the woods and set about learning to use it. He'd chosen a middle-of-the-range set, so it was never going to be perfectly accurate, but then neither was he. Being able to hit a tree trunk at thirty yards would be enough.

Of course, he'd never mention to the others that he'd bought a bow and arrow set. They'd have his life. Alicia would start calling him Katniss and Dahl would conveniently remember that he'd been given one as a young child.

That thought brought a crushing sense of melancholy over Drake. He collapsed in the woods, falling to his knees, alone . . . so isolated he might never be found. The bright blue sky was overheard, the ground soft and lush beneath him, but he saw only darkness and severity. The rightness or wrongness of his decision didn't matter anymore. Family mattered, and that was all. Staying apart like this was safeguarding all of them. After a while he forced himself to his feet and pushed on. The rest of that day passed slowly in a dense, dark cloud.

The night fell hard. Drake opened his bottle of bourbon for only the second time. It was still three-quarters full. Drake knocked back a couple of shots by the campfire before retreating to his nylon tent, determined that tomorrow would be a better day. He was camped close to the edge of a steep cliff and could hear a lazy waterfall somewhere off to the east. It was a nice, monotonous sound and Drake found himself drifting close to sleep in no time.

The blood-curdling scream that rang through the woods came as an intense surprise. Drake shot upright, heart hammering, barely able to believe his ears. *Did I fall asleep? Is this a nightmare?*

But the screams didn't abate. They became a terrified woman's cry for help.

It was unmistakable and very real. Drake shook off the incredulity and delved into his backpack. He found a knife, a flashlight and the gun, grabbed the compass on the way out. It was pitch black outside. The chill night was suddenly silent, utterly still as if every animal was motionless and listening. Drake copied them. Inside the tent, he'd had no clue as to the direction the screams were coming from.

He listened now, head down, eyes closed to enhance his night vision when he needed them. Seconds passed. Drake was starting to wonder if maybe the screams had indeed been the result of some crazy nightmare when they again tore through the woods. He was off in an instant, running to his right and in a western direction.

The first part was easy, he'd scouted a path earlier that night before the sun set, always careful. He pushed past a gnarly trunk and ducked a low hanging branch, crossed a flat clearing and then jumped over a two-foot-wide fold in the ground. His boots hit the other side hard. He kept running. The screams continued, sounding as though they were spilling from a woman on the run. They didn't stay in one place.

Drake estimated the woman was several hundred feet to his right. He switched direction, and ran straight into a tangle of thorn and brush; tried to jump it, and found himself firmly in the middle of it.

Bollocks.

A fitting thought, since the sharp branches reached up to the top of his thighs. Drake jumped again, ignoring the scratches and scrapes. He stumbled on the other side of the impassable mass, coming down on one knee.

The screaming had stopped. There was some crying now and a high-pitched moaning. Drake pushed off a feeling of inadequacy, feeling way out of his depth here. He couldn't even run straight. Three trees blocked his way. He dodged around them, found himself up against a jutting boulder and used its rugged surface to climb.

He found himself about six feet higher in the air.

Ahead, the trees pushed and leaned together like drunks staggering home. Drake thought he saw a light far off through the jumble but wasn't sure. The woman's screams were dying out. He thought he heard a man's grunt but at this distance couldn't be sure.

"Hey!" he called. "Where are you?"

No answer.

"Keep shouting! Hey! I'm here!"

There was one more scream. A terrifying, bloodcurdling shriek that chilled Drake's bones, and then all was silent.

The Yorkshireman leapt down off the boulder and smashed his way through trees and thick undergrowth, sprawling to the ground more than once. He picked himself up, checked his weapons, and kept going. There was nothing ahead but shrubbery and tree trunks and low hanging branches. There were no more sounds, but then a chopper could have passed overhead, and he wouldn't have heard it over the racket he himself was making.

Minutes later, Drake came into a clearing among trees.

He pulled up short, breathing hard and staring. The sight that met his eyes shocked him. He shook his head, hardly able to believe his eyes.

Squat and silent in front of him, dark and menacing, was a cabin in the woods.

CHAPTER FOUR

Alicia, Cam and Shaw decided to stay together. They left Washington DC by train and headed south to New Orleans.

Waiting for the train to arrive at Union Station was boring. Sitting on the train was boring. The journey was boring. Alicia leaned with her head against the window, staring out at the passing scenery as the big train trundled south and west. She didn't feel like interacting. Her life had been turned upside down.

How could Drake leave so suddenly? So easily?

Part of her knew it hadn't been easy, but Alicia chose to ignore that knowledge for now. The fact was, the team hadn't only been ghosted by the government—it had been disbanded by its own people.

Cam saw her despondency and tried to cheer her up. "It won't be forever," he said.

"Fuck off, Camden."

"We're heading to the party capital of the United States."

"Fuck off, Camden."

"Do you want me to leave?"

"Yeah, go and fuck off, Camden."

He didn't. And neither did Shaw. The two newcomers to their team—a team she now once again thought of as Team SPEAR because the Strike Force initiative had ended so badly—preferred her company.

Which she thought was odd.

Cam, originally from Romania, was a struggling bare-knuckle fighter. Brought up with gypsies in his homeland he'd escaped a life of daily battle and dispute by running away with his sister, Ruby. Alicia had later saved Cam's life during her search for the galleon's gold and the Sword of Saint Peter, but they had both seen Ruby killed at the hands of mercenaries. Cam was still living with that, fighting to process it, whilst Alicia felt partly responsible for his welfare. The kid looked twenty-two but was really twenty-nine. He'd never felt love or security or been part of a real family unit. Alicia had been hoping SPEAR might provide that.

Shaw, on the other hand, was a native American knife-wielder whose mother and sister had been executed by the Blood King. Shaw was grieving too. On the outside she was an enigma, wearing a tight ponytail, fancy leather boots with gold tips and lavish filigree, a black leather jacket and the ubiquitous tight black jeans. She'd been taught hand-to-hand and knife combat by an old Delta Force vet who used to trade pretty much anything for a crate of beer back in Shaw's old town. The vet had taught her so well, Shaw now held herself and fought in the way of someone who'd trained with a Special Forces' unit. Her father was killed by a gang of thieves whilst robbing their casino which had later descended into ruin, and her four brothers had fallen by the wayside, alive but basically uninterested and incoherent after their father died.

"Why'd you come with me?"

Cam was seated beside her while Shaw was a row behind, but both heard Alicia's abrupt question. They were silent for a while as if thinking but, just as Alicia was getting impatient, Cam looked down at his still-bruised knuckles and let out a deep sigh.

"You're my last chance," he muttered.

"Last chance? Are you kidding me? You're what . . . ten?"

Cam looked hurt. "I'm twenty-nine, as you know, and have seen more in three decades than most see in their entire lives. But luckily, I've never been alone. I don't want to be alone now. My brothers are fighters and thieves. My sisters are con artists. I don't want any of that life."

"Did your parents hurt you?" Alicia asked gruffly.

"Not with their fists. They once told me that they made me so that they could make money off me. Put me to work fighting. And that's what they did."

Alicia grimaced. Her own childhood *had* seen violence, in a very different way, until she'd fled to join the army. "You wanna hang for a while then?" she suggested carefully.

"No. I want a permanent base. People I can count on in my life."

Alicia saw why he was clinging to the paradigm presented by Team SPEAR. Despite the danger involved in their missions it offered stability and a shoulder to lean on. Alicia turned slightly.

"Your turn."

Shaw was leaning forward with her head between seats. "I've never known what I wanted," she said. "First I was the daughter of a casino owner. Then the protégé of a Delta vet. Then, an outcast, poor, picked over and cast aside. Even my brothers didn't care about me. All I had was my mother and sister for guidance until the Blood King took them away. All that's behind me now." Shaw took a deep breath. "I'm twenty-eight. I can still have the life I want. The only problem is—I don't know what that is."

"And you want a team of Special Forces soldiers to help you find it?" Alicia asked dubiously.

"No, not at all. I want a team of experienced, life-worn, intelligent people with a good understanding of ethics and truth, and the confidence to take no shit 'cause they're so utterly bad-ass, to point me in the right direction."

Alicia blinked as she absorbed that and then nodded. "All right. Well, I suppose you're both here for the right reasons. The only problem is—that team split up and we, at least, are headed for the booze-hazed, laid-back, culture-heavy streets of New Orleans."

"I thought we were headed to Bourbon Street to get totally shitfaced?" Cam asked.

"That's what I said," Alicia replied.

"Something about . . . you've never been there before and wondered how much trouble you could get into," Shaw clarified.

"And you still came with me?" Alicia assumed she'd been in the bottom of a bottle when she'd uttered those words.

"Sounds like a good time." Cam shrugged. "I haven't had many of those."

Alicia slapped him on the shoulder. "Stop crying, Babyface. I guess, if we're headed for Bourbon Street, you two can be my bodyguards."

Cam grinned at that and Shaw nodded her head. Their minds were made up.

Their fates sealed.

They arrived in New Orleans as the clock ticked past 3 p.m. Alicia decided the American train industry didn't have a whole lot of imagination since this terminal was also called Union Station. They shrugged into their backpacks and headed along the platform toward the ticket gates, just three people among a mad, baying throng. Announcements clanged over loudspeakers, horns sounded in the street outside, and roller-suitcases rumbled across the concrete. Alicia surveilled as best she could, but you could have hidden a herd of ninjas in that station and she'd never have noticed.

Thinking of ninjas brought up memories of Mai. She'd never once imagined she might miss the black-haired, opinionated, hugely annoying Sprite, and would never admit it, but felt a touch of melancholy on recalling some of their finer arguments . . . and battles. Those had been good times.

Thoughts of Mai turned to memories of Dahl and Kinimaka, Hayden and Yorgi, and the rest of the team. Alicia found herself leaving the station and stepping into New Orleans for the first time lost in contemplation—reflecting over old times.

"Anyone know where we're going?" Cam asked, wrenching her out of her reverie.

"Cab driver probably will." Alicia nodded toward a line of cabs.

Bourbon Street was a ten-minute drive. Since they didn't have a destination the cab driver dropped them right in the middle of the action. Alicia climbed out into eighteen-degree heat and sunshine; not bad for a southern wintry day. The first thing that hit her was the noise, and then the vast amount of people. Bourbon Street was raucous, an overcrowded splash of multicoloured hues, a cultural assault on the eyes and ears. Wherever she looked there was noise and commotion, color and custom.

"Wow," Cam said. "Where do we start?"

The cab pulled away. Alicia eyed the younger man. "First lesson," she said. "Always start in the pub."

Hoisting their backpacks, they sought out the closest establishment. Inside, it was even louder. Every wall seemed to have dark wooden paneling, and every table and chair looked the same. Three deep-gold chandeliers lined the ceiling.

Alicia threaded her way none too gently to the bar area, found a space and leaned across the smeared surface.

"Three beers," she shouted, not caring what the bar tender brought.

Cam pushed in next to her. "What do you think?"

"Of this place? I could get lost here."

"Is that the plan?"

"For a little while. Until life reveals the next step."

"Nice, but shouldn't you decide that?" Shaw said from the other side.

"Yeah, probably." Alicia swiveled her head between the two of them. "Look. I'm never gonna be the best teacher. I'll never be a role model. You shouldn't look up to me. I make ten bad decisions for each good one. If you want guidance and support to take the next step, to find out where you're going in life, tagging along with Alicia Myles is about the worst thing you could do."

Their beers arrived. Cam paid. Shaw proposed a toast.

"To Alicia Myles," she said, raising her glass. "The world's crappiest role model."

"Alicia Myles." Cam clinked their beers.

"Alicia Myles," Alicia said in agreement. "May the bitch one day get everything she deserves."

As they drank, Alicia started to tune out, to forget the bad, and focus on what was in front of her. This was hardly a new beginning, but it was a start. From Bourbon Street all the pathways of the world lay wide open. You could imagine anything from here, any outcome, any dream.

Who was she to deny herself the chance of changing her destiny? Fortune lay at the junction of every new decision, always open for business. Alicia drank and laughed and enjoyed the moment while it lasted.

Tomorrow would bring new challenges.

It always did.

CHAPTER FIVE

On the second night, after they'd spent the first day finding a hotel and settling in, Alicia decided they would enjoy their first proper night out on the town.

"Where we headed?" she asked Shaw, standing in just her underwear, trying to decide between tight blue jeans and hot pants that felt as if they might cut her in half. "Jazz club to start?"

"I don't do jazz." Shaw was lying on her own bed, tugging up the same pair of jeans Alicia had seen her wearing for the last two weeks.

"You have any other bloody clothes?"

"No. But I so wish I had those hot pants."

Alicia was about to offer them out but then noticed Shaw's face. "You taking the piss? But yeah, you're right. I've seen looser submarine doors."

"You've been on a submarine?"

"I've been on a few sailors if that counts."

Shaw nodded. "It does." At that moment there was a knock at the door to Shaw's room. Cam called out, asking if they were ready.

Alicia regarded the skin-tight shorts she was wearing. "Give me twenty minutes," she said. "And a can opener."

They found Cam ten minutes later waiting for them in the lobby. He wore Wrangler jeans, a white T-shirt and black boots. Alicia nodded her appreciation.

"First one of us to pull gets a prize," she said, heading for the door.

"Pull?" Shaw asked, confused.

"Score. Gets a guy, or a girl, into a compromising position."

"Don't you have a . . . boyfriend?" Shaw asked softly.

"I'm not sure. But until he lets me know, I'm fair game. There's your second lessen, kids—red-blooded women don't fuck around waiting for a guy to make his mind up. They're either all in, or they're all out. Figuratively and physically speaking."

Sunset painted the southern skies, turning them into a stunning fresco of rich, deep, crimson colors. The noise outside hit them like a wall, overwhelming for a moment until they let it sink in and started to move with it, embrace it.

Alicia kept her vigilance high, well aware of why the team had grudgingly decided to split. In addition to jeans, she'd donned a new cropped leather jacket and a baseball cap inscribed with the quote: *has anyone seen my pants?* Her eyes swept the street left and right, hunting for their first port of call.

"The Dungeon," she said. "Sounds perfect."

Twenty minutes later they were entering their second bar and thirty minutes after that, their third. It was shots in all three, followed by some shouted conversation and confused head shaking. When they headed outside, the relatively cool blast of air was a blessing.

"How we doing?" Alicia asked as they joined the flow of human traffic in search of the next bar.

"About half-way to shitfaced," Shaw said.

"Lightweight," Alicia grunted as Shaw nodded.

"Shots are my nectar," Cam said. "The allowance used to be one between each round in the ring and two between each bout. 'Course that was homemade moonshine, of a sort. Blew your balls off."

"Sorry to hear that," Alicia said, already zeroing in on the next liquor establishment. "Let's try this one."

More bars followed, with Alicia leading the way. The party atmosphere along Bourbon Street was intoxicating and, as night fell, sharpened the need for revelry in Alicia's mind, taking the excitement up a notch. They met every manner of merry-maker along their route, from twenty-somethings in groups out for a good time to loners propping up a calmer bar with a faraway look in their eyes. Alicia knew that look only too well. Lost in old memories, they feared more halcyon days were gone forever.

Midnight passed in a flicker. Their area of New Orleans took it up a notch. They visited a live jazz pub whose old-school façade was matched only in spectacle by the diverse and colorful crowd inside. They drank potent cocktails in Lafitte's, which dated back to the early 1770s, making it the oldest bar in America. The Old Absinthe House delivered incredible food along with a flaming absinthe shot that made even Alicia's head spin. There was the Cat's Meow with its gleaming pink and green neon sign and The Swamp where they partied and chanced a bull ride.

At an unknown hour they stumbled out of The Swamp. The cold air, washing across Alicia's face did nothing to sober her up, but the gang of men across the road beating up on each other sent a spear of clarity through her brain.

They were halfway down an alley, their antics illuminated by a solitary, hazy light. Dumpsters lined the walls around them, and a pile of garbage stood at the head of the alley. Alicia first staggered and then stumbled her way across the road, not stopping until she reached the debris.

Barely aware that Cam and Shaw were at her side she peered hard at proceedings. It seemed two men were being beset by four others. They were all young, around the same age, and decked out in the usual designer gear, all drunk and ready to do something they'd regret a hundred times in the morning.

Alicia held on to a wall and walked toward them. "Hey!" she called out. "Hey, watcha doin'? Stop that!"

Even to her own ears her words sounded inadequate. The boys barely gave her a glance. One meaty youth clubbed a slighter kid across the face, sending him to his knees. His friends laughed. The kid's friend shouted at Meaty and narrowly avoided a kick to the groin. Instead, he backed into one of Meaty's friends who gave him an elbow to the ear for his troubles. Both smaller kids were now on the ground.

Even through deep inebriation Alicia sensed a violent change in the atmosphere. The situation had turned dangerous. With the kids down, the bullies sensed a way to vent their frustrations.

"Hey, Meatbox!" Alicia cried, swaying in place about eight feet from the fight. "Pick on someone . . . someone your own size."

Meaty turned to her, big face puffed out to match his biceps. His friends squinted as they tried to focus on her.

"Fuck off, bitch," Meaty growled. "This is none of your business."

"Great intro." Alicia took three more steps. "I congratulate you. But you should walk away now. Stop hitting those kids."

Meaty clenched his fists. "When I wanna fuck an old hooker I'll call one," he snarled nastily before throwing her ten dollars from his pocket. "And if I wanna beat up that bitch afterward, who's gonna stop me?"

Cam and Shaw stepped up, advising the youth to stop talking, but Alicia had gone quickly and unnervingly silent.

She didn't move at all, just regarded the youth with instantly calm and sober eyes.

"Yeah, fuck off." One of Meaty's friends waved a fist from eighteen feet away.

"I really wouldn't push—" Cam began.

But Meaty interrupted him. "You still here?" he jeered at Alicia. "Wanna big sausage to chew on? I'd give you a bunch of—"

Alicia exploded into action so suddenly even Cam flinched in shock. Her first stop was at a lanky youth's side, who received three jabs to the ribs and folded. Her second was in front of a spotty, gum-chewing kid who never worked out how he went from looking hard and sneering to on his ass with a bloodied nose. Her third stop was directly before Meaty himself.

"You wanna hit me? Take your best shot."

Meaty blinked from his fallen, stupefied friends to the smart-mouthed blond now standing before him. Maybe he saw something ferocious and deadly in her eyes, maybe he sensed the vast potential for violence before him. Whatever it was, sobriety cut through and he took a step back.

"Hey . . ." He held his hands aloft. "Hey . . . I get it. Calm down."

Alicia ground her teeth, barely able to hold back. She knew how this went. If she unleashed now and taught the bully a lesson, his posse would call the cops and she'd be the bad guy. But if she let him walk away without recompense, he'd be back at it again within twenty-four hours.

What would Drake do?

Fuck Drake. Alicia settled on a debilitating jab to the solar plexus, showing no effort and no malice, but putting the bully on his fucking arse big time and for as long as possible. When that was done, she beckoned the two terrorized kids forward and sent them away.

"There's always someone bigger and badder," she told the bullies. "Don't forget that, and you might live to see thirty."

She turned and walked away, totally sober now. Cam and Shaw watched her back and then joined her in the street. Alicia looked glumly at the jam-packed, riotous bars.

"You guys ready to start again?"

"I'm done," Shaw said, swaying a little.

"Me too," Cam agreed though he looked perfectly steady on his feet and had a solemn, focused look in his eye.

"Bollocks." Alicia sighed. "A perfectly good night out ruined by a bunch of knobs."

"Not ruined," Cam said. "You saved those kids."

Alicia pursed her lips and nodded. Together, they wound their way back toward their hotel. Alicia persuaded them to grab one more for the road at a quiet jazz club opposite, and then they separated and returned to their rooms.

Alicia fell onto the bed fully clothed. Her window, partly open, admitted a soft, cooling, welcome breeze that wafted her thin drapes. Alicia lay for a while staring up at the ceiling, wondering why violence always found her.

It didn't take long to understand. She, and the rest of her team, were people that walked toward violence instead of away from it. Rather than ignoring it, they faced danger head on. They looked for bad deeds—and knew where to look—instead of gazing in a different direction.

They were the first responders of the military world.

What would they do now?

Getting drowsy, Alicia shrugged her jeans off and turned over on the bed. Seconds later, she fell into a deep, dream-laden sleep.

CHAPTER SIX

Waking the next morning, Alicia felt happier. She texted Cam and Shaw and met them for breakfast. Everyone attested that they felt rough that day—although Cam looked as fit and focused as ever—so they stuck with water and good food and spent the evening chatting over a takeaway meal.

Days passed. Alicia fell into a basic routine where she woke, showered, checked out the morning through her open window with its barely-there drapes, then strolled off for breakfast, sometimes alone, sometimes with her two friends. In the afternoons they found a no-frills gym where they could work out. Alicia joined a rough-and-ready boxing club where the men soon learned to respect her.

A week went by.

They stayed fit and healthy. They didn't repeat their debauchery of the first night save for once a week, when they let loose. Bourbon Street wasn't their main haunt, but they liked to use it as a base, enjoying the diversity, the atmosphere, and the opportunity to people-watch to an absurd extreme.

Nothing came of their clash with Meaty and pals. Alicia hadn't expected any blowback and never saw anyone from that encounter again. She just hoped Meaty might become a better person, though doubted it.

They saw life. Alicia learned about things that hadn't registered on her radar through the years of fighting at Drake's side. She found Reality TV, which she hated;

Instagram, which brought her closer to David Boreanaz, Chris Hemsworth and Sean Bean, which she enjoyed; and Celebrity YouTube, which, like most adults she assumed, she didn't understand at all. Cam and Shaw continued to support her, which made her grateful and a little suspicious. Did they think she needed shoring up?

Maybe I do.

The separation from Team SPEAR had been a tough one. It still was. The hardest challenge of her life. It was all she could do not to contact Hayden or Dahl or even Mai. They'd all gone in different directions. How were they doing? Was Karin the common denominator—keeping track of all of them? Hayden had voiced the possibility, and Alicia did have a way of contacting her, but she left it alone for now, aware that suitable isolation at the beginning would bring them back together sooner down the road.

During the third week, Alicia made a mistake.

Again, the atmosphere and alcohol could be blamed. It was during a long stint around the French Quarter, where they visited their favorite bars twice and ate street food, joined an impromptu parade and earned racks of Mardi Gras beads. Alicia learned from a colorful dancer that purple beads symbolized justice, green represented faith and gold signified power. She collected as many as she was able, her neck eventually fully engulfed by the colorful beads. They stumbled into the final pub around three in the morning, almost ready to start drifting back to their hotel.

Alicia shoved her way to the bar, pushing reluctant bodies out of the way. Once there she caught the bar tender's attention, leaned over and ordered six shots. While the guy made the drinks she turned, looking for Cam and Shaw.

A man caught her eye. She squinted, trying to focus

through the alcoholic haze that fogged her brain. Yes, he looked good—like Drake, Dahl and Mano all rolled into one. He had an easy smile that grabbed her attention and a pair of startling blue eyes that could drop a pair of panties at fifty yards.

Alicia ignored him. Eight seconds later he appeared at her side.

"You wanna get out of here? Give me a shot at the title."

She didn't move. "The title?"

"Of being the best one-night stand of your life."

Alicia glanced up at him, ire and indignation at the ready, but his calm smile gave her pause. Instinctively she knew this man posed no threat. He really was just after a good time. Also, the way he held himself and several tattoos spoke of the military.

"You served?" she asked.

"Yeah, shipping out again in a few weeks. You?"

Alicia bowed her head slightly. Soldiers knew soldiers. That fact alone instantly garnered respect and time. "Yeah," she said. "Maybe. I've been around a bit."

"That's what I was hoping for." Again, the eyes pinned her.

"Look . . ." she said. "I'm not—"

But then he dipped his head and Alicia found a delicious man's face right in front of her. She drew back slightly, but then saw the pacific-blue eyes, the rugged features and the visceral allure of the laid-back soldier and grabbed the flesh at the back of his neck.

"You asked for it," she whispered huskily.

Seeing herself beyond the alcoholic fog she might have stopped it, but caught in the moment, divided from her crucial family, and six hours into a binge, she pulled the guy's head down until his lips met hers. Alicia kissed him at the bar, lips mashed, tongue flicking, her hand holding him in place. Her left hand grabbed his belt buckle and tugged, pulling him in closer. For a long moment, there was no other emotion—no doubt, no insecurity, no frustration, no anger, except a sweeping desire that blocked out all else.

And then a rough hand grabbed her shoulder, pulling her away from the guy.

Alicia grunted and spun, ready to do harm. But it was Cam who'd grabbed her. Cam who'd forced her to stop.

"Fuck off, Cam."

"You shouldn't be doing that."

She knew a lot of soldiers and most of them by now would be up in Cam's face, threatening the lad or pushing him aside, but the man she'd been kissing only stood patiently and waited, which only made her want him more.

"Don't tell me what to do."

"I know it's hard, but remember Drake. Remember SPEAR. Your friends."

"I don't want to remember that."

"You go down this road, Alicia, and you will lose yourself."

She heard his words through the haze and wanted to explain how she'd all she'd needed was a few hours of escape, of feeling nothing but pleasure; a diversion, a distraction. "You're calling this a junction then?"

"Yeah, a devil's junction."

"We've already done that one."

"I know. That's why I think you'll understand. You don't have to take the wrong turn."

Alicia blinked at Cam, unable to understand in that moment how he'd become so wise. Something about him being older than he looked, maybe? Something about his entire life being spent fighting in a metaphoric boxing ring?

It was the soldier she'd been kissing that broke the moment. "Look," he said. "There's more going on here than I'm comfortable with. Don't worry. I'm happy to walk away."

Alicia was left staring at his back, or more precisely at his finely tailored, Wranglered ass, as it rolled away. As an afterthought she shouted: "Hey, what's your name?"

The soldier turned, eyes flashing, and said: "Jericho."

Alicia nodded, and then turned to Cam. "Well, thanks asshole. You just saved me from one fine and sweaty diversion. Hope you're fucking proud."

The drinks came, six shot glasses slammed on the bar. Alicia handed over the money and narrowed her eyes at Cam. "S'pose you're gonna put me to bed now?"

"No. I will." Shaw was at her back, pushing the drinks away. "I think we should call it a night."

Alicia knew in her heart that they were both right but her stubborn nature made her rebel. She reached out quickly, grabbed two shots and downed them. "I'm not done yet."

They waited, saying nothing. Around them the bar heaved; the music was loud, the conversation at full tempo. All manner of toxic fumes infused the air and even the wood-paneled walls were sweating. Alicia found that, even seated at the bar, she could barely move, barely make herself heard.

"This," she said, "is shit. I think I'm done drinking."

"Shall we head back to the hotel?" Shaw asked innocently.

"Yeah, let's do that."

In the end, she was glad she'd made the decision to

leave and return to the hotel. It was the right one. The safe one.

Alicia wondered briefly when she'd become a woman who preferred *safe*.

CHAPTER SEVEN

Hayden and Kinimaka spent some time in Washington DC. First, they wanted to thank Connor Bryant, owner of the private military contracting firm—Glacier—for helping them escape the burning skyscraper, Junction One, without having to talk to the police and then enabling them to plan and execute the downfall of both the Devil and the Blood King. After that, they probed various old sources; gently, trying to learn if their team was under suspicion, had any kind of warrant out on them, and how the Strike Force initiative was currently viewed.

The first two questions were answered to Hayden's satisfaction. Nobody was gunning for them. It seemed enough that two violent, horrible threats to the world had been neutralized, although there was still some concern about the missing nukes and the potential doomsday scenario the deaths of both the Blood King and the Devil may invoke.

The final question went unresolved. The Strike Force teams, along with several other covert Special Forces' units, were truly being ghosted. There *was* no information.

Why the hell would the army, the country, and new president—John Lacey—do that?

Even if you judged them solely by their contributions to world safety during the last few years, Hayden knew their impact was invaluable. Nobody in their right mind would jeopardize such vital contributions.

But the tales she was hearing about President Lacey didn't assure her of his sanity.

The whole debacle was moot. Neither she nor Kinimaka could do anything about it. No matter how hard they tried to push, they were up against a fortress of deliberately raised brick walls.

Staying in DC wasn't healthy. They both knew that. They couldn't go home. They might be targets. DC was the worse place to stay. But Hayden and Mano both felt a duty toward their team, a duty to resolve their problems. Everyone had sacrificed so much to SPEAR and then Strike Force, to keeping civilians safe around the world, that Hayden felt honor-bound to work through this new, dreadful situation and coax forth a solution.

They stayed in a nondescript hotel, making quiet calls from burner phones which they immediately discarded, meeting with contacts one time only in parks, malls and coffee shops, calling in favors and getting nowhere. They risked their lives every day.

Early in the second week something changed.

Hayden was brushing her teeth in the small restroom of the tiny hotel room they were sharing. Kinimaka had already completed a check of the room just in case they'd been infiltrated during the night—it had happened before—and was now headed down to grab breakfast from a nearby bakery. Hayden had kept her old phone after asking Karin to shield any GPS tracking signal it might have, using her new NSA capabilities, and now that phone rang.

Hayden threw her toothbrush in the sink and leapt across the bed. The caller display read: *Unknown Caller*. Not unusual.

"Hello?"

"Hayden Jaye?"

"Who's this?"

"*The* Hayden Jaye? Who helped out the enigmatic and daring LA team to locate the plagues of Pandora?"

Hayden hesitated, eyes narrowing. "My God, Trent, is that you?"

A chuckle affirmed her guess. "In the flesh, so to speak. How are you all?"

Hayden didn't answer at first. Amid their current state of affairs, the danger, the unfamiliar and the unknown, it was typical of Aaron Trent to ask after their welfare first. He was a serious man, rarely cracking a smile, but had a true moral compass and a deep sense of loyalty that Hayden admired.

Trent had been one third of the trio she knew as the Disavowed before they joined the Strike Force initiative about the same time as Team SPEAR. It wasn't long before then that the Disavowed had been considered essential to the front line of the United States' war on evil. Their prowess, cleverness and ability to work as a team had earned them a nickname—the Razor's Edge. The best of the best in the intelligence gathering and covert infiltration field, sought after by every US agency and field office. Then came their disavowing, a terrible cover-up that left them adrift and purposeless.

Much like we are now, she mused.

"Well . . ." She paused. "How are we? I guess we're up shit creek without a paddle. Over in LA, I guess you're more like up shit boulevard without a latte. More or less, though, we're in the same boat. Does that make sense?"

Trent didn't laugh. She hadn't expected him too. "No, but I do agree. Silk and Radford are climbing the walls. It's not all bad though."

Hayden focused. "Did you hear something new about Strike Force?"

"Maybe, but not over the phone. How soon can you all get here?"

"To Los Angeles?" California most certainly hadn't been on her radar. "I . . . I'm not sure."

She was taken aback. They'd stayed in DC for a reason, primarily to be on hand to locate and question new sources of information. DC was where any fresh data regarding the Strike Force teams would surface first.

"Is it a logistics issue?" Trent asked. "I understand we should be keeping a low profile. Once our enemies get wind of the change in our circumstances . . ."

He didn't finish. Didn't have to. Hayden helped him out. "There's only Mano and me," she said. "The others took off for a while for precisely that reason."

"Wise move."

"It sure doesn't feel that way. It feels like a major part of my body's been chopped off."

"Come to LA. We'll take your mind off it."

Hayden saw no reason to refuse and thought they might even learn something. Plus, they hadn't seen Trent and the boys in years. "Are you a good distraction, Aaron?"

"Not me. I'm all work and no play. Radford's the party animal and Silk's the bad boy. But five heads have to be better than two, right? And shit, you guys need someone to talk to after everything that happened."

Hayden wondered exactly how much he knew. Not everyone had died at the Gates of Hell casino. Some had survived the showdown of a lifetime. Maybe those few were already talking around the campfire . . . so to speak.

"All right," she said, making her mind up. "We'll grab a flight and meet you this afternoon."

*

Hayden thought they hadn't changed a bit. Trent was tall with jet-black hair and a serious expression. Silk was shorter with a hard, lived-in face and held himself like a soldier. Radford was pretty, with pineapple-infused hair gel, designer stubble and muscles in all the right places, enhanced by a tight, white T-shirt. They met inside the Hard Rock Café at the Beverly Center, primarily because that was Kinimaka's favorite city haunt. Under the golden light of the restaurant and listening to AC/DC belt out *Back in Black*, the two sundered teams reconvened.

"What happened to Drake and the others?" Silk asked after they'd ordered drinks.

"We're not keeping track," Kinimaka admitted with a sigh, shifting in the booth, knees striking the table with a loud noise that alarmed all those for ten feet in every direction.

"Ah, so it's every man for himself?" Radford asked.

"Not exactly," Hayden said quickly. "Our friend and ex-team member, Karin Blake, now works at the NSA. She's keeping tabs on everyone . . . kind of."

"I remember Karin," Trent said. "Knows her shit."

"And Alicia?" Radford asked with a smile. "How is she?"

Hayden eyed the man. "She's good, but I wouldn't have any designs on her if I were you, Dan. She's basically an unlit fuse, always thirty seconds away from striking."

"I remember," Radford grinned. "She's perfect."

"You guys called us here for a reason," Kinimaka steered the conversation away from their team and toward the point.

"Yes." Trent leaned forward, took a drink of cola and then fixed them with his earnest eyes. "And thanks, Mano. I don't do small talk. I'm sure you know there were seven Strike Force teams at the end when . . . when President

Coburn died. At that time, all seven were engaged in various missions in hotspots around the world, including us. Fortunately, we were in Europe—Italy to be exact. Some of the others were not so lucky."

Kinimaka cocked his head. "Meaning?"

"Strike Force One, Four and Five were—or are—engaged in Syria, Yemen and Afghanistan. They were left out in the cold, abandoned, cut off, cast adrift with no safety rope. Loyal, highly-trained operatives ditched in the hot zone."

Hayden had considered their own situation dire. Now she reassessed. "Are you sure? How do you know?"

"Contacts long cultivated from our days in the CIA as frontline operatives," Trent said, but didn't explain further. "Contacts that want answers."

"Answers?" Kinimaka glanced between the three men.

"As to how and why the new president decided one of his first acts, first orders, was to disavow and dump seven of the best, most dependable Special Forces teams at America's disposal."

"It feels premeditated," Hayden mused. "Like he knew what he was going to do before he took office."

"Which puts an entirely new slant on why the Blood King pulled his trigger," Trent finished quietly.

Even after the build-up Hayden was shocked to the core. The very suggestion Trent was making was utterly abhorrent. "I find that hard to believe," she said.

Trent nodded. "As do we. Which is why we've been searching for an alternative explanation."

Hayden widened her eyes expectantly. "And?"

Radford shrugged. "We're searching," he said. "But we haven't found anything."

Shit, Hayden thought. *This is all we need right now.*

CHAPTER EIGHT

Hayden completely understood why Trent would not want to impart this kind of information over a cellphone. They were under enough scrutiny—or rather would be if they gave those in charge a reason to notice them. When you needed more freedom to act, to plan, you were best advised to draw less attention.

The rest of that night played out amicably. Radford unashamedly chatted up the waitresses every chance he got, with some degree of success. Silk kept an eye on the restaurant, always alert. And Trent explained as much as he was able, himself desperate for help and information.

Hayden felt inadequate when she realized that she couldn't help much and had not kept in touch with any of her political contacts during the last five years. The only people she knew that might help worked at Interpol or MI6. Maybe if Kenzie were here, she could squeeze something out of Mossad, but she wasn't, and Hayden had nothing.

They ate, drank a few beers and agreed to talk again tomorrow. Both Hayden and Kinimaka needed time to digest the new facts and to consider what might be done next. They found a local hotel, rented a room, and headed up for the night. Lying together, they barely slept, staring up at the ceiling and trying to process what had happened . . .

And what would come next.

A few days passed, one blending naturally with the

Voodoo Soldiers

other until Hayden started to lose track of what day it was. Early one morning, Hayden rose, unpacked her rucksack and sat on the edge of the bed. Kinimaka followed his usual routine of heading out to collect breakfast. The habit helped the big guy cope with their new reality and Hayden never turned away hot croissants and coffee before 9 a.m.

Another practice that kept them sane was calling Karin. Today, Hayden waited until the blond woman should have reached her office and then dialed the number, using one of their burner cells.

"How's it going?" Karin answered on the first ring.

Hayden skipped the small talk and told her exactly what Trent had revealed the night before, mentioning no names. Karin, above all of them, would be aware of potential digital surveillance and should have taken steps to avoid it, to Hayden's thinking.

"That's all you know?" Karin asked when Hayden paused.

"All? Isn't that plenty to make a start?"

"I can kick over a few rocks, but I don't have the kind of juice that would reach the Capitol building let alone the White House. You'd be better off searching for people that knew Kovalenko."

"Sure. Do what you can. I believe we've got it good compared to some of the other teams."

"And Strike Force wasn't the only Special Forces unit operating," Kinimaka added. "Some of those other teams don't even have designations."

"An idea of the extent of what's going on would help," Hayden said. "Though I admit, if the leader of the free world's involved, I wouldn't know how to proceed from there."

Karin agreed and promised to investigate further whilst

using caution. It could take some time. After a pause in their chat, Hayden asked the question that most bothered her.

"Have you heard from the others yet?"

"Mai checked in. She's in Tokyo with her sister and Dai. Do you remember a chick called Zuki?"

Hayden nodded as Kinimaka handed her a coffee. "Oh yeah. Crazy, rich Asian babe with a penchant for murder. Used the samurai against us when we were tracking down the Four Sacred Treasures."

"That's the one. Apparently, whispers are building around her from one end of Asia to the next. Mai's looking into it."

"I don't know why. We're no longer in a position to do anything about it."

"Maybe not. But the last thing you want is *her* in a position to do something about *you*. She's worse than bad news."

Hayden recalled it was at the last big battle between samurai, ninja, the Tsugarai clan and Special Forces that Dino had lost a hand. In truth, they were lucky that was all they lost, but Dino had understandably taken the injury badly.

"How is Dino?"

"Good days and bad." Karin sounded frustrated. "Rehab is a bitch, as you know. Sometimes it's clear we lost more than Dino's hand in that cave."

"Hang in there, Karin, and send Dino our love. It will get better."

"I hope so. Anyway, Dahl and Kenzie stayed in DC and have a dinner date with Connor Bryant."

"We thanked him already."

"He owns one of the best private military firms in the world. Maybe Dahl's eyeing that up."

Hayden remembered Bryant well. He'd confessed to them that the sleazeball act was precisely that, a persona Bryant had engineered and could no longer get rid of. Also, it helped him become anti-social when he needed to.

"A dinner date?" Mano was listening to the loudspeaker. "Dahl and Kenzie?"

"Is that all you took from that?" Hayden bit a chunk out of her croissant before it went cold. "I wonder why they're bothering with Bryant?" she addressed Karin.

"Could be the obvious. They want a job."

"Doubtful. We agreed three months before making any moves."

"You did? I didn't know that. Maybe Kenz wants to practice her sword skills on him or he owns a free-running complex that Dahl can use? Who knows?"

It was true, Hayden mused. Dahl and Kenzie were two of the most unpredictable people she'd ever known.

With no more information forthcoming, Hayden thanked Karin and ended the call. She drank more coffee and turned to Kinimaka.

"I wonder how the others are doing?"

The man-mountain turned to look at her, the bed protesting under his weight. "There is a Hawaiian proverb for that, Hay."

"You have a proverb for everything."

"I guess so. But that's because Hawaiians are so wise. It goes: *If you plan for a year, plant kalo. If you plan for ten years, plant koa. If you plan for one hundred years, teach the children.*"

"And how does that answer my question?"

"Well, I guess I'm saying: Have patience."

"Ah, well just say that next time. It's much quicker."

"Yeah, I forgot we're in a hurry." Kinimaka turned

toward the window as if seeking a little bright light to soothe his dismal day.

Hayden closed her eyes and took a breath. "I'm sorry, Mano, okay? It's just . . . this fucking situation has got me reeling." She threw her pastry onto the table and put both hands to her face, covering up. "It's unjust. One man's power play destroying hundreds of careers and lives. It's . . ."

When she couldn't go on, Kinimaka finished for her ". . . Washington. The heart of American politics. There are very few out there that care like President Coburn did."

Hayden couldn't hold back the tears. Mano walked over to her, putting both arms around her shoulders. Nobody in their team had been as close to the president as Hayden. His loss would affect far more than the lives of a few soldiers.

"I hope Trent is wrong," she said finally. "About the new president."

"Either way, I doubt we can do much about it."

"What?" Hayden looked up through her tears, smiling. "With the Mad Swede, Taz and the Sprite? With an unintelligible Yorkshire ass and a sword-wielding Israeli? We could change the world, Mano."

"We already have." He smiled. "And you missed out the heavy-handed Hawaiian and their go-getting leader. And all the evil bad guys on their trail."

"The phrase 'you reap what you sow' was never more fitting."

Kinimaka stood back. "I'd reap a field of terrorists if it meant saving one innocent civilian. You know that."

"We all would. And that's the truth about what makes us so dangerous to . . ." She hesitated, unsure of how to phrase her next words. "To those that might seek to curb our freedoms," she said finally, deliberately declassifying her description. The list might include those that were supposedly on the side of good, as well as the clear-cut bad.

"On the positive side, Kono is progressing well," Kinimaka looked to change the subject.

"I'm sorry we didn't get to see your sister in DC," Hayden said, wiping her eyes. "The pregnancy is okay?"

"Yeah. I only call once every three or four days on a burner, but all is well. Kono is due in two months."

Hayden was about to quiz him further when her phone rang. Thinking it might be Karin, she scooped it up and jabbed the answer button.

"What you got for me?"

"Steady on, girl," Radford said with a chuckle. "I didn't know you felt that way."

"Ah, I thought it was somebody else." Hayden laughed at herself. "Sorry."

"Don't be. I wish I was that guy. Or girl. Anyway, we figured that since you're here in LA you might wanna help us out on a job."

"You have a job?"

"Sure we do. We're the Disavowed, baby. Reps juicier than an In-N-Out Burger's . . ."

"I get the picture," Hayden said.

"Did he mention food?" Kinimaka asked.

"Christ, you're still eating breakfast," Hayden said. "Look, Radford, give us twenty minutes. All right?"

"Sure. Meet you there." Radford hung up.

"Wait, where?" Hayden stared at her phone in disbelief and then called Radford back to get an address. Two minutes later they were tooling up to head out and meet up with the Disavowed.

"Y'know," Hayden said. "I've fucking missed this."

"Radford, Silk and Trent?"

"No, Mano, I mean the action. This is what we do. What we're made for. This is the life that we should lead."

Kinimaka swilled down the last of the coffee. "Lead the way, boss."

"Always." Hayden practically ran out of the room.

CHAPTER NINE

When they arrived at the meeting point, Hayden was surprised to find only Silk and Radford had arrived. She'd imagined Trent being first to practically everything where work was concerned.

"Aaron?" she asked, walking along a baked, gravelly path toward them with Mano at her side.

They'd agreed to meet behind a strip mall in West LA, central to all of them. The area was littered with brown and green shrubbery and comprised of dirt tracks. The sun beat down as if it wanted to cook the scalp beneath her blond hair.

"Yeah, didn't want to say too much on the phone," Radford said. "Trent's been taken."

Hayden gawped at them. "Trent . . . *what?* Taken by whom?"

"Gunrunner from Dallas," Silk said matter-of-factly.

Kinimaka eyed their surroundings with suspicion. "Feels a bit like a Hollywood trailer," he muttered. "We're close to Universal and I loved the new *Dallas*. Especially the blond that told John Ross to go home and—"

"Listen. This is real. This is serious."

Silk's lived-in face was stern, and Hayden couldn't imagine Trent pulling a trick like this. She held out a hand. "All right, tell us."

"Years ago, we took down this guy's brother. He was trying to make moves in LA. The asshole came in hard, almost starting a fucking gang war until we handed him his ass. Literally. He went through a windshield at full speed and hit a brick wall. Wasn't pretty. Anyways, the Dallas gunrunner—"

"It might be easier if we knew his name," Hayden pointed out.

"Yeah, yeah, it's Schiller. Real nasty piece of shit. We didn't check him out too much, him all the way over in Texas, but heard he runs a good part of the criminal activity over there." Silk paused for a breath. "Now Schiller's kidnapped Trent for revenge and has vowed to kill him slowly."

"How do you know that?"

"He told us." Radford indicated his phone somewhat belatedly. "Called us less than an hour ago."

"They're planning to take him back to Dallas to do it right," Silk said. "That's what he said."

Hayden grabbed Silk's hand. "You have to get help right away. The timing is crucial here. Do you have any leads?"

"No. But we do have a friend in the FBI."

Hayden recalled Special Agent Claire Collins. She'd been the Disavowed's handler and it had appeared that she and Trent had a crush on each other at the time they last met. Hard on the outside, a bitch on the interior, Collins was as tough as nails. A fighter to the end, sometimes unapproachable, but after dark—after work—if the music and the mood and the party took her fancy, she was as passionate and wild as any red-blooded woman that managed to let loose infrequently.

"She's looking into it?"

"Yeah, FBI resources fully utilized."

That was something. Hayden took a breath. She hadn't realized she cared so deeply for Trent and his grave but fair and loyal way of doing things until now.

"I'm assuming Mikey isn't aware?"

"Damn right he's not. Trent's son will never know this happened."

It was presumptive but necessary conjecture, reinforcing their faith in themselves. Hayden stood under the baking heat for a moment, squinting against the sun's bright glare, before prompting the two men once more.

"Clock's ticking," she said. "Do you have anything else?"

"Yeah," Both Silk and Radford appeared like two men in shock, unused to losing their leader and not quite sure how to proceed.

Silk took the question. "They got Aaron between his home and Mikey's school. Trent was returning home after drop-off."

"Thank God they didn't take the kid," Kinimaka said.

"God had nothing to do with it," Radford said. "Schiller told us he'd thought about it but taking the kid as well would have been too *messy*. His beef is with Trent. They rammed his vehicle and dragged him away in the street. Transferred rides and were gone in minutes. Overall, the op went without a hitch."

"I wish you had the rest of the team with you," Silk said.

Hayden did too. Even with the Disavowed guys they were vastly undermanned to execute a rescue op against a gang of gunrunners. "The FBI will help?"

"Yeah, but they don't act fast."

Hayden knew it. She wondered if they'd act even slower following President Lacey's actions regarding the Strike Force teams.

"This is the result of ghosting the Strike Force teams," Silk said. "It's what you, we and others were afraid of. Our enemies are tracking us now. You did well to split up because we're easier to track when we stay together."

Hayden glanced at Kinimaka. Splitting up had been Drake's plan and not all of them had agreed with it. Still, they had acquiesced and now it seemed the Yorkshireman had been right. Nobody knew what was around the next bend; nobody could predict what was coming tomorrow. But, this time, Drake's intuition was proving to be correct.

Kinimaka stayed practical. "I guess, since you're going up against a crew of gunrunners, that you have weapons?" He spread his arms to indicate that he and Hayden did not.

"We got a stash," Silk said. "We should head over there now."

It proved to be a good idea. By the time they arrived at a vast warehouse filled with public storage units and started to flick through an assortment of weapons, Agent Collins had called back.

"I got something," she whispered across the loudspeaker.

"Speak up," Radford said.

"Friggin' *can't*. You think this is on the books?"

"Why shouldn't it be? This is a goddamn manhunt."

Collins sighed. "And when we find Trent are you gonna allow the FBI to go in and get him?"

Radford paused, mouth open, suddenly seeing the light. "Ahh . . ."

"Yeah, best close your mouth before I stick something down it, bud. Listen, since Trent was abducted between the school and home and presumably out of his car, we used traffic cams to chart his route. We caught him at La Brea, heading north, followed him through several lights until he turned east on Franklin. Now, that might be heading toward the Hills but it's still a pretty built up area. Anyway, between Grace and Cahuenga there's a UPS store and a Lido Cleaners with a small parking lot. Seems Trent stopped there to use one of those services and he was jumped on his way out."

"You follow them?"

Collins lowered her voice. "Bastards knew where the cameras were. Used backstreets to get away. But we did manage to backtrack and get a partial plate. I matched the model of the car and we got 'em. Car's parked at a warehouse outside a closed-down shop on North Orange."

"Not that clever then," Silk said. "They must be waiting on orders to move. They wouldn't want to drive to Texas, I guess..."

"Or they're hurting Trent right now," Kinimaka said.

"No, they're taking him to Schiller," Silk said.

"We have to get over there fast," Hayden said. "And hope..."

"I'm coming," Collins said sharply. "I'll meet you there. Do not, I repeat *do not*, go in without me."

The connection was cut. Hayden breathed in tension like it had been thickly cut and layered in the air. Silk and Radford kept their heads down, choosing guns and ammo and saying nothing. Kinimaka grabbed a Glock and several spare 9mm cartridges. There wouldn't be much call for anything else. Hayden selected two Glocks and pockets-full of backup rounds. You couldn't be too careful with gunrunners.

They left the storage unit by way of two cars. Radford's new Corvette ZR1 and Silk's truly oversized, pitch-black F150. The journey to the mini strip mall would take eighteen minutes.

Hayden made the trip with the Glock in her hand, hoping that they would arrive in time to save Aaron Trent from a horrible death.

CHAPTER TEN

Torsten Dahl remained in DC with Kenzie. The pair found separate hotel rooms with adjoining doors, and booked in for a week. Their rooms were on Indiana, a stone's throw from the National Mall, but their windows overlooked only a busy office building in which they could observe the many goings on.

"You see that old guy with the well-trimmed beard," Dahl was holding his cellphone up to his ear, talking to Kenzie who stood in the next room, also studying the activity across the road.

"Oh, yeah, he could have been a fighter. A long time ago."

"You think? Look at the way he's holding his lunchbox."

"Old breakages? Arthritis?"

"Both, brought on by boxing. And I'm so glad you're not Drake."

"Wow, thanks and . . . why?"

"Because I just realized lunchbox has a different meaning to the wild animal known as the Yorkshire Bell End."

"And what's a bell end?"

Dahl hesitated, thinking swiftly. "Umm . . ."

"Maybe you could show me?" Kenzie's voice was soft.

"Hey, you see her?" Dahl exclaimed in a hurry. "Long black hair tied in a pony-tail. She's in a bloody hurry. Whaddya think? Deadline?"

"No idea. It would help if we knew what kind of offices they were."

Dahl googled it. "Attorneys," he said. "Boring."

"Not her," Kenzie caught his attention. "Eighth floor up, third from the right. She's on Tinder."

"At this time? It's barely 10 a.m. What's she doing?"

"Lining one up for later," Kenzie said with a knowing catch to her voice.

"Right. Well, on that note I'll meet you downstairs. Say four minutes?"

"Yes, sir. Right on that, sir. Can't wait."

Dahl shook his head and cut her off. It had been an odd week, starting off emotionally harsh with the splitting of the team. Dahl hadn't agreed with Drake, but the Yorkshire twat left anyway and then Hayden jumped on the twat-wagon and everyone else followed suit. To Dahl's mind they were good enough as a team to stay together. Good enough to overcome any obstacle that this new life threw at them.

Dahl had known from the beginning that, if everyone split up, he would stay with Kenzie. For a long time now, they had been skirting something. Finally, they had a chance to explore it. The first week was tentative, and it still was. Adapting to a new way of life meant more than just a change of scene—it was a lifestyle change—your brain needed time to recalibrate absolutely everything that you took for granted.

It could take a while.

Dahl ignored all his initial feelings. They were born of anger and regret, of disappointment and longing. They were all negative emotions and wouldn't serve him well in the long run. The second week his outlook began to improve. He started to view life with a lighter attitude, even a little optimism. It wasn't perfect, this civilian life, but it was all he had.

They ventured out rarely at first, conscious that DC was a hotbed for criminals of all kinds and reluctant to risk some friend of a brother's terrorist contact recognizing them and reporting back to whatever Godfather pulled their strings. It was Connor Bryant's phone call that forced them out of their anti-social, well-veiled space.

"Come to the offices. Let me show you the operation."

"Didn't they burn down?" Dahl asked apologetically for reasons he couldn't understand.

"Yeah, but we got temporary new ones close by. Come on over anytime."

The offer was genuine. Dahl and Kenzie discussed it. Los Angeles was a long way. Where the Israeli was all for it, at the very least to get them away from the oppressive hotel, Dahl couldn't help but remember that their initial meeting with Bryant had been set up by the Devil.

That thought gave him deep misgivings.

The meet was a mere "ends justify the means" kind of scenario, Dahl knew. They had been expecting to meet G, and Bryant had allowed them into the party because he had an appointment with them in a few days—all cleverly orchestrated stuff. But why had the Devil chosen Bryant and his firm Glacier? Was it simple circumstance, a beneficial scenario with no context? Or was there a deeper vein running between the Devil and Bryant?

Either way, Dahl decided the best way to expose it was to stay close to it.

After visiting Bryant's new offices in Los Angeles and learning quite a bit about the way he did business, Dahl was none the wiser. Bryant seemed a genuine, if complex, guy. He hit on Kenzie in front of the employees and apologized in private for no obvious reason. Kenzie went with it, annoying Dahl. When the two seemed close to finalizing a dinner date that would only end up in one place, Dahl pulled them out of there faster than he'd left the burning skyscraper just over a week ago. But they didn't get away scot free. Bryant's last words were to organize a three-way dinner date.

Dahl agreed just to get them out of there. Later, Kenzie and he talked out their feelings in the hotel bar, revisiting all they had experienced through the last few years.

Dawn broke and they were still talking.

Now, three or four days later, Dahl had lost track of time, and the dinner date was looming. He found Kenzie in the hotel lobby and nodded.

"Can we find a way to cancel tonight?"

"With Bryant? The only way you'll keep me in is to pin me down, Torsten."

Dahl led the way to their customary breakfast table and signaled the waitress for a cafetiere of steaming hot coffee.

"Is Bryant worth all this?"

"All this? If you mean a few hours of socializing, then *yes*. Back in Israel in my youth we used to learn stealth by joining stakeouts. All night, no talking, no contact. Day after day. Those stakeouts were more interesting than our new life. We need human interaction. You can't stop living just because someone yanked the rug out from under you. We've had enough time to adjust."

Dahl knew she was right and gave her a slight nod of acknowledgement. Their chat the other night had touched him deeply. Kenzie had confessed to "knowing he was the right one" from practically the first day they met.

Everything since had been her holding back. If that were true, Dahl was a little wary of seeing her let loose.

He reflected briefly on his life and how he'd reached this point. One thing that set his mind at rest was how well the girls were doing back in Stockholm. They were making friends and flourishing at school. Johanna, his ex-wife, was finally happy again.

The knowledge shut a door in Dahl's mind, giving him closure. That part of his life could now be stored in the past—only the girls mattered going forward.

Giving him room to breathe.

Giving me a choice.

"Then I guess we're going to meet Bryant." Dahl exhaled in a rush.

Going out to dinner meant buying new clothes, although Dahl made sure he stayed conservative. Kenzie on the other hand went all out, buying a tight, knee-length black dress that was slit to the waist on the right side, and several items from Victoria's Secret.

"We have to watch the money, Kenz," Dahl gasped when he saw the bills.

"Are we married?" Kenzie snapped. "'Cause I don't remember saying 'I do.'"

Dahl clammed up, taking it on the chin. Truth be told he was looking forward to seeing Kenzie in her new clothes. At least—most of them. Despite their long talk, they still didn't know where they stood moving forward.

Before they met to head out for dinner, Dahl stood alone in his room for a while. The lights were switched off and Los Angeles was enjoying a splendid sunset, crimson and gold splayed out across the western horizon of which he could see brief snatches through the office buildings. His eyes didn't absorb the sunset—they were focused internally.

With the splitting up of the team they had lost more than just companionship. They were a family unit, a unit that functioned better when it worked as a whole. Sundered, it suffered. They were not the same soldiers when they were forced apart. Soldiers that fought together for an extended period of time developed an almost psychic sense of cooperation. It was something no military leader on earth could replicate or teach and, when you reached that level of intuition, you were among the best in the world.

Dahl missed that. He wondered if they would ever recover the best of what they had been. And with every beat of his heart he hoped that somehow, someway, they could one day pick up where they let off.

But, for now, he had a different problem.

Kenzie was knocking at the door.

CHAPTER ELEVEN

Dahl wasn't used to dining out.

He was used swallowing down a soldier's ration on the hoof, tasting nothing, and getting back to the action. Away from conflict, he ate properly, mostly at home, cooking food that helped maintain his wellbeing. But heading out to dinner—especially with Kenzie draped across one arm—was a dismaying prospect.

In the end though, he need not have worried. Bryant brought a lady friend, a woman by the name of Diana, and spent most of the meal either trying to impress her, or impress others at her expense. It was an odd two and a half hours. Dahl enjoyed his starter, sipped his beer, and tried to tune Bryant out by turning to Kenzie.

"Enjoying yourself?"

"I've had worse nights. You?"

"I guess," he grumbled. "But I was probably being shot at."

"You're kidding?" Kenzie gave him a false smile. "Bryant's firing bullet after bullet over there. Thinks he's the world's greatest marksman."

"Yeah, well, I've about had enough—"

"Recount some of your exploits." Bryant appeared to remember he wasn't the only person at the table. "Both of you."

Whilst Kenzie was happy to relate more than one feat, Dahl found himself turning reluctant. He didn't talk about business outside of the team—whom he liked to wind up—and the telling of old tales resurrected memories of lost friends he'd rather keep below the surface. The mere mention of cities brought back heart-breaking memories—Lauren and Smyth were connected to London, Romero to DC. Dahl was a far better person when he held those thoughts at bay.

"Killed a sub, a helicopter . . . and a strip club, technically," he said with a shrug.

"Well, two out of three ain't bad!" Bryant yelled with a lewd wink at Diana, then leaned across the table. "Seriously . . . a strip club? Man, that's cool!"

"Is the Moulin Rouge a strip club?" Kenzie asked. "I don't think—"

"The Moulin fucking Rouge? That was you? Oh, shit, I gotta get you on my team."

Dahl pulled away from the booze-infused breath only to see Bryant wink at him with total sobriety.

"Seriously, dude," he said. "You should come work for me."

If it was a sales pitch, it was a weird one. Dahl ate the rest of his meal as quickly as possible, uneasy at the table, and made a move to leave as soon as he could.

"Thanks for a great night," he said, as they exited the restaurant and its over-ecstatic atmosphere to enter the blessed outdoors. "We'll think about your offer but, if we join, it will be as a team. Not individuals."

"I can probably accommodate that for the most part," Bryant said, tapping a cigarette out of a pack. "Can't promise every mission will be team-based though, man. You should understand that."

Dahl did, to be fair. He nodded, shook hands and watched the couple walk away.

"Future boss?" Kenzie asked.

"I can't work him out. First, he's a sleaze, then he's a likeable kind of guy. Now he's a loudmouth and then offers us an olive branch, a way to carry on working. I don't think I like him, but . . ."

"He kinda grows on you," Kenzie said.

"Really? That guy? You mean you'd . . ." Dahl left it hanging, the inflection obvious.

"Oh, crap, no. The only reason I'd sit on his face is to shut him the hell up for half an hour."

Dahl coughed and turned away as their taxi arrived. "What are you saying then?"

"He's a nice guy fronting a tough exterior, and badly. In his trade, he has to try. Nice isn't normal when dealing with mercenaries, warlords, and the worst snakes in the government. Nice gets you dead."

Dahl considered that, already knowing she was right. They spent the taxi ride in comfortable silence, and it was only when they exited and paid, standing in front of their hotel, that they remembered they were in Los Angeles, on a fine evening, with nothing to do.

"Shit, I wished I'd hired a car." Dahl stared up in the direction of Mulholland Drive and the Hollywood Hills. "Shelby Mustang. GT500, like the one I used around Palicki Airfield . . ." He hesitated, remembering that Kenzie hadn't been with them that day, not like Komodo and Smyth and . . .

"Don't mind me," he said. "Old memories—they sometimes unman me."

"I'm a soldier too." Kenzie came closer, throwing her arms around his shoulders. "You don't have to hide that kind of thing from me. *I get it.* They unman me too. We've both lost friends along the way. We wonder what they'd be like now, what they'd be doing right *now*. It's not unhealthy to remember better days."

This close, Kenzie was bordering on irresistible. Dahl's vision was full of her. When her lips met his it wasn't a surprise, but a welcome relief. When her eyes studied his from inches away it was exactly as he'd always imagined it would be.

And when the passion ignited his body, it was unstoppable.

Stumbling, laughing, they made their way up the steps of the hotel and through the lobby. Enamored of each other, they saw nothing but their own bodies and reflections of themselves. Everywhere Dahl looked he saw Kenzie. They ignored any watchers, any judgmental asshole and, laughing, staggered into an elevator before pressing the button to the third floor.

They couldn't wait. Dahl framed Kenzie's face with both his hands and kissed her deeply. It was as good as he'd always expected it would be. Kenzie didn't melt into his kiss, but came back passionately, driving him across the elevator and into the side. Dahl turned her around, putting her back to the wall. She was exquisite, a dream. His hands slipped down to her hips just as the elevator dinged, the doors sliding open with a hiss.

"Your room or mine?" Kenzie whispered.

"Don't care if it's the floor, just get there fast."

Kenzie grabbed his arm and ran, dragging him down the corridor with a laugh and a coy look back. She opened the door to her room and threw him inside. Dahl stumbled, caught himself and then looked up but she was already airborne. Her thighs locked onto his waist, bearing him backward. Dahl fell onto the bed with Kenzie on top as the heavy door closed behind them.

Without pause, Dahl slipped the straps of her dress off her shoulders. The split skirt revealed her thigh to her waist and Dahl ran his right hand along the soft, smooth skin as Kenzie watched.

"Jesus," she said. "I feel like I'm gonna explode."

The Mad Swede winced. "That's not the best kind of language to use around a soldier, Kenz."

"Well, how about this." She bent down to whisper in his ear. "Fuck me, Dahl. Fuck me like it's your last day alive."

"That's better," he said, and spun her over.

CHAPTER TWELVE

Mai Kitano's first act on arriving in Tokyo was to call Karin and establish a contact. She wanted to be aware of all issues—ranging from the largely immaterial to the emphatically urgent.

Next, she sought out her sister, Chika, and Dai Hibiki, her sister's husband and one of Mai's oldest friends. They lived in a nice house on the outskirts of Tokyo. The ex-ninja arrived by cab and, hoisting her backpack, took her time walking up to the front door.

Which opened before she arrived.

"Good to see you," Dai said conservatively but Chika rushed past him to enfold Mai in a hard, sisterly hug.

"Why didn't you come see me the last time you were here?" She drew away and fixed Mai with accusing eyes.

"It wasn't exactly a family opportunity." Mai recalled chasing mercs, ninja, the Tsugarai and samurai from east to west Japan as they searched for four sacred treasures.

"Really? You spoke to Dai."

Chika's irritation wasn't real, and Mai knew it. She shook her head at her sister, walked past her and hugged Dai.

"Lovely to see you," she said.

"We should talk later," he whispered, causing her fragile optimism to shatter.

"About what?"

But Chika was already at her shoulder and pulling her

inside the house. Mai spent three pleasant hours catching up around the kitchen table with drinks and finger foods, learning that Grace—the girl she'd rescued from the evil Tsugarai, the girl she loved—was flourishing quite nicely in college just across the city. She'd made friends, learned ballet, and had started playing the guitar. Mai smiled to hear how the girl was turning her life around.

They'd already prepared a bedroom for Mai; a small child's room really—Grace's old one. Mai didn't mind one bit, seeing it furnished with Grace's stuff, seeing parts of the girl's personality, thoughts and cherished possessions hanging on the walls, scattered on surfaces and perched on the end of her bed.

Mai relaxed alone in there for some time, drinking in Grace's character, hoping that they might soon meet up again. She was quiet and self-reflective when she emerged to see that the sun had already set. Chika was sitting in a comfy seat, watching the television. Dai rose to greet her.

He grabbed two beers from the fridge and motioned her outside. "How about a catch up?" he asked loudly.

Mai nodded. Chika didn't stir. Dai led them outside onto his porch, placed the two cold beers on a plastic table and offered her one of the seats.

"I heard what happened," he said. "All of it."

"Good news travels fast." She took her seat, wondering what was going on. Dai had left Tokyo's police force over a year ago, but still seemed privy to current information.

"Bad news travels faster," he said glumly. "The US withdrew support for many of its Special Forces teams almost overnight. Even those *in-mission*. I have to say—I was shocked."

"We all were," Mai said, "so we split up for a while. That way, any enemies that get the silly idea of trying to track us down will find only the empty air we left behind."

"I imagine that's hard," Dai Hibiki said insightfully. "And I'm sorry."

Mai took a long swig of beer, wrapping up as a chill wind swept across the porch. "Why the hell are we out here, Dai?"

Her old friend bowed his head. "I am sorry for the furtive signals," he said. "But an enemy you should all fear is making noises."

Mai cast her mind back over the last five years. "Which one?"

"Zuki Chiyome. Leader of what was once the most powerful shadow royal family of Japan. Of the principal bloodline. Zuki Chiyome—the noble brat, the shrewd and ruthless leader. Do you remember what happened to her?"

"After the sacred treasures thing when she sent Samurai warriors to kill us and devastated part of Tokyo, they sent her to a special kind of prison."

"Well, she adapted. She continues to shape affairs from her hostile prison, apparently in between varying bouts of torture and solitary. If anything, she's growing stronger in adversity."

"But the Japanese still have her, right? She's still behind locked doors? Are you saying she's a threat to our team?"

Hibiki eyed her astutely. "Isn't that why you separated?"

Mai knew he was essentially correct. Zuki was a terrible representation of everyone that hated the SPEAR team and, if freed, would be prepared to raze cities to locate them.

"Yes, for the good of everyone. What have you heard?"

"Rumors from reputable sources." He shrugged. "Same as my cop days. You investigate as best you can with the meagre assets at your disposal. Most governments would rather fund a terrorist or a dictator in its search for rare earth materials than bolster and support their domestic police force. It's why I got disillusioned with the entire political masquerade in the first place."

"I know," Mai said gently. "I really do. So, what have your sources told you?"

"Well, first the good news. Zuki is well and truly locked up. It would take a very clever, very resourceful plan to get anywhere close to freeing her and there's nothing of that kind on the horizon."

"And the bad news?"

"Like I said, she continues to be influential. Her family are of the principal shadow bloodline. People *will* listen to her whether we want them to or not. And I mean powerful, influential figures, and not just because she can offer them more of what they crave. Some are beholden to her."

"We should have ended her when we had the chance," Mai mused.

"Certainly, you'd never have regretted that move. Letting her live, however, that's a decision loaded with risk."

"All I've heard so far are generalities. Do you have any specific incidents? Threats?"

"Weeks ago, the guard tasked with her interrogation was found floating in Tokyo harbor, a suicide note left on his computer. A day later, Zuki's clan reinforced their hold in Kabukicho, one of her strongholds. Businesses were strong-armed, infiltrating gangs murdered on the street. And that was just the start."

"It's ramping up?"

"A steady escalation, yeah."

"The police surely caught some of her soldiers? Rounded them up?"

"Harder to crack than a ninja's virtue. No offence.

They're happy to go to prison. Scared of retaliation. I even believe she still has her clutches in the old samurai clan."

Mai was surprised that the clan would continue to ally itself with her. "In what way?"

Hibiki drained his bottle and chewed his bottom lip, staring into the distance. "Reports of gatherings. They're massing, more arriving every day. Increased resources—money, real estate, vehicles, overall reach and infrastructure. I wonder if she's funding them."

"Bad for Tokyo if that's true," Mai said.

"Bad for the world," Hibiki said. "She won't be content with Tokyo."

Mai wondered at the prospect of a half-mad, royal Japanese princess with bad blood and a deep desire to rule the world using a samurai army to enforce her goals, but only for half a minute. "Even if I wanted to act, what can I do?"

"Gather your team. Every passing day makes her stronger."

"Not gonna happen anytime soon," Mai affirmed. "Half of SPEAR aren't even in contact with Karin."

"I guess there are other teams." Hibiki sounded depressed. "Other countries that might help."

Mai looked away from her friend, studying the hunkering darkness that held sway over Tokyo. The deeper it went, the more secrets it held; more atrocities, more complexity. She wished she could see what was coming.

Because their destiny was shooting toward them, she knew, and nothing was going to slow it down.

CHAPTER THIRTEEN

Drake paused outside the cabin in the woods, breathing heavily.

A dark, threatening atmosphere hung over the place. It was a low building, with a peaked roof, a porch and two windows in the front. A dirt track ran past it, leading to a dirt road that appeared to wind its way through the forest. Drake hadn't heard any sounds whatsoever, let alone screams, in a while.

Drake dropped to one knee in a creeping darkness lit only by starshine, removed his flashlight and then his Glock handgun, expelling the cartridge by habit to check the load. Reassured, he rose, left the backpack behind, and approached the cabin from its east-facing blind side. A brief shower had slickened the trees and now the incessant dripping around him was a counterpoint to his own soft movement. He stayed low, cautious, avoiding the worst of the brush. The night hung heavy overhead, but Drake could see well enough.

Reaching the cabin, he turned, putting his back against the rough timber. He took a moment to survey his rear—the dirt trail and shadow-heavy treeline—then, satisfied he wasn't being crept up on, dashed around to the cabin's front. A cool breeze caressed his face. He pressed his face to the window, peering inside, but the darkness gave him nothing, it was all too dense.

The wooden porch boards gave a slight creak under his weight. Drake peered around. Still nothing.

The cabin's door was ajar.

Drake examined the handle, the lock. Nothing was broken. There was a soft sound at his back, making him whirl, before realizing it was the lazy wind susurrating through the trees. He froze, listening, but nothing else stirred.

Alone, he inched the door open and stepped into the breach.

Darkness filled his vision. Drake thought it safe to use the flashlight and switched it on. The thin beam played off the walls at first, illuminating bare plaster, a tired old kitchen unit and a set of enormous antlers, clearly fake, glued to the western side. His initial sweep confirmed that the cabin was just one large room.

Then he turned the beam to the floor.

Shock coursed through his veins. Drake clenched his fists and his teeth, and brought the Glock up. Quickly, he closed the door at his back, not wanting to be surprised.

He turned his attention back to the horrific scene.

A woman's clothing was strewn for almost the entire length of the cabin. Most of it was torn, some of it was bloody. Drake saw jeans, socks, boots and a T-shirt, a ripped pink jacket with blood soaking its sleeve. Undergarments were in separate places as if thrown aside. Close to the center of the cabin, a pool of blood congealed.

Drake moved closer, sweeping the flashlight to left and right. The cabin's floor, where it wasn't covered with blood, was coated in dust. He crouched to see at least two different sets of shoeprints, maybe more. Finally, and with a growing sense of dread, he rose to his full height.

Did a woman get murdered here? Did she escape? Into the woods?

That was what he'd heard. Drake took a few moments to

check through the kitchen units but found them empty. There was little else inside the cabin, nothing except a thick sense of malice and fear that raised the hairs on Drake's neck. He'd found dead bodies before, killed people, but this was entirely different.

Opening the door, he carefully exited. Looking around once more, he breathed in the clear night air, waiting for any kind of movement. Was he being watched? Were they holding her captive out there, a hand across her mouth? Drake waited.

As he stood in silence, his eyes drifted down to the wide dirt trail that formed a clearing in front of the cabin. In the dirt were tire tracks and, judging by the way they were so perfectly formed, they were fresh.

Drake didn't move a muscle, senses attuned, waiting for longer than most people would be able to hold down a struggling woman or keep silent. In the end, satisfied he was alone, he bent to examine the tracks.

They belonged to a big truck, an SUV or maybe a pickup. That was as far as his knowledge went. Drake retrieved his backpack, fished out a burner cell and took as many pictures as he could before stowing everything away.

Then he checked the time: *3 a.m.*

Shivering as the cold started to bite its way through his clothing, he started back toward Coyote, his mind askew and dismayed. Again, he thought, this was completely different than seeing someone killed on a battlefield. This level of death was poles apart; it was cold-blooded, premeditated murder. Drake couldn't get the image of the woman's forlorn clothing out of his mind; the sounds of her terrified screams.

But by the time the world woke up, he'd be in a position to do something about it.

*

When the hour was reasonable, and he was still a morning's hike short of Coyote, he called Karin Blake.

"Ok, so you are still alive then?" she greeted him.

Drake was too shook-up and driven by what he'd heard and discovered to respond to her banter in the accustomed way. "I need your help," he said, staring at the trail ahead. "Something bad happened out here last night."

He didn't stop talking until Karin was caught up. Then he paused, giving her the chance to answer.

"Bloody hell, Drake, you're supposed to be keeping a low profile."

"Can you help?"

"I don't know, to be fair."

"C'mon, Karin, this woman could still be alive." But inside he doubted it. There had been entirely too much blood.

"Call the cops," she said. "They'll get it sorted far quicker than me."

"We both know that's a load of bollocks. Besides, I don't know the local cops. I know you. And I know you can get me an answer in about ten clicks. With the cops, I'd be answering questions all day and under suspicion for a week."

"And all while the real perpetrator gets away." Karin sighed. "I get it. All right, I'm heading in now. Give me thirty."

Drake hung up. He didn't ask after Alicia's welfare, how the others were doing. He didn't enquire about Dino's injury. The stakes were too high to lose valuable time. He needed Karin totally focused and he needed to speed up, get back to Coyote before the sun reached its zenith. Drake checked his compass frequently, following winding trail after trail, pushing until his heart beat fast and the sweat streamed down his face. Drake was fit, but the arduous trek, the speed at which he marched and the burden that weighed down his heart tore strips from his vitality.

When Karin called back, he was about an hour from Coyote.

"Hey," she said. "I really think you should get the cops involved and drift away. Do it anonymously. I assume you got GPS readings for the cabin, so call and let them handle it."

"Karin," Drake said through clenched teeth. "I heard her screams. I heard her fucking *fear*. I was close and I couldn't find her. It was my fault—I was *too late*."

"Not your fault. You did what you could."

"My mind is made up," Drake said. "Can you help, or not?"

"Dammit, you're a stubborn ass. But yes, I can. The tire tracks belong to a Chevrolet Silverado."

Drake groaned. "There has to be thousands of those around here."

"Yeah, but not like this bad boy. It's received one of those third-party aggressive upgrades. They call it the Jackal now. Upgraded shocks, flares, custom hood, axles, springs. The grade three upgrade even gets special thirty-seven-inch, off-road tires."

Drake grinned as he topped a rise, seeing the town of Coyote spread out in the distance. The outskirts were comprised of warehouses, gas stations and, to the north, attractive houses. Approaching the center, suburban areas branched out in a rough palm shape, replete with nicely landscaped verges and clean boulevards. It was a bigger town than he'd initially thought.

"I'm pretty sure those tires and a vehicle like that are relatively rare," he said. "Even around here."

"Yeah, you know what to do?"

"Can't you check the database?"

"That's a big 'no.' Whilst I can bury a tire-track vehicle ID among other cases, I can't hide a personal check on addresses quite so easily. It'd get flagged. Sorry, mate."

"That's okay. You've been a big help." Drake was about to cut her off when she spoke up once more.

"Be careful."

"Will do." He barely heard her. Coyote was sprawled out in front of him. Drake knew exactly what he had to do.

It turned out there were three major tire outlets in Coyote. Drake got their addresses through Google and clicked the closest into his street app. It turned out to be another thirty-minute walk. Drake didn't plan to arrive there looking hot, dirty and tired, so stopped at a local gas station to clean up in the restroom. Once presentable, he grabbed a water and a sandwich before walking a further ten minutes, eating and drinking as he went.

He'd entered the front part of an industrial estate by now, one of two that sat outside the town's main hub. Businesses had their doors and warehouses open as men and women worked inside and out. Drake walked past a carpet merchant, a glass warehouse and a noisy builder's yard before turning into the parking lot that fronted the tire place.

He'd had time to formulate a plan during the latter part of his walk. Avoiding the customer entrance, he walked toward the open warehouse doors and hailed a mechanic.

"How's it going?"

The man, a young, dark-haired youth with black-streaked hands, face and arms looked up. He didn't look friendly and nodded to his right.

"Shop's around there."

"Quick question?" Drake asked, careful to keep the Yorkshire accent from thickening his voice too much. *Enunciate,* he thought. *Enunciate those sentences.*

The youth gave him a pained expression, glaring at the job he was working on to show Drake that this was costing him time.

"Sure. Shoot."

Drake grimaced a little at the choice of words. "I'm researching the town before potentially moving out here in the summer," he said carefully. "Nice place so far. But, mate, I bought a truck." He grinned. "Big mother. A Silverado Jackal. You know?"

He let the question hang, watching the other man's face. "Yeah, that's sick," the tire mechanic said. "Special kind of Gucci."

Drake was up to date enough to know the word had nothing to do with the fashion brand. These days, it simply meant great.

"Tires are big mothers. Thirty-seven inch. Do you guys stock them? Repair them?"

"Figure we could." The youth nodded. "But you gotta check with the shop, man. I got work to do."

Drake nodded, arriving at the final, most important question. "That's cool. I'll check right now. Hey, anyone else got one around here?"

The Yorkshireman tried to look relaxed and competitive at the same time, appealing to the youth's pro-active spirit.

"Yeah, man, I've seen a red one driving around. Blood red. Now I gotta—"

"Aye, get back to work. I know. Cheers mate."

Drake dropped the pretense of a clear accent. It was hard work. He walked away from the youth, the lot and the tire dealer, already googling the second of Coyote's three main workshops.

The second shop turned out to be on the same estate, just further toward the back. Drake made his way there and repeated the process, keeping a low profile for no obvious reason when a police car cruised by, learning that this tire dealer too, didn't attend personally to the red Silverado Jackal, or any other that might frequent Coyote.

Which left the third tire place and that was on the other side of town. Drake hefted his rucksack and followed the sun-blasted streets, dust in his hair, blisters on his feet, blazing a trail to the only lead that he had left. It was after 3 p.m. by the time he arrived.

"Hey . . ." He went through the same routine with a different youth, one that acted like the mirror image of the previous two. All in a hurry, all discourteous, all distinctly unhelpful if they could get away with it. Maybe they were triplets.

"See the guy inside," this kid said, pointing. "The guy that owns that truck's an asshole."

Drake managed to maintain a poker face. "You know him? He comes here?"

"I work for him. Now I gotta get back to work, man."

It took Drake a few second to process that. Of course, it made sense—the guy that owned a specialist vehicle also owned and earned decent money from a business that might help look after that vehicle.

"Where's the Jackal now?" he asked, trying to affect an eager appearance.

"Haven't seen it all day." The youth turned away,

signaling the end of the conversation. Drake backed up, giving the whole place a good once over. It was unlikely that the business owner would leave any evidence on the premises.

Which meant finding out where he lived.

"Hey," he bothered the uncooperative kid once more. "Hey, are there any other Jackals in Coyote?" He blinked twice on realizing what he'd just said.

"Not that I know of." The back stayed in Drake's face.

But the Yorkshireman didn't care. To all intents and purposes, he'd tracked down the vehicle that had been in the forest last night at the same time as a woman was accosted, or worse. It had taken all day, but he was closer.

Drake considered his next move.

CHAPTER FOURTEEN

But as he'd previously realized, Coyote was a big place.

Without resources, Drake saw only two options: stake out the tire dealership in the middle of a busy industrial estate, hoping for a glimpse of the red Jackal, or return to the owner's cabin in the woods.

After a while of mulling it over, Drake saw a third option.

"Karin?" he called his old friend once more. "I really need your help."

"You and everyone else. Now I know what a switchboard feels like. You do realize I'm not your bloody coordinator, controller or handler?"

Drake guessed he wasn't the only one calling Karin for assistance. "This is different," he said. "I've found out where the owner of that Silverado works but there's no time. I can't sit here on my ass for days and I can't scour a town this size."

"Ah, I see. Well, the answer's still no, Matt. The kind of search you're asking me to do isn't just risky around here, it's tantamount to dismissal, maybe even charges. It gets flagged. I'd have to explain it."

"Surely there's—"

"Please," Karin said quietly. "Please don't ask me to do this."

Drake hesitated, taking a step back from the situation. Yes, he could see it from Karin's point of view, especially if other members of the team were bugging her too, but a woman's life was at stake.

"I can't think of any other way," he admitted honestly, almost under his breath.

"Fucksake, Drake," Karin said, taking one of Alicia's old lines. "I want to help but my hands are tied."

Drake closed his eyes and looked up into the blue glare of the bright skies. The sun beat down, laced with a cold breeze. So this was how it felt to be without resources, without help. This was how ordinary civilians might feel day on day, night on night. What could he do?

"Sorry," he said. "It's so bloody frustrating. Normally on the job, we don't hit dead ends. We don't wait around. We act. We attack. We save."

"Yeah, I know, I know. And again, I'm sorry for everything."

"I can't just drop this. She could still be alive, waiting for—"

"Go to the cops."

Again, Drake fought deep reservations. An official report would give away his position, and would undoubtedly hold up his investigation. If the woman was still alive, she didn't have much time. Also, if the bad guy was proficient, the cops would find little remaining evidence.

"If she's still alive," Karin said, "won't he be returning to finish the job at his first opportunity?"

Like a shaft of lightning, her words fused the sparks of understanding flickering around his brain. This whole conversation had ignited the early glimmerings of an idea and now he saw it clearly. Yes, the guy that owned the Jackal would be back to finish the job tonight. If Drake wanted to help the woman, and if he wanted to maintain a low profile, there was only one place to go.

It was 3:30 p.m.

He prayed he had time. Without saying another word, he pocketed the burner and turned around, taking a moment to regain his bearings. Then he hefted his backpack and broke into a run. The stark truth was—if the woman was dead, he'd lose a day. If she was alive—he'd have a shot at saving her.

Soon, Coyote was at his back. The paths through the trees beckoned like old friends. Drake kept his breathing short, his head focused. A thin plume of trail-dust stirred up in his wake, shining in the sun. Soon, the green canopy enveloped him, his vision a cluttered jumble of boughs, trunks and low-hanging leaves. He ducked and switched directions and studied the ground. His muscles sang at last, welcoming the hard going. Drake ran for an hour without slowing and then walked for a short distance before jogging again, eating up the ground. The sun melted away, expiring in one smoldering laceration that caught his eyes and almost made him stumble. A dull, claylike blue replaced it for a spell and then darkness fell in earnest.

Drake had always known he'd have to cover as much ground as possible before dark. When night fell, he was still a few hours away from his destination. He didn't stop, barely slowed. An old phrase kept rattling around his head: *In the darkness, be the light.* He focused harder, worked harder, kept the end goal firmly at the front of his mind. The trees whispered and bent this way and that. The ground worked against him, trying to force a mistake. The night air was a balm caressing his burning hot face.

Before 11 p.m. he reached his destination.

He dropped low, several hundred feet away from the cabin, but now using warcraft instead of piling on the speed. He lay for several minutes on his front, calming his breathing, studying the night, and getting re-accustomed to its sounds.

When he could do so silently, Drake moved forward.

First, he stowed the backpack, taking weapons and two flashlights from it. Using the thicker trees, he approached the cabin until the structure and the clearing in front of it was reasonably visible, its surrounds picked out by a starlit sky.

He waited, at ease now that he was able to embrace the training. This was the typical, common work he was used to. For this, he didn't need extra resources.

Minutes ticked by. Midnight came and went. Drake breathed slow and easy, patiently waiting. Of course, it wasn't easy. He worried that the man he thought of as the Jackal might not turn up, that he had several places where he conducted his foul business, that he'd killed the girl last night. He worried but waited and trusted the feeling in his gut.

A murderer would always return to the place he felt comfortable.

A little after 1 a.m., the stillness was broken by the unmistakable rumble of a powerful engine and the grating crunch of heavy tires. Drake tensed, peering out from deep cover. He rolled an aching shoulder and flexed tired limbs. Truth be told, it had been one hell of a long day and wasn't about to get any easier. If this was what low-profile civilian rambling was like, then give him a dangerous op any day.

The Silverado came into view and chewed to a halt in the clearing, its front wheels turned to forty-five-degree angles. Drake could see a figure hunched over the steering wheel, a large man. Faint light glinted off wire-rimmed glasses. When the door cracked open, the interior light came on, affording Drake a better view.

The guy sported a beard and sideburns, both thick and shot through with gray. His face was set in a grim expression. Drake saw corded arms beneath an overstretched jacket and noted that the man had a way of carrying himself.

Shit, that's not good. He's military.

His opponent could have been worse, but could have been a whole lot easier too. Drake had been hoping for some geek with bad vision and pencil-thin arms. Still, this made no difference if . . .

Drake watched the man walk around the side of his car. Yes, the expected big handgun was stuck into his waistband and, as he walked, he drew a deadly military knife from a holster inside his black leather jacket.

Drake crept closer, aware he'd seen and heard nothing blameworthy yet.

He froze as the guy looked up, testing the air. Maybe he sensed something. Maybe this was habit, a last check before unveiling something terrible. Seconds passed. Drake held his breath, blended with the forest.

The guy grasped the tailgate and opened it, reached inside and grabbed something which he then dragged off the back of the truck, letting it fall and slam onto the ground.

It was big, human size, wrapped in a coarse gray blanket, and it wriggled.

The guy gave it a kick. The human—which to Drake's gaze it clearly was—stopped moving. The guy bent down, grabbed the person's ankles and dragged them toward the front of the cabin.

For Drake, it was a vision out of a nightmare. Yes, he'd seen warfare, but this was pure horror, a scene from Hell. The hulking man dragged the wrapped figure through dirt and gravel, leaving wide trail marks in their wake, and the only witnesses to his unspeakable act were the still trees, the distant stars, and Matt Drake.

The captive squirmed. Drake could hear muffled noises, as if the person had been gagged. He moved warily, stepping when the big guy stepped, the synced movements helping to mask any sounds he might make.

Drake was at the edge of the treeline by the time the guy had reached the set of three wooden steps leading to the cabin's front door.

He paused. No weapons were drawn. The captive managed to get a solid kick in, making their tormentor grunt and step back. Drake dropped low as the figure took an opportunity to gulp air, relax, and give the clearing a slow once over.

The man's gaze passed over him without stopping. The captive still kicked and grunted, the blanket cocoon scraping across the ground. Drake steadied himself, wanting to rush over there and end the prisoner's torment but unable to reveal his position. After what seemed like an hour the Jackal—as Drake continued to think of him—nodded and reached down once more. Drake watched him through layers of tree growth.

Grabbing a handful of blanket, the man lugged the heavy weight once more, bouncing it up the steps until it lay on the narrow porch. He then turned his back to Drake and opened the cabin door.

Drake slipped out of cover and ran for the truck, crouching behind its enormous bulk and using its windows to continue watching.

The Jackal dragged his kicking captive into the cabin.

Drake crept around to the rear of the truck. The Jackal, confident in his isolation out here, left the door to the cabin open. Drake avoided any line of sight provided by the door and approached the cabin from an obtuse angle.

Seconds later he had his back to the cabin's outer wall. It didn't go unnoticed that he carried the same weapons as the guy inside—a gun and a knife. He heard a deep, gravelly voice, the sound of the blanket tearing and then a woman's muffled cry.

Unable to wait any longer, Drake slipped around the door frame, gun held high. The Jackal was bent over at the waist, poised above a barely dressed woman squirming on the floor. Her flesh was badly bruised, her face dark with contusions. Her arms appeared burned; her fingers broken.

But still she fought.

Drake forced down the rush of admiration and aimed his gun at the Jackal's center mass.

"Hands in the air."

The Jackal didn't rise but looked up at Drake from beneath shaggy brows. The grin on his face was evil, his eyes so narrow they might have been slits.

"You better shoot me now, boy. I don't follow orders easy."

Drake nodded at the gun. "See this? It says you do." His gaze dropped briefly to the woman, saw her desperate, hopeful eyes, and looked away.

"I don't hear it speaking, New Meat. And you're alone."

Drake wished, in that moment, he had backup in the form of Alicia, Dahl or Mai, Hayden or Mano. He wasn't about to shoot the Jackal in cold blood, but he did need to subdue him.

"Turn around." He glanced down at the woman. "Come toward me."

But the Jackal reached out and grabbed her ankle. She

screamed, kicking weakly. The Jackal laughed as he lifted her leg in one meaty hand, pulling her spine off the floor, holding her foot close to his face.

"Now what you gonna do?" he growled.

"Let her go, you evil fuck." Drake had reached his limit. He wasn't about to be messed with this way by a sick, backwoods killer. He strode forward, holding the gun steady. Three steps in, with six still separating them, the Jackal surprised him. In a shocking combined burst of strength and speed he hefted and threw the woman forward. Her body twisted on the floor, her limbs striking Drake. He adjusted the Glock, raised it again, but the Jackal was already on him. Hit by a freight train, Drake staggered back.

The twisted face was up against his own, the big body bearing him backward. Drake's face was washed in fetid breath. The Jackal snarled. Drake hit the wall beside the door with a crash. The Jackal leaned into him, an arm coming up and pressing on Drake's windpipe. The gun was caught between them.

"I'm gonna boil your fucking eyeballs," the killer snarled.

Drake still had the knife in his left hand. It too was trapped, but he managed to slip it free just as black motes danced in front of his eyes. The Jackal grinned, spittle flying. Drake rammed the point of the knife into the man's ribs.

His opponent's eyes widened, his entire body stiffening. Drake felt a lessening of the pressure at his throat. In that second, he thought he'd won. Then realization sank in. Under his jacket, the guy was wearing a vest. The blade had glanced off it, the surprise attack giving the Jackal a moment's pause.

Drake used it. He brought a knee up into his opponent's groin, encountering no protection there. He brought his right elbow around in a ninety-degree swipe, striking the big, meaty face and hard cheekbones. The Jackal barely moved, enjoying the pain. Drake elbowed him again and shoved him away, gaining a little space.

"That all you got?"

The Jackal grabbed both Drake's arms at the top of the wrists, holding them down, then unleashed the hardest headbutt Drake had ever felt. Bright red sparks exploded before his eyes. His legs shook, something warm and red ran down his face. The Jackal's forehead struck again. This time, Drake managed to avert his face, but the blow still jarred his brain. He was in trouble. This guy was fueled by deep rage, by back-to-the-wall adrenalin, by madness. Drake was struggling to hold him off.

The Jackal still held Drake's arms pinned down to his sides. It was hard to get leverage. He ducked his skull into the Jackal's next head-strike. The Jackal yowled. Drake yanked and twisted his arms free, staggering to the left.

The Jackal came after him.

It was the woman that gave Drake a chance. She was crawling across the floor, dragging the blanket behind her, approaching inch by inch. Finally, she reached out, grabbed the Jackal's lower legs in a bear hug, and clung on, desperation giving her strength.

The Jackal wavered in place. Drake struck out hard and fast, four blows to the face and two to the solar plexus. The man barely felt them, so Drake jumped at him, using his weight to unbalance him and send him staggering across the woman to the hard floor.

The Jackal came down with a crash that shook the floor and walls. He kicked out, but Drake was wise now. The

Yorkshireman lifted his gun and aimed it at the Jackal's right arm. He fired without pause, blasting a bloody chunk of flesh free. The woman screamed. The Jackal grinned. Drake aimed at the man's right thigh and paused.

"Last fucking chance," he rasped.

The Jackal's glance flicked to the cabin door.

All the hair's on Drake's neck rose in cold warning. His instinct screamed. He dove headlong. The woman hadn't been screaming because of the gunfire; she'd seen a second attacker. Drake hit the floor and spun on his back, gun aimed between his knees.

A man was framed in the doorway, wearing dark clothing and a hood. He held a knife low at his knees and was hunched. The starlight at his back only served to make the figure even darker, more terrifying. He lurched at Drake, limping badly, drool spilling from his mouth. He came fast, grunting, and Drake couldn't recognize or later describe the dark utterances that fell from his mouth.

Drake shot him in the face or, rather, the hood. He jerked backward and collapsed in a heap. Drake took a breath, realizing he was now lying next to the Jackal.

Swinging the Glock around he took aim, but the Jackal was only staring at the still-twitching body of his accomplice.

"My . . . son . . ." he breathed. "You killed him . . ."

Drake leapt up and backed away. He reached out a hand for the woman and drew her upright, sheltering her with his left hand. The gun never veered from the Jackal's face.

The woman's breath was hot. "What . . . next?"

"Your choice. You wanna call the cops? I'd have to grab my phone." He'd left it buried in the backpack.

"I can watch him," the woman said.

"If he attacks you—" Drake handed her the Glock,

pressed her hands around the weapon and gestured. "Well, you know. Are you sure you're okay for a minute?"

She nodded. Drake moved fast, not trusting the Jackal to try something. He stepped over the dead figure and ran across the clearing, quickly finding his backpack. Once he rose with the cellphone and bag in his hand he started back across the clearing.

The gunshot was loud, ringing out of the cabin door and echoing through the silent forest.

Drake raced back into the cabin. The woman was staring at the dead remains of the Jackal with intense hatred, disgust and, most of all, a deep-seated fear. "I shot him through the face to be sure," she said. "I'd never be able to sleep or rest safely again. If he walked free . . . ever . . ."

"Got it," Drake said. "This way . . . you get closure."

The woman collapsed and started crying as Drake called the cops. *So much for keeping a bloody low profile.*

CHAPTER FIFTEEN

Hayden hoped they'd reach the strip mall in time to save Aaron Trent from a merciless death at the hands of Texan gunrunners.

Mano, Silk and Radford were with her. Agent Collins of the FBI was en route. Hayden carried her Glock in her lap, counting down the seconds until they arrived, wishing they could go faster. The gunrunners who'd kidnapped Trent had held him for well over an hour now.

The LA traffic let them through. They used side roads both Radford and Silk knew well. Hayden readied herself as Silk gestured ahead.

"There."

They pulled up, jumped out of their cars, and approached the warehouse as the sun beat down hard on the gray concrete surface of a small parking lot. Hayden held her gun pointed downward. They threaded through a narrow alley between a laundry and a pizza place, coming up against the dark façade of a warehouse building. Hayden paused with her back to the wall.

Running steps approached from the alley they'd just traversed. Agent Collins appeared, looking grim. "I told you to wait."

"Trent's in there," Silk said, the only words needed.

Collins nodded, then acknowledged Hayden and Kinimaka. "Go."

They approached a steel outer door and checked the

lock. It was engaged, so Silk used a leather wallet of tools and his endless years of experience to pick it. Hayden watched him work, wishing she'd bothered to learn that kind of skill. It would have saved her a lot of bother, time and broken door frames through the years.

"Ready," Silk said, crouching.

He was first through into the darkened interior, followed by Radford, Kinimaka and Hayden. Collins brought up the rear, watching their backs. Hayden swung her gun left and right, searching for enemies as they entered a high, dimly lit space cluttered by towers of boxes and crates, lined by half-filled shelves.

It took less than thirty seconds to explore.

"Clear," Hayden said. Everyone else repeated her.

"Shit, they cleared out?" Collins asked.

Hayden studied the place through dust motes picked out by diffused sunlight shining through high-level rows of half-covered windows.

"Empty." Silk cursed, face haunted. "We're too late."

"But they were here." Kinimaka was over in a corner, staring at the floor. He reached down to pick up discarded, blood-smeared duct tape. "Still tacky."

Collins clung to the lifeline. "We have to hope he's still okay," she said. "And we're not out of moves yet."

As she fished out her phone to make a call, Hayden walked a short way through the dusty warehouse, using her own cell to contact Karin Blake.

"We have a major issue here. I need your help."

Karin sighed heavily. "You too, huh?"

"What does that mean?"

"I'm working harder for the divided SPEAR team than I am for the NSA today. Drake's been on the phone. Mai wants info."

"Drake?" Hayden repeated. "What the hell does he want? And where is he?"

"Colorado," Karin said vaguely. "It doesn't matter. Tell me what you need."

Hayden caught Karin up and told her about Schiller, the Texan gunrunner. Karin responded in horror and with concern, but pointed out that Agent Collins had all the resources she needed.

"Understood," Hayden said quietly. "But I don't want some asshole above Collins tying this up because he once had a beef with Trent or something. It happens. You know it. He's a good man and deserves every chance, Karin."

"I agree." Karin promised to call back as soon as she had any information.

Hayden turned back to Collins, noting that the agent had finished her own call and was watching her. "NSA," Hayden said. "We have a contact."

Collins nodded, a mix of emotions flickering across her face. The group took one last look around the warehouse and then started back toward their cars. Between Silk and Radford, and hanging over them all like a pendulous storm cloud, was Trent's horrible absence.

But by the time they reached the cars both the FBI and Karin were back on the phone. Hayden whipped her cell out as she sat down in the passenger seat of Silk's big F150.

"Yeah?"

"I checked out the warehouse," Karin said. "It's registered through two shell companies, owners hard to trace. But the second shell company was hidden by an amateur—it's owned by a guy called Sheppard. Josh Sheppard. I'm sending you his Los Angeles address right now."

Hayden cut the call and turned to Silk just as Collins

shouted out the exact same thing from the back seat. Hayden smiled grimly at the special agent and received the same back. Collins' face, like her nature, was set as severe as stone on the outside, yet her eyes blazed with an inner passion. Hayden was confident she'd burn down the entire gun-running operation to save Trent.

Fifteen nerve-wracking minutes later they were parked outside the place where Sheppard worked. He ran a photocopying firm out of a big strip mall in West LA. When they arrived, they parked up and ran across a sun-drenched courtyard surrounded by shops and restaurants of all sizes, looking for the right place. Kinimaka spotted it, and sweating heavily he ran straight for the door, narrowly missing smashing into a brown planter three times his size. He grabbed the door handle and yanked it open.

Collins, Silk and Radford were through in a blur. Hayden went next. The contrast in light as they entered made them momentarily blind. But then Hayden saw three hesitant looking dudes blinking at them from behind a low counter.

"Josh Sheppard." Collins flashed her FBI badge.

One of the dudes jerked a thumb toward the back. "In his office."

They barged in. Sheppard looked up in alarm. At first glance he was a short, skinny guy wearing thick glasses and sporting a comb-over, not the sort they'd been expecting. His first act, standing up with his arms in the air, didn't exactly paint him as a hardened criminal either.

Collins slapped down a piece of paper with the warehouse address clearly printed on his desk. "This your place?"

Sheppard blinked, rattled, but finally sent his eyes down toward the piece of paper. "What is it?"

"You tell us." Silk moved closer to the man, his bulk and deadly expression grabbing Sheppard's attention.

"Explain this is or go to jail," Collins added.

"I-I don't know. *This* is my business, where you are now. I rent it. What is this address?"

Hayden threaded her way between Silk and Collins, sensing the guy was as puzzled as they were. "Look," she said. "The warehouse is registered to you. It's been used for weapons' storage. And worse. You're looking at ten years in state prison."

Sheppard gawped and then started to retch. Kinimaka reached down, grabbed a trash can and placed it on the desk before him.

"Shit, Mano." Hayden grabbed it and moved it out of reach. "It's made of mesh."

Kinimaka looked sheepish. Sheppard managed to control himself, then leaned forward, both hands resting on his desk.

"I know what this is," he said finally. "I'm so fucking *sick* of his shit. I knew he'd drag me into his mess."

Hayden perched on the edge of his desk, effecting a sympathetic aura. "Who?" she asked. "Who are you talking about?"

"My brother. Well, half-brother. Dropped the family name before he was fourteen to go by *Pearl* for unknown reasons. Different fathers," he added.

"We get it," Collins said. "Does Pearl belong to a gang?"

"Yeah, real bunch of assholes they are too. They intimidate, strong-arm, offer protection around West LA. But they really just smuggle firearms for some big Texan asshole you people can't touch." Sheppard shrugged. "Hey ho."

"Hey fucking ho?" Collins grated, stepping into

Sheppard's face. "Those fuckers have my friend. They're gonna kill him. And you are gonna give me some goddamn relevant info or I'm gonna feed your ass to federal prison. You get me?"

Sheppard almost started blubbering. "P-Pearl," he said. "Must have used my information to rent the warehouse. He . . . he lives in Downtown. I can give you the address."

"Not good enough," Silk snapped. "He won't be home. What car does he drive? Which places does he frequent? Names of people he hangs with. Girlfriend? Real, registered name?"

Armed with as much data as they could collect, the team left Sheppard for now and returned to their cars. By mutual consent, both Hayden and Collins made calls for urgent assistance. When they'd done that, there was nothing to do but hope.

"I hope to God that we're not too late," Collins said to the silent car, her tone revealing doubt and fear and profound anxiety. "Please, Trent, stay alive . . ."

CHAPTER SIXTEEN

Hayden wasn't prepared for it all to go crazy but, ten minutes later, it did. They got a location for Pearl's car—a deep blue, '99 Firebird—and peeled out of the parking lot to investigate. Silk's F150 bounced from the curb to solid asphalt, the reinforced springs taking the shock, and swerved into traffic. Horns blared. Radford's Corvette, with Kinimaka in the passenger seat, followed closely.

"Eight minutes." Hayden had jabbed the location into the vehicle's satnav.

They arrived in six, screeching up to the curb, leaving their vehicles splayed haphazardly. They leapt out, unholstering weapons. Hayden shook off a feeling that they were already too late. It had been hours since they took Trent. How slow could his captors be? Why would they delay so long?

Focus.

Ahead, a vacant lot led to a dusty brown field that had been crudely fenced off. There were more holes in the fence than chain links and the single gate hung askew. Pearl's Firebird was parked in front of the gate.

"Wide open space," Collins said, peering around the corner of the building that backed on to the lot. "I see three men in the middle of the field. Dark-skinned, maybe Cuban. They're sitting on deck chairs, smoking and drinking. Looks like a smoke break."

"Could mean Trent's close by," Hayden said. "Let's take them."

Collins didn't need asking twice. She moved out with Silk and Radford. Hayden checked that Kinimaka was ready and then followed. Using Pearl's car as cover, they moved to its flank and then crouched down, peering around. Hayden checked the doors and windows of any buildings that overlooked them.

"Clear."

Collins moved fast, staying low. She ran through the broken gate. Silk and Radford fanned out to her left and right. All guns were pointed at Pearl and his drinking buddies.

"Don't move, hands up!" Collins yelled. "FBI!"

Pearl uncoiled, going for his gun. The other two copied his move. Collins fired into the ground at their feet so that the bullets kicked up dust onto their boots. All three men hesitated.

"Don't do it," Silk growled. "We got you covered."

Hayden and Kinimaka extended their cover by spreading out. In a rough half-circle, they held their guns pointed at Pearl and his accomplices.

"We want Trent," Collins said tightly. "That's all. You got a chance here, guys. I recommend that you take it and walk away."

Her words pierced their taciturn nature, causing glances to pass between all three. They didn't play dumb; they wanted a way out of this.

"You true?" Pearl asked, holding on to his gun but with the barrel pointed at the ground.

"Yeah, I'm fucking true. Now, last chance. Drop your guns in the dirt and answer my goddamn question."

"Trent? Yeah, I seen him. He alive. For now." Pearl let go of his gun first; his friends then followed suit.

Pearl wasn't about to show fear or gratitude. His

defiance wouldn't be diluted by guns or aggression or leniency. He looked like a soldier rooting for his cause.

"Where do they have him?"

Pearl gritted his teeth, glancing from under his eyebrows at his colleagues. They offered him nothing, letting him make the decision and shoulder the responsibility.

"He been prepped to be moved. They takin' him away."

"To Dallas? To Schiller?"

"Yeah, yeah." Pearl didn't try to hide his surprise. "He goin' there. You think you know everything—why you askin' me?"

"Tell me something I don't know," Collins growled.

"And then you cut us loose?"

"We never seen you," Silk imitated.

"All right. It's not for Schiller. Yeah, this guy Trent, he smoked Schiller's brother. But Schiller don't care. Hated his fucking brother . . ." Pearl laughed. "Bet you didn't know Schiller is in bed with the Russians, did you?"

He waited for the surprise to crease Collins' face before laughing again. "Oh, yeah, you like that don't you? You lookin' like that. I see you. Anyway," he hurried on in response to Silk's threatening step forward, "the Russian owns Schiller. She a big boss, one of them oligarchs. She want Trent to pay for killin' *her* brother a few years ago."

Hayden sifted through what she knew of Trent and the Disavowed. She recalled they had been instrumental in bringing a Russian named Blanka Davic to justice after a major terrorist attack on Los Angeles. Davic had died at the end of it all.

Collins asked the question.

"Maybe." Pearl shrugged. "This oligarch is a woman and pissed off at Trent, that all I know. Picked up the rest by accident."

Hayden knew what that really meant—he'd listened to conversations that didn't concern him.

"They're taking him to Schiller under this Russian's orders," Silk repeated, eyes narrowed. "Then, I assume he's not been harmed."

"Not much." Pearl grinned arrogantly.

"One last time." Collins tightened her grip on the handgun. "Where is he?"

"Two blocks west." He nodded. "The marina."

"You mean Marina del Rey? That's a big place," Collins said. "Give us the name of a fucking boat."

Pearl looked uncertain. "Don't know. *Imp* . . . *Imper* . . . *Impy* . . . it dark blue at the end of Tahiti Way."

Anger seethed through Hayden's veins and was evident in Collins' face. The idiot clearly wasn't bluffing. When he shrugged, looking both smug and stupid, Silk stepped in and delivered a bone-crunching blow to his face. Pearl went down, lights-out, as his friends gawped on.

"Make a move," Silk dared them, flicking his handgun toward their faces.

Both men raised hands and stepped further back. Collins hesitated. Hayden knew she wanted to step in and cuff all three, leave them there for patrol units to pick up, but there was no time. Hayden showed the example by starting to back away; the others followed.

Seconds later, they leapt into their cars.

"How long?" Hayden asked.

"Ten minutes minimum," Collins told her. "But prepare for a fight. Russians don't go down easy."

Hayden nodded wryly. She knew that, having tackled one or two in the last few years. Kinimaka was sitting forward and looking grim in Radford's Corvette as the yellow sports car blurred past them. Silk sped up in its wake. Streets and pedestrians swept by on both sides, mere distortions from the corners of her eyes. The asphalt roared as the engine fired hard, mufflers growling. The F150 was a beast, bullying smaller cars out of its way.

Five minutes into the journey, Hayden's phone rang. It was Karin. "Shit," she said. "I have to take this."

"You got a minute?" the Blake woman asked.

"Barely," Hayden said edgily. "We're on our way to reacquire Trent."

"Okay, just listen. I thought you might be interested to hear that data is starting to filter through from the local authorities in Nevada. The Blood King and the Devil were found together, along with their men, several days ago as you know. Don't worry, they're still dead. There are suspicions that their killers were members of a certain Special Forces team, but no proof and, since those teams were disbanded, no official mandate to search for or bring you in. So, unless they find anything highly incriminating, which they won't, all is well."

Hayden felt relief on hearing the news. "That's awesome. God, I wish I could share it with the rest of the team."

"I'll try my best to do that. The larger issue arising out of all this—and what most are focusing on—is the Blood King's initial declaration—that he stashed three nukes to use as leverage. Obviously, we have no idea where, or any idea what he meant by that."

Hayden closed her eyes for a moment. "I remember. Why the hell can't that bastard just go away and die? Leave us all alone?"

"We're two minutes out," Collins said.

"I have to go," Hayden told Karin. "And thanks for the update."

"No worries."

The car slowed. Hayden tried to put the bad news out of her mind, but it wasn't easy. Somewhere on this planet three nuclear weapons had been secreted by a madman; weapons capable of vast damage. What happened now that he was dead?

Hayden shut the door to that train of thought.

They were here.

CHAPTER SEVENTEEN

"Marina del Rey." Collins pointed ahead. "Playground of the rich."

Hayden could only see a little of the famous harbor, but knew it was a series of docks and walkaways where hundreds if not thousands of expensive boats were moored, all manner of shapes and sizes. The larger ones were moored at the end of each dock, partially blocking in their lesser rivals.

"I'll give Pearl some credit," Silk said bleakly. "If he hadn't told us Tahiti Way, we'd never have found it."

"Don't speak too soon," Collins said. "We haven't found it yet."

They exited the car and cast around. Radford had a map of the dock on his cellphone. A small blue dot marked their position.

"Three streets that way," he said. "We're close."

It was the first bit of good luck Hayden could recall. They started forward, hiding their weapons but still looking out of place striding along the dock area. Only Radford, with his designer gear, cargo shorts and lightweight jacket fitted in. The others wore long jeans, boots and cheap T-shirts or shirts.

"Hay." Kinimaka nudged her as they approached the wide street named Tahiti Way. "I just spotted a Cheesecake Factory ahead and to your left."

Hayden shook her head. "You and your friggin' food."

"Nothing comes between me and my Orange Chicken," the Hawaiian said. "Most definitely not evil Russians."

The street spread out to their right, projecting into the water. Thirty or forty jetties then held roughly twenty anchorages and Hayden counted dozens of boats to either side with a larger vessel at the far end. Most of the paintwork was white, causing significant glare as it threw back the glower of the waning sun. They spent some time searching for a boat that matched the details Pearl had given them.

"Dark blue," Kinimaka said. "Far end. You can't miss it."

"Had to be the biggest," Collins said. "We are dealing with Russians after all."

It was an ocean-going yacht with a skylounge, several interior cabins and, most likely at least two staterooms. There was quite a bit of activity on deck, two or three men wearing tight T-shirts and stubble stalking around as if getting the boat ready to sail. When they bent down Hayden could clearly see the guns holstered in their belts.

"It's the *Imperator*," Kinimaka said.

"What?" Collins asked, still approaching.

"The name of the boat is *Imperator*. It's Latin, meaning 'to command.'"

"When the hell did you eat a dictionary?" Hayden asked. "Though it wouldn't surprise me."

"Never," Mano said. "It's from *Mad Max*."

Hayden kept her concentration. They were twenty feet from the boat now, the men aboard focused on their tasks. Collins led the way, with Silk a step behind. The sun to the west was settling across the horizon in a bloated haze of red and gold, gilding roads, high-rise office buildings, beaches and boats so that they resembled painted ingots. The rescue team almost reached the boat before they were seen.

"Hey." A man stretched from his task, seeing them approach. "You shouldn't be here."

"Is this Dmitri's boat?" Hayden called out. Her question obtained them five more steps.

"*Nyet,* now fuck off."

"How about you fuck off, asshole," Collins drew her handgun and trained it on the man. The other two were also watching now. Hayden and the others covered them as they reached for weapons.

"Don't do it!" Collins yelled, seeing the first man going for his gun. "*Do not* do it!"

He hesitated. Collins climbed a short ladder to the deck and stepped aboard the gently rolling vessel. Hayden and the others followed, never letting the enemy out of their sights. The Russians didn't move.

"On your knees," Collins said.

Hayden was already scanning the rest of the boat. With no activity on the outside, she tried to peer in through the various windows, but saw nothing. Was Trent on this craft, being prepared to set sail? To leave the Californian shores never to be seen again? Or was he dead already?

Collins marched toward the first man, pulling cuffs from her belt. Silk and Radford got the other two, producing black zip ties. Hayden, watching the cornered men, saw their intentions before the thoughts had fully formed.

The first leapt up from a crouch at Agent Collins, smashing her in the chest and headlong across a fitted storage box. The second and third jumped at Silk and Radford with far worse results. The second struck Silk's elbow solidly with his throat, crushing his own windpipe, something Hayden couldn't ever remember seeing before. The third ran into Radford's bare knee with his groin, folding like a bad boxer. Hayden lined the first man's skull up in the sights of her Glock.

"Stop!"

But he didn't, and tugged a gun from his belt. Collins was still rising, blood streaming from her skull. Hayden opened fire before the Russian, felling him. She'd already spied an open door and ran for it.

Silk and Radford ran for a second. Kinimaka backed up Hayden. Collins pulled herself to her feet, placing a hand to her head to staunch the flow of blood, grimacing in pain as she followed the big Hawaiian.

Speed was everything now. Hayden entered a darkened lounge area, saw steps leading downward. A bald man was rushing up. When his eyes met hers, he brought his gun up but Hayden was prepared and shot him through his shining pate. He fell backward in a gout of blood that smeared the walls to left and right. Careful to watch her footing, she raced down to the lower deck.

When she set foot on the floor, Silk and Radford were ahead, coming from the front. Silk shook his head to indicate they'd encountered no enemies. Hayden turned left to find herself in a narrow corridor that traversed the remainder of the ship.

Together, they started along it.

A figure stepped briefly out from a doorway ahead, firing. The bullet ricocheted above Hayden's skull; the shot badly aimed in haste before he disappeared again. This time, Hayden and the others crouched, waiting for him to return. Instead, a second Russian slid out from another doorway, semi-auto rifle loosing several bullets that rattled into the woodwork before Silk shot him through the chest.

"Keep moving," Collins said.

Hayden was already advancing along the narrow corridor. The man who'd fired first, emerged just as she reached his doorway. She threw out a hand, grabbed the wrist that held the gun, and forced it down just as he opened fire. The bullet slammed into the deck. Hayden wrenched down on the wrist, pulling the guy out into the corridor.

Kinimaka shot him through the head.

Further along, they passed two small bedrooms. Both were empty. The staterooms were at the far end of the corridor. Hayden carefully approached the first with Kinimaka a step behind.

She paused at the doorframe. Ahead, part of the interior of the second stateroom was visible through a half-open door. Nothing moved. A set of wooden stairs then ran back up to the deck. Hayden paused for two seconds before stepping past the doorway of the first stateroom, peering inside as she went.

A gunshot rang out, plowing through the air she'd just vacated. She spun, crouched and nodded at the others.

Trent was inside; lying face down on a bed with his hands cuffed behind his back. A Russian heavy stood at each side of the bed and another man—dressed in a suit—was standing in a far corner. All three held weapons. Hayden had only managed to see two handguns but didn't have to guess for long what the third man held.

Automatic gunfire ripped through the wall, splintering timber just above her head. Hayden ducked, jabbed by shards. Everyone dived to the floor. The stream of bullets didn't let up. Hayden kept her head down, wincing, showered by splinters, the bullets passing through both corridor walls and slamming into the side of the boat.

Even prone on the ground, Kinimaka was still the tallest of them. A bullet seared just above his skull, making him cringe. It was Silk, once a soldier, who scrambled forward, rolled into the doorway on his stomach, and returned fire.

There was a deep, guttural yell. The automatic fire stopped. Silk rose to a crouch. Hayden leaned into the doorway's gap too, lending support. The first Russian was down. The second, standing on the left side of the bed, was aiming his gun at Silk. The third guy hadn't moved.

"Back off," the second man cried out. "You back off or I shoot."

Silk calmly advanced into the room. The others followed, guns aimed and unwavering, spreading out along the interior wall. Hayden couldn't see Trent's face or how much damage had been done to him, but he was moving.

Thank God.

"Guns down," Collins said. "FBI."

"You're not FBI," the suited man in the corner sneered.

Hayden studied him, noting a slick, tanned, well-dressed individual with a composed air of confidence. Could this be Schiller, working for his Russian bosses? Or someone else?

"I'm reaching for my badge." Collins' left hand inched toward her belt.

"I don't care about your badge," the well-presented man said. "I have three. You killed my men and will pay for that."

His accent was American. Hayden opened her mouth to ask a question when he waved at the last standing Russian on the other side of the room. "Karl, kill them."

To his credit, Karl gawped back at his boss as if to say: *All five, really?* But then brute intellect must have set in for he whipped his gun up to fire.

Kinimaka shot him through the center of the forehead.

"Great move," Collins said sarcastically. "Now. Do you wanna shoot us too?"

"You're Schiller aren't you?" Hayden took a gamble. "Who do you work for?"

Collins either didn't understand that Hayden was trying to catch Schiller's attention and put him off guard, or was far more interested in Trent's welfare. That was what happened when your team hadn't had time to gel or, rather, when your team broke up.

"Trent," Collins yelled over Schiller's reply. "Are you hurt?"

The figure grunted and tried to roll, not an easy task with your hands tied behind your back. Hayden heard Schiller say: "Madame Davic," just as Trent finally turned onto his back to face them. His face was covered in blood. The sheets were soaked in blood. His shirt had been torn open, grooves carved across his chest. Everything bled.

"You *fucker*." Collins ran around the side of the bed, putting her gun down on the sheets and reaching for Trent. Silk and Radford had murderous looks that made Hayden uneasy.

"I'd lower your gun if I were you," she told Schiller.

"Why? Madame Davic is evil incarnate. She will literally see me eaten alive for this failure. I may as well take my chances."

"You have no chance," Kinimaka said equably.

"You're wrong," Schiller replied, his voice soft.

The boat gave a great rumble as its engines started and then a sharp lurch as it maneuvered away from the jetty. Hayden staggered. Everyone was thrown off balance except Schiller.

He'd been expecting it. As the boat powered forward into the channel, he held his ground, aimed his weapon, and fired.

CHAPTER EIGHTEEN

Three shots. The first hit Silk square in the chest, making him fold. The second glanced past Silk's falling shoulder, drawing blood. The third smashed into Radford, spinning him in place.

Hayden reached out to steady herself, instinctively going to ground. As Schiller switched targets, a radio squawked.

"The ship is just five minutes out! Five minutes! Get yourself safe, sir!"

Several thoughts ran through Hayden's mind in a blur. They were transporting Trent to a bigger vessel, probably well-manned. Probably belonging to this mysterious Madame Davic. Probably Russian. And they didn't have long to take action.

But Silk? Radford?

Hayden locked the questions away. Schiller darted forward. He fired at Kinimaka, narrowly missing. Collins was standing over Trent, trying to protect the bloodied man. Hayden rose as Schiller sighted on Collins, and threw herself at the Texan gunrunner.

She hit him at chest-height, sending him staggering against the side of the boat. Schiller struck and then fell to his knees, the gun flying away. Hayden already had her weapon aimed at his head and was fully committed.

The bullet turned the left side of his face into pulp.

She whirled. Kinimaka was rushing toward the door.

"I'll stop the boat," he rumbled.

Hayden didn't doubt it. As Collins turned back to Trent, she ran to both Silk and Radford.

The latter had taken a bullet to the shoulder, and gripped the wound with a grimace. But even in his pain, he was reaching for Silk, riddled with worry for his friend of many decades.

Silk lay on his back, unmoving. His eyes, open, stared at the ceiling. Hayden gritted her teeth and bent over him. There was no blood.

Silk's eyes flickered toward her. "Ow," he said.

Hayden's body flushed with relief. Reaching out gingerly, she touched Silk's chest, feeling the hoped-for body armor.

"So happy," she murmured, placing a hand to his cheek. "Thank you for living."

Silk nodded, gasping: "Trent?"

"He's hurt, but he'll live," Collins said from the bed. "He'll recover."

"Just . . . wait . . ." Hayden said, realizing something. "You three have body armor, right? Where the hell's ours?"

"Only . . . had . . . three . . . jackets," Silk gasped and grinned.

Hayden shook her head in wry amusement as she rose and headed out the door. Kinimaka might need backup. The boat hadn't slowed. She raced along the corridor and up the stairs, coming out once more into the deep ceramic-blue dusk brushing away the daylight one stroke at a time.

The main cabin was at her back. She turned a corner to see the big Hawaiian throw a much smaller man through the glass window that wrapped around it. The guy landed badly, breaking his neck. Hayden whirled to look for the larger ship she expected to see on the horizon.

There it was. Just a mile or so distant. Golden lights twinkled all along its sides and deck, belying the danger lurking within. Hayden couldn't squint hard enough to make out the name so pulled out her phone, snapped a photo and zoomed in: *Freya*.

Wasn't Freya something to do with old Norse mythology?

Hayden suppressed a shiver, feeling that the bruised, hanging drapery of the night skies might be offering some menacing portent to the future. She hoped not. She was done with Odin and his goddamn bones and wanted nothing to do with someone called Madame Davic. She heaved a sigh of relief when their boat shifted course, heading back to Los Angeles.

Kinimaka called through the broken window: "Is Trent okay?"

Hayden kept her eyes on the enormous ship they had narrowly missed joining and answered: "Yeah, he will be. He got lucky."

"His face didn't look lucky."

"Nah, well, it could have been far worse," Hayden's attention was still mostly focused on Madame Davic's ship. "Far, far worse . . ."

CHAPTER NINETEEN

Alicia was past caring.

During their last night out, Cam had saved her from the promising attentions of the soldier named Jericho, not the kid's best move. But Alicia understood where he was coming from. Yes, their team had broken up. Yes, Drake had gone his own way; but the future still held potential. A night with Jericho—however satisfying—might have scuppered all that.

Alicia had spent a few days in reflection, hating it. She considered what might come next. After all, they couldn't haunt the bars and streets of the French Quarter or other fun parts of New Orleans forever. Shaw seemed happy to pause her life for a while and so did Cam. Why then did Alicia feel the need to derail hers?

Old issues. Past battles. Ancient wars. *That's why.* She'd been scrambling to victory her entire life; in fact, she thought, that sentence *defined* her life.

Scrambling to victory. Always late.

The night was young, pretty and held a southern kind of promise. Alicia met it with open arms. She dragged Cam and Shaw along for the ride, warning them both against looking out for her virtue. Cam in particular argued against another bender, but Alicia was going anyway and the young man, she thought, came along mostly to keep an eye on her.

Ironic really . . .

Bourbon Street was alive, the music deep and captivating, the people more fascinating than anywhere she'd ever been. This was her kind of place. Here, there was no one judging her or trying to kill her. Here, she could be the full-on Alicia Myles.

"Drink," she told the bartender, slamming her shot glass on the bar. "Make it stiff."

The guy threw her a glance. She held his eyes and grinned. When he overfilled her glass she nodded in appreciation, then grabbed her drink and walked away. Tonight, she wore tight pale-blue jeans, a black sweater that showed her midriff and nothing else. She wended her way back to Cam and Shaw and leaned across the small, round table they were oppressing with their elbows.

"To drinking the memories away," she said and downed half the glass in one gulp.

They didn't respond. Cam was staring into space. Shaw was trying to avoid the attentions of a muscle-bound thirty-something whose rippling abs made him look like he'd swallowed six copies of *War and Peace*.

Alicia explored the bar with a considered gaze. It was too hot. The DJ was louder than his music. It was time to move on. Once outside, they saw that the day was done, and darkness had arrived. A full moon held sway above, pure and picturesque against the gloomy backdrop.

Alicia headed for another bar. Halfway, she thought she saw Jericho and sharpened her gaze, but the unknown figure was lost in the crowd and never reappeared. Alicia nodded at the doorman who recognized her, and strode inside.

The atmosphere within grabbed her attention. Almost every bar on Bourbon Street brimmed with an aura of raucous delight. This one, normally one of her favorites, tonight held an underlying tension between its deep-rooted, timeworn walls; a restlessness.

They threaded their way to the bar, ordered drinks and looked around. Alicia saw nothing untoward. The place was packed, the music loud, the sweat-level high. The three corners she could see were shadowy, full of indistinct figures. She shrugged and turned to the others.

"Find a table. See you in a few."

She headed for the restroom, already feeling the alcohol buzz in her brain. When she came out, the narrow corridor was blocked by a large, unassuming stranger with a steady grin and deep, wistful eyes.

"Sorry," he said when she paused. "I'll try to get out of your way."

He squashed back against the wall. Alicia couldn't see a way to get past without making contact so didn't even try. She pressed her left arm into his body as she squeezed by, feeling everything from chest to groin.

"You'll do," she said, turned and grabbed a handful of T-shirt. She offered up her mouth, which he quickly covered with his own. Alicia kissed him deeply, ignoring someone's earnest plea to get past, preferring to lose herself in a few moments of pleasure. It meant nothing—a guy she didn't know and would never see again in a forgettable bar in a city she was unlikely to ever revisit.

Harmless. Wasn't it?

Then Cam was at her side, pulling them apart, the young kid feeling protective and hurt. Probably thinking he was doing the right thing. And, oddly, this time it turned out that he was . . .

The quiet, unassuming guy turned vicious. He snarled, shoving Alicia against the back wall and turning on Cam. A fist lashed out, surprising the bare-knuckle boxer. Cam took the blow without flinching and stepped away, hands up in apology.

Alicia blinked, spine jarred from hard contact with the wall.

"Hey—" she started to say.

"*Fucker,*" the guy snarled at Cam in a southern accent. "You'll pay for that."

The sudden violence shocked Alicia. The guy unleashed like an Uzi, firing knuckles at Cam's head as fast as he could, grunting and growling and drooling spittle. Cam covered up, bowed by the blows. And, in that instant, up and down the corridor, Alicia saw men and women recognize the man and back up in fear.

What the hell is this?

They knew him. It stood to reason then that he was a local and so were they. Alicia snapped to. The guy was raining punches on Cam and enjoying it. Cam was backed into a corner, fists at the sides of his face for protection, body half-folded. Alicia saw fear on several watching faces as the man pressed his advantage.

The malevolent grin on his face was shocking.

"Hey." Alicia grabbed his shoulder. "He was only—"

The man whirled quickly and slammed a fist into her face. Alicia felt pain explode in her right cheek. Though she hadn't shown it, deep down she'd been relieved when Cam had stepped in. Now, she was elated.

She rolled her shoulders, preparing to fight, but Cam had taken advantage of the sudden distraction. He'd been waiting for it. As the guy turned to strike Alicia, Cam unleashed from the corner.

Clenched fists, hardened to fighting, smashed into the guy's eye socket and split the skin. Blood spattered the floor. Cam's left jabbed out fast, sending three draining strikes to his opponent's ribs and sternum.

The man's head dropped.

Cam came in like it was a title fight, punching high and low, concentrating on the face and then the ears and neck, the ribs too. The man, stunned and in agony, held up a hand to ward him off. Cam grabbed it at the wrist, twisted and broke it.

The sudden explosion of violence caught even Alicia off guard. It all happened in a matter of seconds, and it happened an instant after the guy attacked her.

Did Cam really take advantage of the moment, or is he fighting for me?

When the man fell to his knees, Cam maintained the assault. Bones broke. Blood rained down onto the floor, making a puddle. Alicia saw people she thought were locals backing up, real fear making their eyes go wide and shiny.

"Stop it," she told Cam. "He's had enough."

Her words penetrated, proving that Cam hadn't given in to anger; he was fighting well within his limits. The young man straightened up and stepped back, leaving the guy prone on the floor, breathing but unable to move.

Alicia started looking for a back way out.

She needn't have bothered. There was a flurry of movement at the door that led back into the bar; locals and tourists thrown aside. Alicia saw several heavyset, dark-skinned men approach, faces and bodies as hard as carbon.

Crap, that's not good.

She readied for a fight, signaling Cam, wondering briefly where Shaw might be. The men came quickly, elbowing people aside or throwing them to the floor. Their bulk blocked the corridor and the wall-lights, dimming the whole area. The leader locked eyes with Alicia and then studied Cam.

Without a word he reached down, grabbed the fallen

guy by the collar and hauled him upright, ignoring the yell of pain and protest. Another man squeezed by and helped support him. Then, dragging the man between them, they turned and marched back the way they'd come.

Cam raised his eyebrows at Alicia. "You okay?"

Alicia let out a long breath. "Dammit, Cam, we need to discuss boundaries. I thought we were gonna get pulped there."

"I was trying to save you."

She thought that an interesting choice of words. *Save,* not *help.* "From myself?" she asked. "Yeah, you probably did the right thing but I'm a big girl, Cam, and I can deal with my own mistakes."

Cam didn't look convinced. "They didn't look happy," he said, referring to the muscle that had dragged the fallen man away.

"My thoughts exactly. Let's grab Shaw and get lost before they come back. But Cam, listen—you're not my bodyguard. You're not with me to watch out for me. Understand?"

The young man lowered his head. "You saved me," he said. "Saved my life. I feel that I owe you a debt. An obligation. For the rest of my life."

"Are you fucking kidding me?"

"No." Cam looked deadly earnest.

Alicia gave in to a more pressing concern; they really should get the hell out of there. If the guy Cam had mushed-up was local, then so were his friends and other locals might help them. She didn't want another fight tonight.

Which struck her as a bit odd since she'd barely struck a blow . . .

It was Cam who was causing the disquiet. She grabbed

him and started back toward the bar, thinking that he'd really gotten under her skin. The last thing she wanted was someone watching out for her. There was nothing else in life quite like making your own major fuck ups and then owning them.

"You and me," she whispered as they walked. "You and me. We have to find a way to sort this out."

They burst back into the bar which, oddly, appeared a lot quieter than it had been when Alicia headed for the restroom. Heads and eyes turned to look at her. Alicia quelled an unsettling shiver.

Who exactly had they injured?

Shaw was seated where they'd left her, a content expression on her face, looking none the wiser. She did narrow her eyes a little when they came stalking up together.

"Whoa," she said. "Share a cubicle?"

"You wish." Alicia kept her eyes on the exit doors and signaled for them to move. "Don't hang about," she said. "Just go."

"Why? What—"

"I'm just being careful. But something happened back there . . . something we don't fully understand yet. And truth be told, I really don't want to."

Though cryptic, her words galvanized Shaw into action. Seconds later, they were out on the street.

Again, the night seemed quieter, the partygoers more subdued. Shadows held sway in the doorways and alleys, casting an arcane and impenetrable menace out onto the street in long, hungry fingers.

Alicia turned toward their hotel, having no desire to investigate them.

CHAPTER TWENTY

Marinette lived in the swamp.

She was a sensual being, lewd and beguiling, a mesmerizing princess who, legends declared, was over one hundred years old and hadn't aged a day over twenty-five. She was well-read, sophisticated and wiser than her years, whether it be a quarter century or a whole. She was dark-skinned and dark haired and black-eyed, a vision of dusky beauty holding the lives of hundreds in her vicious, revered hands.

In the dark, haunted hours of early morning, Marinette made her way from her bedchamber to her meeting hall. The dusty hallways were barely lit by flickering candles and chilly, but the cold didn't affect her. She wore a black silk robe and nothing else, slinking through the house like a deadly panther, confident that she controlled everything around her for many miles, mind focused on the forthcoming meeting. Her hair, unfettered, fell below her waist, luxurious and glossy-smooth. Marinette's big eyes were naturally wide, her nostrils flared, her lips full and dark. Wherever she walked, her staff gazed up from their knees in awe.

The meeting room was wide and vaulted, a large arena. Marinette took her seat atop a raised dais, three steps above the main floor. She crossed her legs and settled back into an oversized, plush throne, looking over the floor which had seating to either side of a wide aisle.

"What have you brought me?" Her voice was soft and musical, belying the nature of its owner.

"Roppolo, my queen," a man said, advancing up the central aisle.

Marinette stiffened slightly, narrowing her eyes. Roppolo was her primary bodyguard, chosen not only for his prowess in battle but for his unassuming, easy smile that often put her enemies off guard.

Marinette raised an arm, bringing the small procession to a halt. Usually, that arm would look alive, half-covered in bracelets and charms, but tonight it was bare. The only charm she wore hung around her throat: a tiny skull.

"Can Roppolo not approach his queen himself?"

Her guards, of which eight currently filled the aisle, all huge black men bearing guns, machetes, knives and the tattoos she had ordered carved into their bodies, stopped walking. Those supporting Roppolo let go. The man slumped to the floor, head-first, groaning when his forehead struck timber with a loud crack. Marinette watched the blood leaking from a deep gash.

"Speak," Marinette said evenly. Roppolo had served her well through the last half dozen years. She figured he should be allowed a chance to explain.

Roppolo looked up. She saw his blood-slick face, bruised eyes and broken teeth. She saw, by the way he held his right side and winced, that his ribs were broken. She saw an odd tilt to his mouth, which made her speculate that his jaw might have been dislocated. It was a fascinating, remarkable look.

"My . . . my queen," he said with difficulty and through obvious pain. "I . . . I . . . was waylaid. So many men I couldn't . . . count."

Even accounting for Roppolo's stunted speech, she

could tell he was lying. "You should know better than to feed me falsehoods," she snapped. "What happened?" Her eyes bored into the other guards.

"He got into a bar fight," the man who'd been carrying him—Lott—growled. "Started kissing this blond and then some kid started punching all da shit outta him. Proper laid him low."

Marinette blinked, still watching Roppolo. "Kid? Why do you use that description?"

"Kid." Lott shrugged. "Can't have been much past twenty."

Marinette tapped lacquered nails on the arm of her throne, the sound a death-knell countdown through an otherwise silent hall.

"My prime bodyguard," she said. "I have seen you crush six men, fighters all. I have seen you beat down all that stood before you. And yet . . . one *kid* does all this?" She gestured toward his body.

"Jumped me," Roppolo gasped. "From behind."

"Actually," Lott said, "he was beating the kid up when the kid decided to fight back."

Marinette raised a finger for silence. Her body felt unusually cold beneath the silk robe. Usually, the balance was right. Her world, and everything she ruled, was generally in order. The ceremonies streamlined. The rituals precise. The zombies fastened in their cages. Deep, debilitating fear was her weapon of choice, enforced if required by her army of terrifying aggressors.

Something told her the scales had shifted imperceptibly tonight. The only sound in the chill hall was Roppolo's blood, dripping unrelentingly into the puddle forming around his knees. Marinette knew the scales needed rebalancing.

There was a sour odor in the air. A persistent bite of frost that shouldn't exist. A fog stealing past the corner of her eyes. Marinette saw all the signs; and knew how to interpret them.

"Strip him," she said. "He will join those in the Wetlands and pay hard for his betrayal."

The words struck Roppolo like a machete to the brain. Striking up like a viper he started to scream: *"No, not that! Please not that!"* Blood flew in streams all around his protesting body. As Lott and other guards ran to restrain him, Roppolo held his hands out beseechingly to Marinette.

"My queen!"

"Maybe if you hadn't lied to me. Maybe. But this business has revealed a weakness in you, Roppolo. Revealed to me that you are a vessel suited only for possession. You will now serve me until you rot."

Despite his grievous injuries, Roppolo struck out and struggled and fought until the breath was kicked from his body and the rest of his teeth knocked from his mouth. He scrapped and clawed even as men planted their boots on his back. In the end, Lott held him as the other guards stripped him down.

"Stand him up," Marinette said when they were done.

Roppolo was hauled to his feet, clamped in place by two men whilst another looped a length of rope around his neck and held it tight from behind. Marinette uncoiled her body, rising with a graceful ease. The silk robe fell to mid-thigh, revealing long, supple legs as she started forward with a carnal, fluid flow of movement.

Naked, Roppolo faced her, eyes bulging with terror, face a slick mask of blood and pain. Liquid crimson still ran from his scalp, down the length of his back, dripping to the floor. Roppolo, her long-term, hard-as-nails bodyguard, was trembling in fear.

Reaching him, she leaned in close, her body brushing his. "Get complacent, did you?" she breathed in his ear. "Arrogant? Comfortable? We'll see how your ego holds up in the Zombie Fields."

Roppolo shrieked, a high keening sound. His captors held on grimly, gripping with every ounce of strength they could muster. The guard controlling the rope around his neck tugged it until Roppolo's air supply was cut off, but still the man fought.

Marinette laughed in his face, glancing up and down his body with disdain. "You are weak," she hissed. "A sack of flesh that is mine to control. The Wetlands will love you."

With blood clotting but still seeping from the head wound, and at the end of his strength, Roppolo sank to his knees. The rope stopped him at first, but then slackened, allowing him to fall. He stared up at Marinette, his eyes beseeching.

"Please, my queen. *Please*. The hallucinogen instead?"

Marinette laughed harshly. "The hallucinogen is for initiates. Newcomers. Recruits. Not for those that believe in the power of Voodoo, whose belief is strong in their culture. You do not believe that you will be the subject of psychosis and overwhelming psychological assault do you, Roppolo?"

Her bodyguard's face told her that he did not.

"Good." Marinette stepped back. Whisper-silent, another guard stepped up in Roppolo's blind spot and jabbed a syringe into the man's neck, expelling the black liquid in a matter of seconds. Marinette watched her ex-bodyguard's face crack hopelessly, his shoulders slump with resignation, his bladder empty in absolute terror.

"Is the hole dug deep?" she asked.

"Yes, my queen," Lott answered.

"The coffin ready?"

"As you ordered."

Marinette watched the vitality drain from Roppolo's eyes. As the last of it faded, she said: "Then bury him." His final look of horror sent an ecstatic shiver through her.

The rope was loosened, the guards now holding Roppolo only to support him. Carefully, they led him out the door. Marinette didn't need to follow to make sure they would throw him inside the casket, nail it shut and bury him alive in a hole in the ground. They had done it countless times before.

"And now it is too late to rest," she sighed before drawing her robe around her and stalking back to the throne. The odd chill persisted though, even with Roppolo consigned to his fate. She sought to dispel the worry by beckoning the remainder of her men forward.

"Tell me," she said simply. "Of my worshippers."

"Content," one man said, knowing never to meet her eyes. "Their dwellings suffice. The rituals consume them. The sacrifices excite them. They live for your presence, your touch, my queen."

"Expansion?" she asked.

"We are proceeding with caution," the same man answered, still studying a patch on the floor with interest. "Whilst disappearances here in the South are numerous and unsolved, too many would attract the wrong attention."

Marinette nodded, understanding. "Proceeding with caution is good," she said. "It instilled in me the wisdom of restraint. And my other businesses?"

"The Baron reports a new shipment, the biggest yet, in

the next two weeks. Mage needs more resources. And Cimetiére . . ." A pause. "Remains unruly."

Marinette repressed a twitch of amusement. Cimetiére was indeed a law unto himself, but never disrespectful. It was his way. And, when you took his job description into account, Marinette had decided a little margin for willfulness was not necessarily a bad thing.

Cimetiére harvested body parts for her from the fresh graves of the recent dead.

The Baron ran her gun running operation. Mage was in charge of her most dangerous and toughest enterprise— human trafficking. All three men deserved a certain flexibility to function well.

"Give them all they need," she said. "What of the Wetlands?"

A graying, bare-chested, stooped man shuffled forward. "Your slaves wait inside their dwellings awaiting orders."

"The concoction governs them entirely?"

"The dosage is working. That and their unshakeable faith, their unspeakable 'death.'" He spoke the latter word whilst making speech marks in the air with his fingers. "We have the blend dead right."

If the last sentence had been designed to amuse her, it didn't. Marinette took her beliefs, her faith and her cultural expectations very seriously. She came from a long line of *caplata,* the female version of the *bokor* witch doctors.

"I've heard enough." She waved them away. "Leave me now."

It was only as they started to turn, to traipse toward their rooms, that a thought struck her. "Wait," she said. "Wait. Roppolo was bested by a youth, you say? A *kid?*"

Lott had recently returned through a side door, the grisly task of burying his ex-boss delegated to others, and spoke up. "Yes, my queen, a blond-haired kid with quick fists. Not at all daunted by violence."

"Blond, you say?" Marinette had few blond worshippers on her property. "And did he have companions?"

"A blond woman. That is all I saw. It was the woman he fought for."

"Interesting. I would like to meet these two blonds, Lott."

It wasn't a request. Lott nodded and backed off, exiting the same way he'd come. Marinette waved the rest of her court away.

Could it be that these blonds were the ones upsetting her steadfastness, her soul? Could they be the ones upsetting her spiritual weighing scales?

The chill lingered in the air. Marinette knew a restful warmth would never come unless she reset the balance.

CHAPTER TWENTY ONE

Alicia woke, snatched abruptly out of a deep sleep, staring up at a cracked and peeling ceiling.

What . . .?

A noise had woken her. Something scratching. Nails, knives or claws on the outside of her door. A quick leap to the right got her to the bedside table and she seized a knife without looking down. The see-through curtain flapped in the breeze admitted by the slightly cracked window but that didn't matter.

Only the sound of claws mattered.

There was a soft knock.

"Housekeeping?"

Alicia let out a loud, pent-up breath. What on earth had prompted her extreme reaction? A dream? Alicia couldn't remember anything but called out: "Not now," and sat down heavily on the edge of her bed.

Last night had been kind of surreal. The guy she'd chosen had proven to be an absolute maniac, and then Cam took him down without breaking a sweat. And who were the goons who dragged the guy away? Alicia didn't know but this morning, even more than last night, the entire business unsettled her.

More so because she was the direct cause of all the trouble.

No change there then. But what am I supposed to do? I can't wander the wilderness like fucking Matt Wolverine. I need interaction . . .

In more ways than one.

Shaking her head, she showered, dressed and made a decision to buy new clothes later that day. They'd all been wearing the same casual gear for entirely too long now. Even the Bourbon Street crowd would judge them. She sent a text to the others requesting a breakfast meet downstairs in ten. When she arrived, both Cam and Shaw were already seated with coffee and pastries laid out before them.

"Shit, am I too late?"

Cam slid his plate across. "Share mine."

"Cheers, boy. What did I miss?"

"Nothing," Cam said glumly.

Alicia looked from the kid to Shaw. "I know what you're thinking," she said.

"I'm happy hanging with you," Shaw said. "I want to learn. But this place isn't where we should be."

"You wanna move on?"

"I want to move on—*mentally. Spiritually. Tangibly.* And, as a soldier. I want my chosen mentor to pick herself up off the floor and grow a set, as she might say."

Alicia came close to choking on a pastry. In a way, she'd been expecting something like that. Not those words exactly, but similar, more reserved. The fact that Shaw spoke so directly showed how frustrated she was.

"We leave tomorrow," she said. "Take the day to get sorted, pack, buy clothes and decide on a destination."

A hopeful light came into Shaw's face and, Alicia noted, Cam's too. She understood then that she'd been repressing these two, inhibiting them by insisting they remained locked in party central. She drank a gallon of coffee, polished off three pastries, then rose to her feet.

"Catch you back here this afternoon," she said.

Turning away, her eyes drifted over two men loitering at the far side of the room. They captured her attention for several reasons. They both stood severely upright in the exact same pose. Patrons of the hotel and serving staff gave them a wide birth, not interfering with or attempting to engage them in conversation. Waiters and waitresses shied away from them as she watched, and kept their gazes averted. And, predominantly, both sets of eyes were locked on Alicia and her companions.

Unwavering.

Alicia tried the "turn away and quickly re-engage" trick, but it had no effect. She pretended to dally, giving it twenty seconds, and then looked over again, but still they watched. It was unnerving and reminded her of her odd, rude awakening that morning. When she sat back down, she felt their eyes boring into her back.

"Watch yourselves today," she said quietly. "That guy last night—he had friends. He was local. Don't wander or stray off the well-traveled track. And stay in touch."

Without explaining herself she left her friends, returned to her room, and followed her own advice, grabbing a burner cell, a knife and other supplies. You couldn't be too careful no matter what you did for a living. Complacency got you killed faster than a sand spider's snapping kiss. She locked the door behind her and ventured out into the day, enjoying the natural warmth and sunlight on her face.

Hours passed. Alicia didn't do much, just enjoyed wandering alone without responsibility. One shop blended into another and when the crowd started to oppress her, she left them to it, seeking out quieter corners.

Even as she left the crowd behind, she saw two tall black men following her progress from a shop doorway. Taking a longer look, she studied the unwavering, unblinking stare of the men and the way that when the passing crowd was comprised of locals, it veered sharply wide of them.

Alicia left Bourbon Street, wandering aimlessly. The shopfronts became less gaudy, the neighborhood a little more run down. She used a couple of tricks to find out if anyone was following her but needn't have bothered. Two more men were openly tracking her from the other side of the street. Alicia saw more than one set of shutters rolled down in their wake.

She called Shaw. "Hey, you seen any suspicious activity today?"

"I have," the native American answered. "Cam's shopping for swim shorts. I'd say that's as shady as it gets."

Ordinarily, Alicia would have agreed and cracked a banana-hammock joke, but this wasn't the time. "I'm serious. I got at least four guys watching me. There's no threat, but . . . just watch yourselves okay?"

Shaw agreed and ended the call. Alicia found a park and sat down to eat a snack. She chose a position from where she could monitor all directions and had access to various escape routes. Her fears began to feel unfounded when nobody spied on her.

At least no one she could see.

As she ate, a prickly feeling rose at the nape of her neck. Turning around, she re-checked her surroundings, spotting no evidence of surveillance.

But I am being watched, she thought.

Uncomfortable, she finished her lunch and walked away. It was only when she skirted the children's play area that she noted the expressions of the mothers and older kids standing there watching her: A mix of fear and pity charged their unwelcoming expressions. Alicia stared at them open-mouthed, never having felt so deeply spooked before.

What is going on?

Without looking around, she left the park and returned to Bourbon. The sun broke clear of the clouds, blazing its undiluted heat straight down on her, but she barely felt it. For the last month or so, New Orleans had felt like a place of happy refuge. Today, there was a sense of menace in the air like death, torture and dark promise all rolled into one.

When she arrived at her hotel the sun was waning. It felt premature to her, as if some unseen presence was advancing the onset of night. Wanting it. *Needing* it, to conceal the nature of its impending, savage performance.

Alicia found Cam and Shaw in the lobby. On seeing them she took a deep breath. "All good?" she asked, forgoing a wealth of questions.

"We saw those guys," Cam said quickly. "Keeping tabs on us. I didn't like the look of them. Reminded me of men who've spent too much time in the ring. Punch drunk."

For Alicia it was something different, but she couldn't quite put her finger on it. "We leave at first light," she said. "Until then, stay on guard."

"You think we should all share a room?" Shaw asked.

Alicia cocked her head, the feisty light returning to her eyes for a second. "See the last night out with a bang?"

"No, no, I meant for security." Shaw colored up just a little.

"I know what you meant. Let's just see how the next few hours pan out. We still good for that restaurant?"

"Yeah, it's quiet," Cam said. "Should be able to spot a tail."

"I don't think that's the problem," Alicia said as they prepared to depart, wishing with all her heart that they'd left yesterday and that the rising sense of foreboding she was feeling was purely down to the odd day she'd had.

But something wasn't right.

In fact, it was deeply, profoundly *wrong*.

CHAPTER TWENTY TWO

Their last meal, although excellent, flavorsome, juicy and large, grew increasingly inconsequential for Alicia.

She couldn't stop watching the entrances, the bar, the back door to the kitchen, the people all around her. Pitch black pressed against the windows, the street outside quite dark, and it might have been comprised of a million tiny eyes for all she knew. They were seated in a corner, with their backs to the wall, their eyes well and truly on a swivel.

"Maybe we go tonight," Cam said as they waited for their mains.

Alicia drank water, the change from alcohol as much a signal of her uneasiness as anything. "Can't," she said. "Already looked into it. The last bus, and train, to Clearwater left an hour ago."

"We don't *have* to go to Florida next," Shaw said.

"I'm not one to go running with my tail between my legs," Alicia said. "We'll face tonight, and whatever it may bring, and leave on our own terms tomorrow."

It was engrained in her nature. She didn't know how to back down or run away. When the mains came, she didn't look at her steak. She studied the restaurant's other patrons, the serving staff and managers. She peered through at the murky street outside.

"We're on our own," Cam said after a while, chewing through a juicy steak. "I haven't seen a weirdo since late afternoon."

Alicia nodded, agreeing. Every table was filled, tourists and locals enjoying the fare. The rowdy sound of liquor-fueled conversation held sway in the room. She finished off her steak and sat back, emptying the water bottle. The watch on her wrist read: 21:47.

"Early night?" she said.

Cam and Shaw looked like they wanted dessert and eyed the menu hopefully. Alicia sighed. "Shit," she said. "Now I know what it's like to have kids."

Cam reached for the plastic-coated list of options. Alicia tried to relax. There really was no danger inside the restaurant. As she sank in her seat, eyes going to the ceiling to seek calm for the first time that day, she sensed a change in the atmosphere around her. Some conversations stilled; others hushed.

The room became charged with tension.

Alicia glanced around. Nothing had changed, at least nothing physical. Then she noticed that the serving staff were absent, the chefs no longer cooking behind the far counter, the bartender missing.

As if by telepathy, 40 percent of the restaurant's customers rose hurriedly and left, leaving half-eaten meals and bottles of wine behind. Alicia tensed, putting a hand on her knife. She swung her knees out from under the table, ready to move.

A manager ushered out the remainder of the patrons, mostly tourists, citing a kitchen fire that, mysteriously, hadn't raised alarm bells or appeared to have any flames.

He didn't look over once at Alicia's table, but left by the front door.

"Umm, that's odd. We're alone," Cam said. "I think we should—"

"Get the hell out?" Alicia finished. "Yeah, me too."

Shaw was looking incredulously around the restaurant. "I don't believe what I just saw."

The abrupt silence was oppressive and dangerous. They were utterly alone, left with the food, drink and takings of the night. Alicia didn't know what kind of power made those things happen in a New Orleans tourist district and didn't want to wait around to find out.

She pushed away from the table. At that moment, the restaurant's front door opened. A large black man held it as a smaller, slinkier figure stepped through. Alicia, Cam and Shaw rose to their feet, still behind the table as dark figures also started to fill the back room, blocking their only other way out. They were silent, hulking shadows, standing unmoving like disturbing, ritualistic statues.

A woman approached them. Dark-skinned and black-eyed, she was a vision of dusky beauty. Pitch-black hair fell below her waist, swaying left and right in time to her sensual, steady gait. A floor-length, tight black skirt hid her legs, a red tunic barely covering a black bra revealed more than covered most of her upper body. Alicia found herself transfixed by a navel ring in the shape of a skull.

"I am Marinette." The woman sat down at the table next to them with a musical chime, the bracelets and charms she wore on both wrists striking together in tune. Even her voice was harmonic. "I am pleased to meet you."

Both Cam and Shaw stared. Alicia noted alert guards at the front door now as well as those not-so-animated ones in the back.

"Is there a problem, Marinette?" she asked evenly.

"No problem," she said. "I wanted to meet the man who obliterated the best bodyguard I've ever had."

Obliterated? Alicia thought. *Odd choice of word.*

"Sorry about that," Cam spoke up. "He was being disrespectful."

"Yes. Damballah is in my head," she answered. "And showed me."

Alicia didn't know what to say to that. "Is the apology enough?" she asked cagily.

"Roppolo is taken care of," Marinette said. "I assure you, he is very sorry for his actions. But that does leave me a bodyguard short."

Her subterranean stare fixed on Cam. The young fistfighter looked shocked at first but recovered quickly and shook his head. "Thanks," he said. "I think. But now, I'm moving on."

"Are you?" Marinette glanced over her right shoulder, toward the door, and then her left, toward the back room. "I have never been denied and I don't recall asking a question."

Alicia cocked her head. "You're fucking with the wrong bitches, baby."

Marinette looked momentarily confused and then sincerely interested. She gazed over Alicia, Cam and Shaw as if sizing up a new, rare delicacy.

"It has been a long time since somebody challenged me," she said softly. "I had forgotten the kick, the surge of decadence it offers. I think that I will enjoy this."

She made to leave. Cam coughed to catch her attention. "We don't want trouble," he clarified. "What is it that you do?"

The question was far more loaded than he intended. Alicia winced. Shaw bit her lip. Marinette took it with casual acceptance, offering no outward emotion. "I run several businesses in the Deep South," she said. "The bayou is mine. The Wetlands are mine. Ask around; but be aware that those that talk might get their tongues cut out, spit-roasted before their eyes and then fed to them. I will speak to you soon."

Alicia remained still, not wanting to provoke anything further. Seconds later, the restaurant was empty, first Marinette and then those silent statues in the back disappearing without a sound. Alicia went for the door.

"You see her?" Cam asked, approaching.

"Oh, yeah, I see her. I really wish I didn't though."

It was the strangest phenomenon. Marinette walked at the head of her entourage, guards a step behind, wending her way along the street outside. The entire crowd parted before her as if she was a giant snake flicking poison from her forked tongue. Once she passed, the crowd reformed as if nothing had happened. Alicia saw several locals cowering in shop doorways and fleeing down an alley.

"Let's get out of here," Cam said.

But Alicia wanted answers. Who the hell was this Marinette and how did she appear to hold so much power? They waited. As expected, the manager was first to return, a fearful expression on his blanched face.

Alicia had been waiting in a chair, her legs up on a table. When the man's frame came through the door she rose fast.

"I don't want any trouble." He turned to flee but Cam was waiting behind the door. With a kick he shoved it closed.

"Please..." The manager looked ready to cry.

"Hey." Alicia raised a hand. "I get that you're scared, I do. I have one question, that's all."

"I know," the manager almost whimpered. "She is *a bokor*. Powerful. She controls the mind. The body. Even the dead."

Alicia wasn't interested in the many superstitions Marinette had somehow managed to instill in the minds of the locals.

"My question . . ." she said pointedly, "is this: Exactly what businesses does she run?"

"Businesses?" The man blinked. "Her home is a no-go area, even for the police. There are legendary terrors. People that visit are never seen again. Except . . . except as . . ." He couldn't bring himself to complete the sentence and forged on: "Her power comes from the old gods—Damballah and Legba and Baron Samedi—and she is over a century old."

Now it was Alicia's turn to blink. "Damn, she's lookin' good for a hundred. I gotta get me some of that voodoo juice."

"Don't say that!" the manager hissed viciously, whipping his head at her like a striking snake. "Not *that*. Do not even say her name. She . . . hears . . . and she listens."

Alicia noted that Cam and Shaw were lapping it all up, their concentration rapt on the manager. She allowed herself a small inner smile, thinking on the gullibility of the young.

"What does she do?" the Englishwoman asked simply.

"Guns," the manager said, looking trapped. "Drugs. Prostitution. And people . . . she trades in people."

Alicia nodded. "Sounds like the same kind of parasite we used to eat for breakfast. Shame the team's not around."

"She has many men," the manager said. "And women. And other things. The swamp where she lives is riddled with danger. You cannot go there uninvited."

Alicia nodded. "Yeah, yeah, perfect cover, well established. I get it, I do. Now, can you tell us her location?"

At that the manager folded, falling to his knees and

holding his hands out beseechingly. When his eyes teared over, Alicia had enough.

"Oh, for fuck's sake," she said. "Leave him. Let's go."

Once outside, they took in the night air, breathing deeply. It had gotten tense in there for a few moments. Alicia had sensed something in Marinette, something wholly wrong and entirely corrupt. That sense didn't come from superstition or hearsay, it came from years of military experience.

"Are we staying?" Cam asked a little fearfully. Alicia was reminded that Cam was a Romanian gypsy and might harbor a few traditional myths of his own. Hadn't he once mentioned something about a *Carnival of Curiosities?*

"Don't worry," she said, indicating the detritus of their meal. "I still got garlic sauce and silver crockery. I got you covered."

"This isn't vampires—"

Alicia didn't have the heart to keep leading him deeper into a pit of embarrassment. Instead, she shook her head.

"Nah," she said. "We're outta here in the morning. Florida is calling."

Both Cam and Shaw looked relieved. Alicia walked with them back to the hotel, itching to place a call to Karin.

Twenty minutes later, she did.

CHAPTER TWENTY THREE

In the small hours of the morning, in some parts of the world, it is said the dead walk at night, drawing sustenance from people's sleeping nightmares and power from their waking fears. Alicia didn't shiver in the early hours, alone in her room, but she did keep the light on and double-lock the door.

And the curtains . . . flimsy as they were, she drew them to obliterate the persistent gap at their center.

"What do you think?" she said after thirty minutes on the phone with Karin.

"Do you know what time it is here?"

"Sorry, but this is important."

"Yeah, and so's my beauty sleep. I'm not getting any younger."

"Can you check into her, this Marinette?"

Karin acquiesced and promised to get back to Alicia early the next day. The Englishwoman signed off, thought about getting undressed, then decided that tonight might be a good night to sleep fully clothed. Maybe she was unnerved but she preferred to think of it as caution. It wasn't every day the voodoo queen of New Orleans threatened you.

She laid her head down on the bed, then rose to check the door once more and stare out the grim window. The streets were slicked with rain, wet and black and starkly lit by pools of lamplight. Dark figures ambled through her field of vision. It was clear to her that she, Cam and Shaw couldn't take Marinette on alone and yet . . . she couldn't seem to let it go.

Cam rolled restlessly on top of the sheets, fully clothed and wishing for the break of dawn to hurry the hell up. Despite New Orleans' vibrancy, traditions and whole nights of freewheeling fun, he was looking forward to quitting her at first light. Most of that anticipation was to get Alicia out of the way of temptation, a weighty desire he didn't fully understand.

When Rose was murdered you lost your only dependent. Was he now deflecting that lost responsibility onto Alicia?

It wasn't like she needed it. Or did she? Cam thought of Alicia as a highly capable, vastly experienced, lost soul. Despite everything she'd gained and overcome, she was still looking for something.

And the debt he owed her for saving his life could never be repaid.

Cam lay sleepless, thoughts drifting to younger, crueler days. A hard upbringing, endless days in the ring and bad treatment at the hands of his parents, brothers and sisters had all led to this. Were we all the sum of our past experiences? Did life offer junctions of hope that only those with hard-won knowledge might recognize and grasp?

He shrugged it away, wondering what adventures Florida might have to offer. Tonight was not the time to dwell in old memory. Hopefully, he'd never see his family, his home or even Romania ever again.

A gust of wind flailed past the window, rattling the

pane. It had been loose since Cam rented the room, but he'd never gotten around to getting it fixed. Now, he barely noticed it. He'd heard far worse noises piercing the night.

And on that subject, was that a rustle outside his door?

At first, he shrugged it off, linking it to his thoughts. But then the noise came again and, with it, this time a definite scratching.

Metal on metal.

Lock pick!

Cam knew the sound, he'd used them a hundred times before. He shot up in bed, twisting toward the door just as it flew inward, bouncing against its hinges. The first thing he saw was a tall black woman rushing in and then three more. All wore leather bottoms and lace shirts; all wore colorful decorative bracelets; all their necks dripped with charm necklaces. Cam faced them, heart pounding.

"I'm not—"

They didn't want to hear him talk. They rushed at him in an unnerving, synchronized assault, all four hitting at the same time. Cam, still kneeling on the bed, covered up. A fist struck his head, an elbow his left bicep, a foot his ribs, a knee his spine. They threw their weight on top of him, bearing him down. Worst of all, they didn't speak or grunt or laugh or shout. He couldn't even hear them breathe. But they came at him hard and viciously, hands targeting all his weak spots.

Cam pushed back, using the mattress's elasticity to gain space and heave upward. A woman fell away. The other three pressed in. Cam threw a punch, striking a midriff. The punch was soft, weakened by the lack of space. They forced themselves on top of him, staying close. Cam was finding it hard to breathe.

A hip crushed down on his face. A pair of knees weighed

on his ribcage as if trying to break it. An arm drove at the side of his neck so hard Cam thought he could hear bones creaking. As one, the women compressed him.

Cam kicked and punched, the bed's softness working against him. He couldn't gain traction, couldn't pivot for a telling hit. There was no sound, only the nightmare flitting of their unflinching, determined faces before his eyes. He smelled sweat and mold, old clothes and something fetid. He jabbed and writhed to no avail.

Then, an opening. A woman's head appeared directly before him. Instantly, he delivered a fight-winning headbutt, knocking her senseless. Blood flew. Her eyes slammed shut. Cam used every ounce of his strength to rise from the bed, the women still clinging to him. His movement shifted them. One lost her grip, another held fast only by gripping on to a handful of loose shirt.

Cam breathed fresh air again. The weight eased. He struck out hard, bruising an attacker's eye socket, bloodying another's nose. They barely flinched. They held on. The woman at his back jammed both knees into his spine, grabbed his hair and pushed hard. Cam cried out, and then wondered why he hadn't been shouting for help this entire time.

The women reacted severely as he opened his mouth to shout again. They jabbed at him, targeting neck and eyes, trying to wrap themselves around him once more. Cam gasped and ignored the pain, drawing a deep breath.

The woman lying before him, face dripping blood from where he'd butted her, opened her eyes. They fixed on his, her lips drawing back in a snarl. Her right hand shot out, closing around his balls like a vice. Pain rocketed through Cam like a missile as she twisted, a sickening surge traveling the length of his body. The other women jumped on top too, striking with hard blows.

Cam instinctively brought both hands down to his groin even as he knew he should be using them to target the woman causing him such intense pain. That left the rest of his body unprotected. Cam saw black spots dancing before his eyes.

"What . . . is . . . this?" he grunted.

They didn't answer, didn't emit any kind of noise. They were focused on their job like nothing he'd ever seen before. When he saw past the bloodstained woman in front of him, he saw four more of them standing in the doorway.

Didn't even use all their number.

That was cold. Cam couldn't dislodge the woman at his groin. The one at his back climbed on top of him, spreading her legs across his neck and bearing down on his face. Cam's eyes, mouth and nostrils were filled with the sight and smell of black leather. He couldn't breathe, couldn't move. Waves of agony swept from his toes to his scalp. On the edge of consciousness, he clenched his fists once more.

Ignore the pain.

It was what he'd been told since the day he could make a fist. That was his father's voice, closely followed by his father's knuckles. Cam held on to that memory and fought; bucking and striking out and kicking his legs to free up some space.

The women were weakening, not holding as tight as they once had. Two slipped away, gasping heavily. Cam saw light. It galvanized him. Knowing his strength was ebbing he threw everything into one last, mighty heave.

And dislodged them all. Finally, he was free. A few seconds passed where he drank in air and allowed his muscles to regain some strength. And then he clenched his fists.

Cam struck out.

But four more women arrived, all holding syringes full of a suspect black liquid.

They fell on him, jabbing needles in his flesh. Cam felt one break off in his skin, another glanced off, drawing blood. But two more pierced him, injecting their unknown venom.

Cam didn't see what happened next.

CHAPTER TWENTY FOUR

Alicia woke suddenly, snatched from an unspeakable dream.

She sat upright, on the edge of her bed, glancing from side to side. Nothing was different to how she'd left it last night. Her backpack still rested on the door handle by a strap for extra security. Her curtains were still fully drawn. She checked the time and found it to be *07:01*. They had plenty of time to catch the train.

She showered quickly and dressed in long-journey clothes: loose leggings and a well-used T-shirt, then grabbed her leather jacket. She brushed her hair with her fingers before heading down to the restaurant.

Shaw was seated at a far table, alone.

"The boy still asleep?" Alicia asked.

"Not his keeper," Shaw said. "Or his lover."

Alicia signaled for coffee and pulled out a chair, scraping its wooden legs across the polished floor. "Sleep like crap, did we?"

"I guess," Shaw admitted. "Couldn't switch off."

"You and me both." Alicia nodded as a young waiter topped up her coffee mug. "I'll be glad to see the back of this place today."

"I thought I saw that look in your eyes last night," Shaw said, leaning forward.

"What look?"

"That something was gnawing at you. Something you couldn't let go of."

"I'm only like that with men," Alicia admitted. "And I'm ready and waiting to go to Florida."

They ate in silence, constantly flicking glances toward the far bank of elevators where Cam usually appeared. By the time they were finished Alicia felt the slightest tinge of worry.

"You think he overslept?" Shaw asked.

"Never happened before," Alicia said. "Maybe he's enjoying some *special* time with his one-eyed wonder weasel."

Shaw pulled a face. "Now there's an image I don't want to think about."

Alicia pushed her plate away, drained her mug and rose. She left the restaurant quickly and headed for the bank of elevators, punching the number for Cam's floor. Shaw was with her. They rode up in silence and made their way to Cam's room.

Alicia saw the door handle first, and scratches around the keyhole. She'd thought it quaint that this old hotel still used door keys when they arrived. Now, not so much. But then—any intruder could bribe a member of staff to duplicate a swipe card too.

When Alicia looked closer, moving in front of the door, she saw that it was slightly ajar.

Fighting the surge of dread, she dashed inside. The room was a mess, bedsheets and mattress in disarray, tilted off the edge of the bed. Alicia's eyes were drawn to the splashes of crimson decorating the sheets.

"Shit, shit, *shit*."

She ran in while Shaw checked the bathroom. The blood wasn't fully dry. Alicia guessed something had happened to Cam in the middle of the night. They searched the room quickly, finding little else of note.

"Boots are still here," Shaw reported. "Suitcase. Clothes. Toiletries."

Alicia stared at the mess. "I'm liking that bitch, Marinette, for this."

"Could be anyone," Shaw said. "Random attack maybe?"

"Cam would've pulverized them," Alicia said. "Only Marinette would know to send the right kind of attackers."

"Which are?"

"Big motherfuckers and lots of 'em. And Marinette told us to our bloody faces that she wanted Cam."

Alicia rebuked herself for not acting sooner. They could have left yesterday. Last night. Could have changed their plans.

Shaw saw it in her face. "Don't blame yourself," she said. "None of us saw this coming."

"But we were being *followed,*" Alicia said angrily. "For a day. And then that bitch—" She bit her lip, knowing that anger and criticism would get her nowhere. After a moment's thought she yanked the mattress back onto the bed and shook the sheets.

Something bright flew out.

Alicia watched it settle then picked it up off the carpet. "This," she said, holding it up, "is a charm bracelet and not one of your touristy knock-offs. I saw Marinette wearing something similar. Don't you see? It proves my theory."

Shaw nodded. "We need help," she said.

Alicia agreed and once, where she might have called the team together, she now whipped her cell out of her pocket and dialed a single number.

"Karin," she said. "We got some serious trouble here."

"Bloody bollocks," Karin exclaimed. "Can't *any* of you guys stay out of trouble?"

Alicia would have loved to explore that comment but

didn't have time. No, *Cam* didn't have time. After taking Cam's key off the nightstand and locking the door, she talked to Karin while they headed back to their own rooms.

"And this Marinette, she's got everyone thinking she's some kind of witch doctor. Surrounds herself with voodoo bullshit. I'll admit she's got some real weird dudes on her payroll but they're all part of the number she's doing on this city. I *knew* she needed taking down just yesterday. If the team had still been together, we'd have done it. If the team . . ." Alicia tailed off, burdened by sorrow and finding herself in the previously unheard-of position of not knowing what to say next.

Karin stepped in. "I can get right on this. Missing persons, ex-military . . . kind of. I can say one of my sources brought it to me which is, basically, true. Give me an hour."

Alicia and Shaw used the time to pack their belongings in preparation for a move. They couldn't stay in a compromised place. Alicia kept her weapons handy before meeting Shaw down in the lobby.

After checking out they spent forty minutes walking, making sure they weren't being followed. Alicia saw nothing like the activity she'd spotted the previous day.

Just before the hour was up, they ducked into a back-street hotel, paid cash and ascended three floors to their rooms.

Karin rang back after fifty-nine minutes. Alicia had been keeping track. She answered the call sitting on her new bed with Shaw at her side. "Hey."

"I hope you're sitting down for this. Marinette—one word—is a suspected gunrunner, people trafficker and enforcer based in Louisiana. She's a drug baron too, and her bad reputation stops even the *cartels* from messing with her. You seem to have gotten yourselves into some heavy shit, Miss Myles."

Alicia grunted. "How'd you know my bedroom name? Anyway, where's she live?"

"That's part of why she's considered untouchable. She lives in an area called Black Snake Swamp. Makes no bones about keeping undesirables out with force. When the cops want to speak to her, they ask to meet at a diner in town. There are a shitload of . . . stories, fables, legends about Marinette."

"Yeah, I can imagine. We met her, remember? You have a locational map. Coordinates?"

"It's a major no-go area, Alicia. You can't be serious—"

"The cops gonna help me? The feds? You know damn well, Karin, that if anyone gets in trouble the team go in. That's what we do."

"The swamp . . . it's dangerous. Remember Mordor? Full of orcs and death traps and spiders? Well . . ."

"You calling me a hobbit?"

"No, no. Marinette has that place locked down like Fort Knox. And she has an army like Camp Pendleton's. You won't get past her security."

Alicia answered without pause. "Then we die trying."

"I'm asking you to wait, that's all."

"Every moment . . ." Alicia sighed. "You know what I'm thinking. Every moment she has him—"

"I do know. but running in there half-assed isn't gonna help."

"I don't go anywhere half-assed. You should know that. It's full-ass or nothing. And my friend Cam deserves the full-ass . . . so to speak."

"Are we still talking about rescuing him?" Shaw looked confused.

"Oh, yeah, that shit's definitely happening. Ping me those coordinates across, Karin. I have a plan."

The sigh on the other end of the phone was highly expressive and indicative of Karin's earlier conjectures.

"Don't fight me," Alicia said. "Help me."

CHAPTER TWENTY FIVE

Alicia and Shaw searched the bars, seeking out one certain individual in the hope that he might help them find Cam.

At the first four they struck out. After that, they separated, Alicia taking establishments on the left, Shaw on the right. By the time they'd explored Bourbon, Toulouse and Dumaine—their main haunts—they were still coming up empty.

"What next?" Shaw asked.

"We go again," Alicia said.

But by mid-afternoon, as the sun blasted hazily through a sky diffused by volatile storm clouds that cast a heavy, turbulent atmosphere across the city, they had completed three circuits and were still no further forward.

"He might have already left the city," Shaw said. "Or he's a night owl."

Alicia knew she was right, but refused to give in. They were standing on the corner of Bourbon and Toulouse, a sign proclaiming *Old Opera House, Live Music*, hanging above them, the Tropical Isle to the right, the Sheraton French Quarter hotel at their backs, when a familiar face sauntered out of the crowd.

"Well, bollocks," Alicia said. "All that exploring, and he walks right up to our bloody noses."

Jericho nodded from across the street, recognizing them, then came over. They faced each other in the middle of the road, surrounded by buildings that slept by day and came alive at night. And luckily so, for the tired-looking daylight façades all around them were anything but inspirational.

"Afternoon," the soldier said.

"Wasn't sure you'd still be here," Alicia said. "Glad you are."

"Ship out in two days. Why, you want another kiss? Was it that good? Where's your bodyguard?"

His friendly, winning smile caught her off-guard again. "Well, I wouldn't say no to a quick—"

Shaw gave her a nudge. "We have bigger issues."

"Yeah, yeah. We do. Raincheck. Look, we're all soldiers here, at least we were." She didn't explain Shaw's history. The way she carried herself spoke for her training. "We're in the shit, mate. Can you lay your hands on any hardware?"

Jericho's grin faltered. "Is that a euph—"

"No, for once it's not a euphemism. I'm serious. Some bitch called Marinette abducted Cam and we're getting him back."

"Cam? The punch-thrower, Cam?"

"She's gonna hurt him, or worse."

Jericho's grin had vanished at the mention of Marinette. He regarded them both with earnest eyes.

"I know of her, of course. Everyone that frequents this part of town has heard of the voodoo witch lady in the death swamp. The good stories and the very bad." He shrugged. "I hear she has a snake as thick as my arm and possessed by her god, Damballah. And I've heard worse—"

"We don't need the stories," Alicia said. "Just the help." She didn't specify again.

Jericho's mouth twitched up into a small smile. "Sure," he said. "Sure, I can hook you up. I've been here long enough to know people. Reliable people. Of course, I wouldn't do this for just anybody."

"Kin," Alicia affirmed.

"Yeah, you served. That's a start. What else can you give me?"

"Well, if you're suggesting a gobble you're out of luck, pal."

Jericho looked confused. "Money," he said. "They'll want money."

"How fast can you work? Time is critical."

"I get that. Let me make a call and we'll go from there."

It turned out that Jericho could make it happen in less than an hour. Alicia nodded gratefully whilst Shaw made a withdrawal from a bank using the fake IDs they'd set up before leaving DC. When she returned to Alicia her face was grim.

"That left a sizeable hole in our balance," she muttered.

Ninety minutes later, Alicia possessed a two-year-old Glock with silencer and spare mags, an obsolete but still effective comms earbud, night-vision binoculars and a Kevlar jacket. Shaw acquired the same. Jericho then drove them to a well-traveled road bordering the outskirts of Marinette's property: The Black Snake Swamp.

"You won't encounter resistance for a while," he said. "She forced the original landowners to the swamp's edges and keeps them at bay. It was a clever move, because all anyone sees are genuine local landowners. Her domain is past the center and the lakes toward the Gulf of Mexico. You sure your GPS is good? You'll die hard and alone without it."

Alicia was confident in their geolocation software. It was one of the better things they'd managed to purloin from the Strike Force HQ.

"We're good." She nodded and reached for the door handle.

"See you on the other side," he said. "You got my number. Call me when you need me."

"*When?*" Alicia turned slightly.

"I got skills," he said, with that boyish, disarming grin.

"Tell you what," Alicia said. "I'll make a deal. If these weapons help save Cam's life, I'll call you and we'll see if you can do more than smile."

"You got it." Jericho sounded enthused. Alicia climbed out of the car and joined Shaw in the mid-afternoon heat. The two-lane blacktop vanished ahead around a long curve lined by lush trees, bordered by a steep bank. They waited for Jericho to leave before consulting their satnav systems.

"Due south." Shaw was studying a colorful display. "There should be a path, kind of."

Alicia nodded, made sure her backpack was secure and her gun close at hand. They crossed the road, skidded down the bank, and found a trail between trees. Alicia wiped the sweat away as a heavy, humid curtain of weather settled over them. High trees concealed the bright sun. Clouds acted like patches of murky night, dappling and disrupting their steady progress.

Alicia smelled fresh grass and decay, the scent of hard-baked earth and a lush fragrance cast by nameless flowers. The green canopy was regularly broken by green fields and narrow rivers where tiny islands of verdant green and cracked logs floated, their broken bodies resting places for birds, frogs and, occasionally, alligators.

Alicia eyed the first she saw warily from the bank, making sure she never broke eye contact. After that, she was constantly searching for signs of the wily, toothsome predator.

The pair didn't speak much. Surveillance was king, which kept them at a steady pace and between trees when a path would have been far easier. Any shacks or moored boats they found soon grew less frequent and the going became harder. Their GPS found paths through the bayou as it became denser and the watercourses more common.

The sun dipped, passing through darker cycles until it was a burnished glare on the horizon, spotted intermittently between foliage. They stopped and drank water and ate when Alicia noticed they'd been trekking for more than two hours.

"Just over thirty minutes to the coordinates," Shaw noted.

"Which, as Karin said, is the general *area* where Marinette lives," Alicia said. "Nobody knows the exact location."

Neither of them mentioned keeping an eye out for guards. It was a clear concern from here on in. When night fell, Alicia eyed the surrounding gloom with distaste.

"Shit, you'd have thought they'd plant streetlamps in here, or at least fix bells to those bloody gators. We're no less than a walking, talking buffet line . . ." She didn't finish, shivering.

Shaw kept it real, studying the GPS. "Track leads southeast now. We could do with some light."

Alicia broke the night-vision goggles out. "Go green."

"Yeah, thanks."

Further into the swamp, with impenetrable night all around them, Alicia could only think about Cam and what might be happening to him. Her chest was tight, her blood pumping hard. Every stumble, every dead-end, every anonymous sound, wound up her anxiety another notch.

An hour passed. They crouched under cover of thick

foliage, peering around one corner across an area of flatland ahead. Fully dark, it made for a mysterious plain, but the ghostly glow of the stars highlighted certain features.

"On the far side," Alicia said. "Pretty sure I can see buildings."

It was indistinct and unlit, but a vertical structure stood out in the bayou. She thought the plain might be dotted with odd trees, bushes, or low-slung dwellings. "That's odd," she mused.

"The pig shelters?"

Alicia squinted. "Is that what they are? Marinette keeps pigs?"

"Corrugated, round domes," Shaw whispered. "I guess they could house anything."

"Thanks," Alicia said wryly. "You ready?"

Both women drew their handguns and entered the dead of night.

CHAPTER TWENTY SIX

Alicia Myles was a world-class operative, an integral part of one of the best Special Forces teams that had ever kicked serious terrorist ass. Some of her past feats were legendary.

But she never saw the enemy coming.

Silent as corpses, they emerged, shrouded in shadow. They were pale and slow-moving but were upon Alicia and Shaw within seconds.

One moment, Alicia was gazing ahead, planning her advance, the next a body was pressing up against her right side. A high, keening sound slipped from her throat. She jerked away, seeing a tall, white figure dressed in rags. It stank too, reeked of filth and despair and festering decay. It came after her, but in a shambolic way, as if guided by sub-standard remote control. Alicia had time to stand, draw her gun and point.

"Get away from me."

Shaw shoved another to the ground, pointing her Glock in warning. Both weapons were silenced.

Then Alicia got a good look at her surroundings. The bushes were being pulled aside by multiple figures, the trees threaded by body after body, all deathly silent and focused on one thing.

"Look at their eyes," Shaw whispered.

Alicia couldn't look anywhere else. Wide and unblinking, every face identical, they approached their quarry with mindless folly, ignoring the weapons. Alicia clubbed the first across the face, breathing an enormous sigh of relief when he collapsed to his knees, bleeding.

"They're alive," she said.

"Duh," Shaw hit back.

They stood back to back, facing a growing number of combatants. Alicia was reluctant to open fire, but the sheer number of their enemies was overwhelming.

"Run," Alicia said.

"Run?"

"They're not too quick on their feet. We can easily outdistance them and, if they're on some kind of drug, they won't be calling home in a hurry. We still have a chance."

To her credit, Shaw set her jaw and nodded. Alicia batted her closest antagonist away and set off at a fast run, Shaw at her side. Their boots hit the loamy ground surely and they increased their pace.

Ahead, the dark plain extended. As they approached its edge, the shambling figures meandering after them, Alicia saw a row of large, crawling shapes, like human-size worms. They had stayed low, creeping across the plain ever so slowly, but now rose like white ghosts, reaching out for their victims. Alicia and Shaw slowed, taking stock.

"Fuck," the Englishwoman said.

"We got 'em in front and behind," Shaw said. "And we don't have enough bullets."

Not for them and Marinette, Alicia thought. "We can break through," she said. "Keep running."

They darted forward. It was clear now that these people lived out here, probably in the corrugated huts. Their clothes were covered in dripping, hanging filth; their faces too. They crawled on their knees or staggered drunkenly.

"This is crazy," Shaw breathed. "I've never seen anything like it."

"Yeah, closest thing I've seen is chucking out time on a Friday night."

As she spoke, Alicia's left foot struck a solid clod of earth. She fell headlong, scraping across the ground, hitting the oncoming figures like a bowling ball and scattering them left and right. Ropy grass and shale bit at her skin. Her ribs shouted in protest as they barreled into a man's lower leg.

She picked herself up quickly, but figures were already gathering around her. They reached out with desperate, hooked fingers, snatching hold of her hair, her jacket, her trousers. They pulled and jerked her, upsetting her balance. They'd already surrounded her, hands grasping from every direction.

Alicia fired a bullet into the ground.

Silenced, it still went off like a gunshot up close. Alicia expected someone to flinch and create a gap, but the noise only fell on deaf ears. Hands were everywhere, at her neck, her skull, her ribs and legs, even in the crack of her ass. She pivoted, elbow out, breaking a cheekbone, and then jabbed three times. Noses were broken, blood sprayed. She kicked a man in the chest. Still they crushed her, reaching, grasping, compacting her space. Their blood coated her. Their putrid breath washed her face.

Soon, she could no longer pivot.

Alicia struck out, then fired her Glock in desperation. Bullets thunked into bodies but made little difference that she could see or feel. Flesh pressed in from all sides, but they weren't hurting her, trying to disable her. Nobody was punching, kicking or nipping. It seemed they wanted to smother her into submission.

She caught a quick glimpse of Shaw battling ten feet to her left and saw the Native American on her knees, knife drawn, whipping the blade from side to side in a deadly semicircle to stave off her attackers. But even as she held them off, more piled in from behind.

Alicia pushed hard, summoning every ounce of aggression in her body. Two women fell at her feet. She used them to gain a little height by climbing on their backs. She threw two elbows downward, into upturned faces. They fell away to be replaced by two more. The women beneath her rose. Alicia used that movement to launch herself headlong, like a crowd-surfing rock star, arms out as she landed atop the crush of heads and shoulders.

They didn't know what to do. Still, they grasped, hands everywhere. They yanked at her clothing, ripping her leggings, her jacket and, as the clothing loosened, at her flesh. Three sets of nails scratched her stomach, at least one drawing blood. A filthy, ragged hand scraped at her face, grazing her cheek.

At the edge of the crowd, Alicia saw light.

Or rather, the absence of it. Just the long, flat plain, devoid of attackers all the way to the square structure in the distance. Even now, even amidst this nightmare, she was still focused on rescuing Cam.

"Break free!" she cried. "It's clear ahead."

Shaw's reply was muffled. Alicia somehow found a burst of momentum that carried her across the heads of the crowd and sent her tumbling at their backs. She rolled, coming up on one knee. Amazingly, she still held the empty Glock. The freaks at her back were staring stupidly at each other and up into the air, wondering where their prey might have vanished to.

Alicia didn't dare attract attention. Every inch of her still crawled from their dreadful, invasive touch. Just watching them right now; their mindless, crowded, random shuffling sent chills to her very core.

Zombies? The word was a fiction, the world it encapsulated a fiction. But . . . it was the perfect description.

What would make people act this way?

She was out of time. Shaw was crawling through legs and bodies to reach her. Three from her group had already spotted her. Alicia rose in the darkness, took a deep breath, and thought of Cam.

Coming for you, kid.

Shaw barged her way through a final pair of legs. Alicia threw a fist at their owner, knocking the guy sprawling. Shaw stood. Her attackers whirled, snarling.

Alicia sensed it was now or never. She hit the plain running, heels kicking up dirt. Men and women howled at her back, stunning the night with their vitriol. Alicia glanced back to check on Shaw . . .

A figure rose right in front of her; a large, slack-jawed black man.

Alicia shouted out in surprise, not only in shock but because she recognized this individual all too well.

Facing her, blocking her way, was Roppolo, the man she'd kissed outside the restroom, the catalyst to all this, the man Cam had beaten up.

Only this wasn't the Roppolo she remembered. His eyes were glazed, his face sagging. He was naked and covered from head to toe in thick dirt as if he'd been buried alive and only recently risen. His gait was that of a drunken man, both feet barely keeping him upright, knees folding back and forth. And when his mouth opened, she expected a defiant phrase, curse words, anything . . .

But all she heard was a keening, rasping, pained croak: *Help meeeee . . .*

Alicia screamed in his face, letting go of nervous adrenalin. From somewhere she could hear Shaw shouting for help but her mental acuities were entirely overwhelmed. This was a man she'd kissed, interacted with, just two days ago. She couldn't process the being that snarled and swayed before her.

"Are you—"

But then it was over. Her attention diverted, the pack had caught up. They swarmed over her, pushing her down and piling on top. They thrust her face in the mud. They sat on her back, her legs, crushing, smothering until Alicia saw black spots dancing before her closed eyes . . .

Then she saw no more.

CHAPTER TWENTY SEVEN

Hayden Jaye climbed off Mano Kinimaka, breathing heavily and sweating hard.

"Hey Mano, when I said: 'Take me for a ride,' I meant in the damn car."

"I thought you'd enjoy this more."

"Well, you got that right at least." Hayden rolled over and pulled the silken bedsheets up to her throat. The aircon, although welcome a minute ago was now starting to chill droplets of sweat on her body. "Was that our victory celebration?"

"Sure it was. We just saved Trent from the hands of some crazy Russian Madam *and* supported Silk and Radford, even ghosted as we are. We're fucking awesome."

"Disavowed is what we are," Hayden said, staring at the ceiling glumly. "Just like them."

"We'll bounce back," Kinimaka said with his usual optimism. "I got faith."

"Don't hit me with another proverb. And I can't see that happening without a change of president."

"First we should find out why he ghosted the Strike Force teams."

Hayden reached across the nightstand for a Styrofoam cup of coffee, which was now cold. "That could be our next project. It'd take finesse, guarded support, and constant vigilance but it's doable. Maybe Trent and the boys could help."

"I'm sure they would want to."

Hayden gulped the coffee, eyes straying toward the shower. She felt good, her mood more upbeat than when they'd left DC, her focus healthier. As she swung her legs out of bed to get moving, her cellphone rang.

"It's Karin," she told Mano, picking it up. "Yeah?" she answered, tapping the speaker icon.

"I don't want to alarm you, but—"

"Oh, that's a great start," Kinimaka said dryly.

"I can't get hold of Alicia or Shaw, and whilst that wouldn't normally bother me, there's some potentially dangerous background to this."

"That doesn't sound like Alicia at all," Hayden said with a fond smile.

Karin took several minutes to explain the context around Alicia's recent troubles.

Kinimaka cursed angrily when she'd finished. "She lost Cam and didn't tell us? What the hell? We could've helped."

"I think speed was key," Karin said. "Something's badly off with this Marinette and Alicia didn't want Cam exposed to it."

"So now *she's* exposed to it," Hayden said, "potentially. Listen, just send us everything you have. We'll get on the road right now and call you once we arrive in New Orleans."

Without chatter or hesitation, they both got up, dressed and packed. They left the hotel and grabbed a taxi to LAX. The first flight out would take almost four hours, but it was the best they could do. The plane was cramped and lifted off late. Hayden suffered every lost minute, worrying for Alicia, Cam and Shaw, wondering what might have happened to them. The faint hope that the trio might still contact Karin after a heavy night out on the town diminished rapidly the further they got into the flight.

Hayden reviewed an email from Karin that contained all the pertinent information. The first two hours of the flight were lost in catching up and passing the intelligence on to Mano. By the time the plane's wheels squealed as they touched down on a Louisianan blacktop runway, they were both up to speed.

A short taxi ride put them on Bourbon Street, at the heart of the chaos.

"We have the coordinates but don't know exactly what we're up against," Hayden said. "And neither did Alicia. She ran in half-cocked."

"I'm guessing she'd have something enjoyably interesting to say about that comment," Kinimaka said, squinting up into a cloudless azure sky.

"Let's hope she gets the chance. Come on, we gotta canvas this place."

Between them, they trawled New Orleans' popular tourist districts. They asked directly about Marinette, the gunrunning and people smuggling. They used old sources to find a weapons supply. They filled backpacks with useful items like smoke grenades and comms systems. Then they returned to the bars and fought for information.

But the mere mention of Marinette caused a dozen different reactions. From guarded fear to outright terror to utter speechlessness. From memory loss to obvious misdirection. Even Hayden's old CIA friends offered nothing clear cut. Marinette, it seemed, was a subject best left alone.

Three hours after they arrived, both Hayden and Kinimaka knew they were being watched.

It wasn't subtle. Men and women slouched close by, in

doorways and on car hoods, eyes tracking their every footstep. These individuals were given a wide berth by the locals. Hayden paused at the entrance to a bar, lowering her head so that nobody could read her lips.

"Are you thinking what I'm thinking, Mano?"

"I dunno. Did you enjoy *Night of the Living Dead*?"

"No, I mean regarding the chumps eyeing us up. We should grab one and make him talk."

"Candidate number one." The big Hawaiian nodded over her right shoulder.

Hayden turned to look. A white-haired, whip-thin woman with the body of a thirty-year-old and the face of a pensioner studied them from the head of a dark alley. "I'd feel better if it was a guy," Hayden said. "A big one, but I guess beggars can't be choosers. She'll do."

They started walking. True to form, the woman watched them openly, not bothering to shy away. Hayden wanted answers but didn't fancy accosting such a frail-looking stray. Her experiences had told her these souls were strong-armed or blackmailed into serving vile masters and mistresses rather than working for profit. It was only when she saw the woman's scrawny hand twitch toward her dress that she saw the outline of a machete hanging under it.

"Yeah, she's definitely a candidate." Hayden waited until she was level with the woman before lurching sideways, striking her at chest level. When she backpedaled into the darker shadows cast by the alley, Hayden and Kinimaka crowded in.

"Who do you work for?"

"Why are you watching us?"

"Get your hands away from that."

The last was directed when Hayden saw her right hand

drifting across the front of her dress toward the machete's outline. Kinimaka blocked the alley as Hayden pushed the woman against a wall.

"Just tell us who you work for and you go free."

When she spoke, her voice was a susurrating sizzle. "You cannot touch me. I am protected."

"Good," Hayden said. "Who protects you?"

"*Marinette!*" The name was uttered like a great revelation, a charm, a curse.

"Tell us more. Why are you watching us? What does she do?"

"You speak her name all around. You gain her attention."

"What, like *Beetlejuice?*"

A blank look greeted that one. Hayden pressed forward. "Who is this Marinette?" Trying to garner information on her dealings, her workforce, associates, bodyguards . . . anything that might help.

"The deadliest snake in the swamp," came a harsh, rustling answer. "The queen of New Orleans. The spirit that crawls in the black and lies with the king of the dead."

"Well, that's pretty clear then. And what do they do?"

"Debauchery. Disruption. Obscenity . . ."

"We're getting nowhere," Kinimaka whispered, "and I see others closing in."

Hayden shook the woman. "Talk to me about Marinette!"

She stared in amazement as the woman fell apart, crying helplessly, tears rolling down her face, her entire body trembling, convulsing, her legs practically folding beneath her. "I cannot, I cannot, I *cannot!*"

Hayden stepped back. The woman grabbed her legs, not in anger but in pure, unadulterated terror. *"Please!"*

Kinimaka nudged her in the back. Hayden needed no more convincing. Together, they jogged away from the head of the alley toward the far end, leaving the woman and her cohorts behind. When they emerged into the next street, Hayden slowed and turned, facing Kinimaka with an uneasy expression.

"What the hell has Alicia gone and gotten herself into now?"

"Whatever it is, it's as noxious as that friggin' swamp, and deadly."

"She has great timing."

"I wasn't meaning that we should hang around and get shaved ice. I'm ready to go save her ass."

"Judging by all the activity and agonizing around here, I don't think we should wait too long."

Kinimaka indicated his backpack, full of the gear they might need. "Ready and willing."

"You sound like Drake. I'm sure that's an old Dinorock reference of his."

"The Yorkshire boy rubs off on you. I wish he was here with us on this highway to hell."

"All right, Mano, that's enough."

"Actually, I'm serious." They used Google maps to locate a car rental depot and started toward it. "This whole day has felt like a long trek leading us down to the Devil's lair. I'm not looking forward to what we might find, but if we save Alicia and the others, it'll be worth it."

Hayden nodded, wishing they could call the cavalry. They couldn't wait, but they could let Karin know. Caution and habit made her check the roads and sidewalks in front and behind.

At least eight pairs of eyes were tracking them.

"This bitch has some serious juice," she said. "But then so do we."

CHAPTER TWENTY EIGHT

Under cover of darkness, they entered a vast and dangerous territory.

Hayden progressed carefully, following the GPS route they'd mapped out on the way here. Easy going at first, after an hour or so it grew more arduous, the foliage denser and full of pitfalls. The night air was cool, a playful breeze nipping at her extremities. A field of stars threw light across the landscape. Trees groaned and the marshes sucked, and what might have been an impressive panorama by daylight had now become a nightmarish, nocturnal vision.

"You good, Mano?" she asked as they followed a path that wound through tall trees.

"I'd prefer to be acquainting myself with a juicy Hard Rock steak to be fair."

Presently, they found another path that bordered a meandering, narrow river and followed its bends in the right general direction. They ate and drank water whilst they walked and kept the conversation to a minimum, both aware that Marinette wouldn't have survived out here for so long without employing some pretty serious protection. Still, all they needed to do was extract three people—an act they'd accomplished countless times in the past.

Were they being overconfident? Arrogant, even?

To that end, Hayden had asked Karin to contact Drake and the others earlier. If they couldn't reach Alicia tonight, they'd decided to retreat, reconnoiter and wait for backup. The plan was about as sound as they could make it in their situation and scouting the area tonight would save time tomorrow.

Then Drake called.

Hayden plucked the softly vibrating phone out of her pocket and stepped away from the path, bending her head to whisper. "Matt?"

"Ey up. What's all this bollocks about Alicia and voodoo? That girl's a fucking trouble magnet."

Hayden knew a little of Drake's adventures, and a lot of her own, during the last few weeks, but didn't mention it. "We're reccying the place right now."

"Shit, you're kidding. Just wait. I'll wang it right o'er."

Hayden frowned. "What?"

"I mean, I'll set off now to join you. But, crap, I'm a day away."

"We doubt that Alicia, Cam and Shaw have a day. There's some seriously weird and very bad shit at large down here, Matt."

"Did Alicia join the Mardi Gras?"

"As much as I would like to see that—no. We've passed on all the info to Karin. Get up to speed and meet us here tomorrow."

Drake signed off. Hayden remained in a crouch for a minute, studying the compressed tree cover around her. Were hooded eyes watching right now? Were silent, ice-cold feet tracking them?

Kinimaka rustled the brush at her side, making her jump. "You coming?"

"Yeah, just don't walk us into a friggin' tree."

The big Hawaiian looked hurt before nodding his acceptance. It was entirely possible. They stuck to the path as it wound away from the banks of the river, arrowing straight across a marshy field before threading through a sparse stand of trees and then another field as the moon waxed brightly above.

Mano Kinimaka abruptly froze in place, face blanketed in fear, hands clenched and body utterly rigid.

"I . . ." he whispered, voice strangled and disbelieving. "I . . ."

Hayden took two steps around his bulk and squinted across the field to see what had upset him so much. A terrible jolt of disgust assailed her body.

"Are those . . . oh, my God."

Four-foot-tall metal spikes had been driven into the ground, set in rows and ranks across the field. Fully pressed down on top of the spikes so that the points emerged were dozens and dozens of severed heads, in varying stages of decay. The fresher ones still had hair and eyes, or what was left of them after the crows had feasted, the older ones were just cracked, bleached skulls.

"*What is this?*" Hayden croaked.

"Burial field. Warning site." Kinimaka looked nauseous. "Catastrophic legacy."

Hayden noted that the path ran right through them. "They only prove that we're on the right track," she said. "Is this voodoo?"

"Not that I know of, but then I know very little."

There was a joke there, but Hayden's head was in entirely the wrong place. She checked the GPS for an alternative route but only came back to the path that led between the severed heads.

"Just go, Mano," she whispered.

They'd seen worse, just not presented as callously and openly on this level. Clearly, nobody unconnected with

Marinette ever visited this area and if they did . . . nothing ever came of it. A knowledge that set Hayden's nerves even more on edge.

Side-by-side, they traversed the grotesque field, eyes focused ahead.

At the other side, the track swept back in a long arc toward the river. They continued, checking the GPS and noting that they were approximately thirty minutes away from Karin's coordinates.

"Remember, stay low. Eyes only," Hayden whispered.

Kinimaka nodded, his big presence reassuring at her side. The narrow river flowed to their right, rippling along at a fair pace, and masking any sounds that they might make. The far bank was a world of twisted shadow, an immeasurable realm of secrecy, nightlife and ferocity.

"Do you hear something?" Mano asked.

Hayden stiffened, listening. The flowing river rushed past, eclipsing all other sounds. "Like what?"

"I dunno. A—"

They came out of the trees. Impossibly tall, elongated shadows, stick-thin giants of terror. They capered forward, dark shades under the glaring moon and stars, sweeping across the trees and silvery light cast across the river.

"Fucking hell. What are—" Kinimaka began but never finished.

From out of the darkness, narrow river boats emerged, long and pointed, brushing hard against the riverbank. Several men were seated in each one and now they leapt up brandishing machetes and crossbows and blood-stained knives. Even in her stunned fear, Hayden fought off a dreamlike sense of unreality. Could this really be happening? Her attention, consumed at first by the marching stick-shadows, switched to the new arrivals.

"Heads up, Mano."

She drew her Glock, lining up bare-chested men as they clambered out of their boats. They gathered at the top of the bank, chests moving up and down, eyes fixed unblinkingly on the interlopers.

Hayden brandished the gun. "Stand down."

From the corner of her eyes, the stick-figures grew larger. They lurched and staggered and swayed, shadows across the trees, pitching forward as if striking like snakes and then enlarging to impossible lengths. "What *are* those things?" Hayden whispered.

"Voodoo gods," Kinimaka said. "Maybe."

"Oh, that really helps."

Before she could focus on escaping their predicament, the new arrivals attacked. No words were passed, no signal seen; the group of twelve men just brandished their weapons and rushed forward. They were vocal, alert and single-minded.

"Kill them," Hayden heard. *"Take off their heads!"*

Without options, she used her gun, firing six quick shots into the oncoming crowd. Kinimaka did the same. Men fell, impeding their colleagues. Men sprawled. Blood sprayed and soaked into the ground. A machete swiped past Hayden's cheek, so close she felt a slice of wind in its wake. She fired again, shooting into the attacker's armpit. He shrieked, collapsing away. Another took his place, but then that man was roughly smashed forward by another coming up from behind. Hayden could do nothing to prevent the impact.

Both men barreled into her, pitching her backward.

Kinimaka battled under a horde of attackers. At least six had targeted him, swinging weapons that he avoided and then just leaping carelessly at his body. The big Hawaiian was an unshakeable boulder at first, bouncing them off, a steadfast rock before rough waves, but as more threw themselves at him he found it increasingly hard to maintain his balance. And those that fell wrapped their arms around his meaty legs, pulling.

He went down like a felled tree, toppling with his full weight on two men. Neither had time to yell out first or breathe much afterward. A man leapt knees-first onto Kinimaka's stomach, raised his machete, and swiped it down at his face.

Mano clapped his hands together, catching the blade between them just inches away from his nose. The barechested attacker pushed down with his full weight, snarling a curse, but Kinimaka twisted the machete and threw him aside. Three more snarling, spitting faces replaced the first.

Hayden put her hands under her as she crashed to the earth, pushed and rolled backward onto her feet. The acrobatic rotation gave her space, but it also gave her enemies room to mobilize and raise their various, steel-edged weapons.

Hayden swapped the mag in her Glock.

"Come on, fuckers," she grated.

Her hair hung like a muddy rag, coated in blood; her clothes were torn. Her face was a smudged, daubed mess. But everything inside, her, everything she was, wanted to get past these killers and find her friends. Because these killers, by just being here, represented the immense peril Alicia and the others were in.

Men rushed her. Hayden opened fire point blank. Gunshots slammed through the bayou. Blood, brains and broken faces filled her vision. She backpedaled. Only two men survived the bullets, and both reached her at the same time. Hayden swiveled, dropped the gun, and threw one man past her shoulder. The other struck her side on, slamming her to her knees.

And he was quick. By the time she realized she was kneeling fully upright, open to attack, his machete was cleaving the air toward her neck. It was a short swing, barely two feet, with no time to stop it. Hayden saw moonlight glinting off an incoming blade, blinked, and then realized she was about to die horribly.

The blade hit her hard, sending her heart into overdrive. Fully expecting to see the world spinning end over end as her head whirled away from her body and into the underbrush, she felt a dull pain in her chest and then realized only the blade's flat side had struck below her neck. Its wielder had lost his grip when Kinimaka blew the top of his skull into the surrounding shadows.

Hayden let out a long gasp and a look of gratitude. Mano was still beset, three attackers circling him. Hayden found her Glock, reloaded and turned to help, but those lost seconds had put her man between the gun and the enemy as he circled slowly.

Get out of the way . . .

Her attention reverted to the high wall of trees that bordered the far bank. The nightmarish stick figures were still there, marching from right to left, spidery legs extending, stretched arms and elongated fingers waving to and fro. Their heads were almost triangular, as black as the deepest trench, and had mouths filled with pointed teeth. Hayden tried to look away.

And then froze in horror, legs like jelly.

Because every stick figure stopped, turned and regarded her at the same time. Motion stopped. They stared. Hayden's mouth fell open. The attention she wanted to give Mano faltered. *What the hell were they doing? And how . . .*

Figures emerged from the far trees, seemingly *real* figures. She could see men and women with bare chests and wild masks, swaying to some unknown beat. A dozen of them, spread out, only they were impossibly tall, standing over twelve feet. They held weapons too, mostly blades but two carried machine guns slung over their shoulders. They advanced to the edge of the bank, outrageous, oversized forms standing before the even wilder silhouettes outlined on the trees at their backs.

Kinimaka took a blow to the head, sinking to one knee. An attacker circled behind him, dipping a hand inside a pouch at his waist. When Kinimaka whirled and struck, the man blew powder straight at the Hawaiian's face, coating it in white dust. Hayden switched her gaze between Mano and the new arrivals, torn between choices. Moments later, Kinimaka staggered, choking and coughing and throwing both hands out in front of him to arrest a fall.

Hayden shot the powder-blower as he turned to her. The other two men ducked behind the Hawaiian's bulk, but then Hayden's already overworked nervous system received another intense jolt as *the twelve-foot-tall masked, machine-gun carrying figures waded across the river.* She forged on, reaching Mano and ducking down, grabbing his face.

"Are you okay?"

He wasn't. His eyes had rolled up into his head. His face was slack, his breathing shallow. She couldn't hold him up as he collapsed to the ground like a felled rhino.

She bit her bottom lip, looked up and saw the tall figures covering her with their guns. Belatedly, she also noted that the bottom six feet of their legs were made of wood—stilts.

"Kneel," one said. "Face to the ground. Hands behind your back. If you struggle, I'll start putting bullets in you, one at a time, until we get some goddamned cooperation."

CHAPTER TWENTY NINE

Alicia Myles regained consciousness gradually, realizing her face was pressed against wood only when she tried to move. It wasn't easy. The stupor inside her head was all encompassing, a thick miasma of lethargy, limpness and procrastination. It took an age to stretch her arms to bring her fingers close to her head, another age to waggle them. The problem was, she thought, there were twenty fingers on that one hand.

Is that right?

It didn't matter. Her legs slid steadily under her. She wanted to rise. She decided it would be better to focus first, find out where she was. Her mind was a blank, her thoughts floating in a warm and comfortable mist. *Where am I?*

The thought, errant, bounced away like a dart hitting a battleship. Minutes or hours later, she knew not, her eyes finally focused on her surroundings.

Interesting . . .

She lay upon a two-foot-wide, raised wooden ledge that ran all the way around the circular dwelling she appeared to be inside. The middle of the dwelling was a grass and dirt ring, filled with pointed stakes.

So falling off the ledge wasn't a great option . . .

Alicia scrambled back against the wall, feeling fear for the first time. The panic pierced the fog somewhat, slightly reviving her system. This wasn't right, or good. And what were those shapes across the ring—two more people lying huddled on the ledge maybe . . .

It took several more minutes for the jigsaw to assemble. The trouble was, the more she remembered the more she wanted to move, to act, to take the initiative, but her limbs remained mostly limp, her brain unresponsive. It could think, but didn't seem to be able to transfer thoughts into actions beyond shuffling around.

What did they do to me?

The recollections kept coming, firing at her until she remembered everything: A swarm of people crushing her and Shaw to the ground. Roppolo looking like some damned over-enthusiastic extra from *Shaun of the Dead*. Except, it hadn't been a joke, it had been horribly, terribly real. What had happened to him?

More importantly, what were they going to do to *her*?

Alicia had been in an enemy camp many times. She was no stranger to the stresses, tortures and humiliations handed out by a malicious captor believing both he and his lair were the center of the universe. All those other times though, she'd had people coming to save her.

Shit.

She started crawling around the ledge, circumventing the odd room. The first of two shapes she came to turned out to be Shaw. The second was Cam.

Mission accomplished then. Best not celebrate yet though. In fact, she might never celebrate ever again. Celebration was what had gotten them all into this predicament. And *she'd* talked them into it.

Shoving the guilt into some deep compartment, she shook Shaw awake. The Native American girl groaned and tried to sit up, instantly recognizing Alicia—thank God— but succeeded only in almost slipping off the ledge onto the pointed stakes. Alicia stopped her with an impromptu burst of adrenalin, finding the sudden surge of gusto improved her vitality. Shaw shuffled away, back to the wall, eyes wide and flicking from side to side.

"Hey." Alicia hadn't realized she could speak until now. "You remember what happened?"

Shaw nodded, groaning, and then pressed both hands to the side of her head as if trying to stop it from falling apart. "They . . . caught us."

"We found Cam though."

Shaw noticed the figure to her left for the first time. "Is he . . . okay?"

A question that covered a range of possibilities. "Haven't checked yet."

Shaw swung her legs back to allow Alicia room to get past. She reached out and shook Cam's shoulder, unable to see his face from this angle and, for some reason, dreading what she might find.

"Hey," she said. "Cam, you okay?"

It took a minute for the young man to respond, but then he rolled over to face her. "You came? Thanks."

Alicia nodded. "What did she do to you?"

"Nothing," Cam said. "I've been locked up in here for a while. I think . . . I think they were waiting for you."

That sounded worse than she'd imagined. "Can either of you stand?"

Cam managed to climb to his knees; Shaw used the wall to support both her legs. Alicia used every ounce of strength to stand, shaking with the effort. "Some bloody getaway this is gonna be."

As they tried to maintain their balance, the effects of whatever drug they were under receding slightly, Alicia heard a key rattling in a steel lock. A moment later the door opened, and she received one of the biggest shocks of her life.

What . . . the . . . fuck?

Four guards shoved two figures through the door and positioned them on the ledge. The figures were unsteady, crawling forward. One of them could barely fit on the ledge. The guards laughed and then re-locked the door, their receding laughter filtering through the cracks in the wood.

"Hayden? Mano?" Alicia felt as though she should rub her eyes like they do in cartoons just to confirm she wasn't seeing things. "I . . . what . . . bollocks!" She shook her head.

"Yeah, it's us," Hayden said. "We're here to rescue you."

Alicia had hoped to reunite under better circumstances. "Well, your rescue sucks balls," she said, realizing now that Karin had probably sent them. "Are the others here?"

"Nah, we didn't wait for them."

"Fantastic." Alicia saw that their faces were covered in bruises, dried blood and cuts. "Are you okay?"

"Feeling A-plus actually. Whatever drug they gave us produces a major high."

"Among other things," Alicia said darkly. "Ours is wearing off."

Hayden nodded, staring at the deadly stakes that made up the middle of the room. "Am I seeing things?"

"No, it's all real. We got ourselves into some seriously freaky shit this time. Wouldn't you prefer a chronic terrorist or die-hard megalomaniac? Give me a Kovalenko over some perverted, black-magic wielding witch any time."

Nobody answered, which was probably just as well. Alicia heard footsteps then, a lot of them. "Heads up," she said, and tested her limbs, evaluating just how much resistance she could dole out.

The wooden door creaked open, the bottom lip catching on the concrete step with a loud scrape. Men entered, stepping lightly around the ledge. The first person they came to was Cam.

The first guard, a large brutish-looking guy with fat jowls and lank hair dripping sweat, reached out, grabbed Cam by the arms, and pulled. Ordinarily, the young boxer would have fought back but tonight he could barely lift his head. For good measure, another guard jabbed him with a syringe, injecting more dark-colored liquid into his system.

Alicia lurched toward them, her system barely functioning. "Leave him . . . alone."

She fell to one knee, caught herself, and crawled harder, desperately wishing that her limbs worked better, her head was clearer, her choices easier. She stumbled as she reached out for Cam.

The brute threw Cam behind him, dropped to a seated position, grabbed her and yanked her across his lap. Alicia felt a sharp jab in the arm along with an almost instant infusion of something potent, something both debilitating and controlling. It sapped her will, her resolve.

"Grab the other one," the brute said, indicating Shaw. Alicia was aware of three more guards converging on the young woman with syringes raised.

Across the way, both Hayden and Kinimaka were subjected to the same treatment. Alicia was still lying face forward across the brute's lap, unable to summon an ounce of willpower. It was only when he told her to stand that she realized she could.

What was this stuff that stripped her of her free will? That suggested she should obey. That circumvented any kind of concern she may have for herself. It made her compliant and, for Alicia, that was a fate worse than death.

Acquiescent, she waited for further orders. When they came, she moved immediately, following Hayden and Kinimaka outside. She saw darkness and felt the gnawing cold, heard the night creatures thrumming in the surrounding trees, but couldn't stop walking along a well-trodden path that led from the hut, between other small, squat buildings, to a larger structure with thick log walls and a thatched gable roof.

"Stop," the brute said.

Alicia fought the compunction, battled against it with every obstinate bone in her body. But, as much as her spirit struggled, her body obeyed.

"Once you are inside," the man spoke to all five of them. "You will meet our queen. Your will is hers to control. Your body, your mind, all hers. She will decide how and when you eat, breathe and move from now on. If you are good, and show enthusiasm, you will thrive in her service."

Alicia wanted to protest, to scream, but nothing worked. This wasn't a drug that turned you into a barely living zombie like the others she'd seen earlier; it was a drug that caused changes in thought, emotion and consciousness, in will, something like a hallucinogen. It governed all your actions.

"Our queen owns you," the brute said. "But smile as you comply. Work hard to fulfil your task. She will see and she will reward."

They were directed to approach the front door, a wide ingress with two steel straps for strength, and wait for it to open. Alicia stood in line, raging inside, but when the door opened and a man beckoned them forth, she put one foot in front of the other, following Cam inside the building.

The interior was a wide space, set up almost like a church with rows of wooden benches and seats that faced a raised platform at the far end. Alicia's eyes were fixed on that platform. She saw a large chair—a throne—covered with crocodile skin, and boasting curved horns and a mirror along the top. Resting at the base of the mirror, above the user's head, was a bleached skull. Underneath the chair lay an alligator head, also bleached. Symbols and odd emblems had been painted on the wall behind the throne, most in a crimson color that appeared to have dripped before drying.

But that wasn't what caught Alicia's main attention.

It was the sight of the woman seated on the throne, the voodoo witch queen of New Orleans.

Marinette.

CHAPTER THIRTY

Crawling through Alicia, more insipid than a slithering snake, was a rising sense of awe.

Marinette was beautiful; a dark-skinned goddess seated upon her throne. A black silk robe did nothing to hide long, supple legs that were crossed, one foot resting lightly on top of the crocodile's head. Alicia saw a mix of intelligence and mesmerizing charisma in the smile on her face and a sophisticated, cultured lean to the set of her body. She found herself responding.

What the fu . . .

"Papa Legba sent you here, bringing you into my fold. Damballah will help nourish you. The gods look down on us and smile. Will you smile too?"

Alicia cursed inside as the corners of her mouth turned up. She couldn't turn her head to see the others, but assumed they were doing the same.

Marinette smiled. "The gods, they do love us."

Alicia was aware of others entering the building at her back, mostly by the sound of shuffling feet, by the guard's stares, and by the sight of their shadows capering in the lights of flickering wall sconces.

"You are mine now," Marinette told Alicia and her friends. "And you will do anything for me. But, like Papa Legba, I am wise and prudent. I understand that, inside, you may still be trying to resist. Because of that I will now divest you of those dissatisfying illusions."

Alicia braced.

"Kneel. All of you."

Could be worse . . . Alicia had full control of her thought processes, but her personal jurisdiction ended there. She fell heavily to her knees, the impact jarring her body through her spine.

"And to prove your subservience, to show *you* that I own your every ounce of flesh, you can start by licking my feet."

The struggle began in earnest. Alicia threw her entire being into it, every scrap of experience, as she tried to force herself not to comply. But, like sublime suggestion, something in the mixture of the drug was controlling her body, her mind. She could see the others struggling too. Kinimaka managed to throw himself sideways. Hayden's face was a twisted mask. They gasped and let out thin-lipped keening cries of defiance.

By now, even Alicia knew it wasn't going to work. Resistance wasn't an option. Marinette sat easily on her throne, enjoying the show, a supercilious, haughty, exceedingly *brattish* smile on that beautiful face. Alicia knew exactly what she wanted to do to that brat, she just couldn't regain enough control to do it.

Cam had been here the longest and he was the first to reach Marinette, crawling through dust and then climbing over the edge of the wooden platform to bow his head before the voodoo queen. He reached out, hands shaking, took hold of Marinette's right foot and dragged his tongue from the tip of one toe to the ankle. Marinette grinned triumphantly, casting her gaze from Cam's uplifted eyes across the entire hall.

"You see," she said softly. "I am irresistible."

Shaw was next, long dark hair splaying across

Marinette's shins as she bent to lick both of her feet. When she and Cam were done, they knelt to the side, facing the onlookers. And though Alicia knew there was no resisting she fought as hard as she would against a platoon of Special Forces soldiers.

But, minutes later, following Hayden, she found herself dipping her head, lifting Marinette's smooth, almost delicate right foot and licking it all over. The sensation wasn't unpleasant, it was the act. Alicia hated herself even as she strained to please her new owner.

When they were all done, they knelt to each side of the throne, facing outward like new pets being shown off.

"Now it begins," Marinette said.

From somewhere, music filled the air.

CHAPTER THIRTY ONE

Despite her wild, wayward past, that night was one of the craziest of Alicia Myles' life.

They were led outside and behind the building to a huge area of flatland the size of two football pitches. Alicia saw the flames before she got there; flickering, leaping fires that painted the trees with dancing shadows of black and crimson. At least three big bonfires blazed in the field. People danced and capered around them—at this distance merely shadows—but all were plainly naked and incensed—their minds taken, brains addled by one of Marinette's drugs. Drums were banging, as well as a rock guitar, xylophones and more drums. It wasn't real voodoo, Alicia knew that even in her hypnotic state; this was Marinette's evil twisted version of a much misunderstood and maligned culture.

Smoke billowed across the area and swept in clouds up to the sky. Fire chased it. Alicia and her friends were pushed and shoved to the center of the field where they were allowed to watch.

Wherever Marinette walked, worshippers turned to wring their hands, supplicate and fall to their knees. They scrambled to kiss the ground in her wake, to garner a nod or a favor. All they needed was to be noticed.

The beat of the drums deepened, forcing its pounding, rhythmic beat through Alicia's head and out through her toes. Despite everything, or perhaps because of it, she could feel her body swaying. Their guards were nodding along. They removed their shoes, and then Alicia's, so they could feel the intense, musical cadence sweeping through the very earth.

Bonfires raged. Naked figures fell to their knees. The skies were drifting, smoky clouds, the dark surroundings shot through with red hot flames that cavorted and played with the night. Figures crawled in Marinette's wake, a terrifying, undulating human snake. The thin stick figures were back, shadows leaping around the blazing conflagrations and then into them, re-emerging from the opposite side. It was theater, but it was incredible theater, and with the perfectly potent mix of drugs, it was proof of Marinette's descendancy from the realm of voodoo gods.

When she raised her arms, the music stopped; when she lowered them, it began anew. She danced with her disciples, got naked with them, lay down and coupled with them. Alicia and her friends were close, unable to look away. The writhing mass of bodies was a new, many-limbed sweaty, gleaming monster, a scene from Hell. Fire coated the scene: raging, violent, fierce. Without being asked, the guards began to remove their clothes . . .

Then so did Cam.

Oh, fuck, I can see where this is going.

Shaw started to follow suit. Alicia fought the pounding ecstasy in her body, the increasing arousal. Sweat coated every inch of her skin. The sensation of lust infused the air. When Cam was naked, Alicia reverted to type, but only in her head.

Oh, for God's sake, put it away, man.

But Shaw was imitating him and then Kinimaka started to grab at his own jacket, his belt and then his trousers. Alicia realized that her own hands were at her waistband.

Wait... what?

The seething mass of bodies piled between the three bonfires broke, slithering apart like a net of eels deposited on a deck. Marinette emerged from the center of that pile, the only one standing, and Alicia gazed on her in awe, transfixed. Her dark body shone in the firelight: nude, slick and inviting.

"Come to me," she said. "Approach now if you desire my mark."

Alicia held back desperately. It wouldn't have worked but, luckily, Marinette hadn't given her a direct order. It was a request. Shockingly then, Alicia saw more than half a dozen men and women line up to Marinette's right, gazing in wonder at their revered and stunning icon.

This is fucking insane...

But it was about to get much worse. Marinette, standing in all her splendor, held out her right hand, palm up. A tall, strapping black man clutching a glistening machete passed her an object. Alicia squinted through drifting smoke, her ears now assaulted by the lack of sound rather than the volume of it.

What is that?

Distracted by Cam redressing and Shaw pulling her jeans back on, and then Kinimaka fumbling with the button-fly of his Levis—all noble distractions, if you asked her—Alicia missed seeing Marinette fix the object to her hand. But she saw her hold it up to the flickering light.

A cold surge swept through her. Marinette had pulled on a black leather glove. Where the fingertips should have been were holes, and jutting over those holes were five long, thin blades. Her glove was a cat's claw, only sporting deadly slivers of steel.

The first supplicant stepped up before her. Marinette

placed her hand on his cheek, meeting his gaze and holding it still for several seconds before slashing the glove at a downward angle. Instantly, the knives were coated in blood. When the man turned, his cheek streamed with it. Marinette had left her mark.

Alicia watched as the voodoo queen violated the skin of all the subjects who'd risen up. Around the wide area the musicians sweated and stood ready, bell mallets poised to return to drum skins, rock guitars slung over shoulders. Others sprawled or knelt or sat in place, elated expressions on their faces. A sense of hot, fiery excitement filled the area that had nothing to do with the raging bonfires—*they* were the mere physical manifestation of the celebrants' inner exhilaration. It was infectious, contagious, and scarily authentic.

The sound of crackling, snapping timbers consumed the night as fully as the blazing bonfires. Alicia sensed a change coming before it happened, knew the ritual was about to return to full swing. She worried for her friends and herself, and over what they might be made to do.

Marinette threw her hands at the air, a challenging gesture. The music started up; people jumped back to their feet, swaying and cavorting. Alicia's attention was then taken as, through the middle of the bonfires, six goats were led by six unclothed men.

The goats were lined up before Marinette and then, in turn, their throats were slit, blood surging across the ground and washing over her feet. She danced in it. She chanted in it. She lifted her arms and weaved like a snake through the air, shining in the night, a personification of pure madness.

The drum beat intensified, heading toward a crescendo. The rock guitar ground out resounding tunes. The

Voodoo Soldiers

believers danced and copulated as smoke billowed all around and elongated, nightmarish shapes flitted from burning pyre to pyre. Alicia thought more than once that she'd died and gone to Hell.

The worst was when she caught sight of Cam and Shaw, Hayden and Kinimaka. They were looking at her, and at each other, unchanged inside and all too aware that their ability to make decisions was no longer their own. How long the drug lasted, Alicia didn't know, but she was pretty sure they'd get a new dose before it ran out. Marinette was clearly an accomplished jailor, unlikely to make mistakes.

Marinette was slinking toward them. Alicia found her body falling to its knees, her hands held up in solicitation at the merest whispered word from a guard. Marinette didn't stop advancing until she was so close that Alicia could smell and feel her intense body heat. The heady aroma made her nostrils flare.

She looked up, meeting the voodoo queen's eyes.

"I want you to do something for me."

Alicia's mind resisted but sensed her body was ready to comply.

"But first . . ." Marinette said. "I want to show you what happens to those that displease me."

It was just Alicia, her four friends, two guards and Marinette in a circle. But then a guard dragged a figure from behind, directing him straight to Marinette. Alicia recognized the familiar figure, clad only in filthy rags—it was Roppolo, the man who'd accosted her in a bar on a night that seemed a distant memory now.

Slack-jawed, devoid of all emotion, slumped and broken he had lost all hope, or all vitality, or any desire to do anything other than what his mistress commanded. Alicia's immediate thought was: *Zombie*.

"I know what you're thinking," Marinette said unnervingly. "And you are right. To this end, Roppolo was drugged with my own concoction, buried alive and left for about eight hours. Then, he was dug up, subjected to an ancient voodoo rite, and reanimated for my pleasure. He serves me until he rots now, with the knowledge that the process can never be reversed, that he sleepwalks forever, that his gods loaned me his empty shell to do my bidding. This is the worst torment that I can offer. Is it so abundantly terrible that you will now beg to serve me? To avoid it?"

Alicia answered the question without consideration. "Yes, my queen."

And in that moment, she thought she'd lost her mind forever.

"Good, because now you can prove it. There is a job I need undertaking, something that will require your special skills. Now, listen . . ."

CHAPTER THIRTY TWO

Matt Drake arrived in New Orleans with little knowledge of what he was up against. When he left Coyote in his rearview, Hayden and Kinimaka were just getting started. By the time he arrived in New Orleans, they were no longer answering their phones.

This place was sucking up too many ex-SPEAR team members.

"I got it, love, I got it."

He was standing on a grass verge overlooking the vast expanse of the mighty Mississippi river, at a place he didn't know, the well-paid cab driver waiting for him half a mile away. A soft wind blew off the water, not cold but refreshing. Karin was listening at the other end of a cellphone. "I'm finding it hard to get my head around their disappearance, that's all," he said. "I mean, *five?*"

"Three plus Cam and Shaw. They're pretty young."

"Mebbe, but they know their way around a fist fight and a gun battle." But those facts were immaterial. "Where are the others?"

"Dahl and Kenzie will touch down in few hours. Mai's leaving now but she's a full day away. Just don't go in there alone."

Drake nodded, staring across the waters. "Aye, sure. I'm not that daft. What time did this guy say he'd be here?"

"Midday."

"Yeah, he's late." Though they'd discovered a significant

amount of information relating to Marinette's business dealings, it was still mostly speculation. What they needed was a gritty New Orleans detective, a man with contacts, not unused to getting the job done the hard way.

It said a lot for Marinette's reputation that the detective had insisted on meeting at a quiet, unsupervised area way out of town. Drake saw a figure approaching down the pathway that ran along the grass verge. "He's coming now."

The detective was white, rough-looking and clearly annoyed. "I got a thousand things to do," were the first words out of his mouth as he reached Drake.

"You and me both, pal. How about some professional courtesy?"

The answering grunt was noncommittal. "I don't mind depositing favors for later," he said. "If the NSA promise future goodwill for information, I'll bank that. I'm Kirk."

Drake nodded, checked their perimeter once more and told the man exactly what he wanted.

"Marinette," Detective Kirk said, "belongs in that gray area between enigma and crisis. She's both. Mysterious, powerful, secretive, vengeful. That's an area where I would tread very lightly."

"And if I preferred to use my size tens?"

"You'd probably get dead. Or worse."

Drake raised his brows. "Worse?"

Detective Kirk frowned. "Hey, you're on my soil. You'd better listen good. I'm a fifteen-year veteran. San Fran before that. If I say *worse*, you better believe its goddamn worse. The things she does . . ." He shook his head, staring down at the ground. "She's a fucking evil witch, man. Yeah, we're basically aware of what she does but . . ." Kirk's face went through several pained expressions as he struggled to voice his feelings.

"I get it, mate. I do. Some of your guys are super religious, eh?"

It was a gentle way of needling toward the truth. Karin had researched the process of so-called "zombification" and had passed her findings along to Drake.

Kirk nodded unhappily. "I guess."

"The stronger the belief, the easier she can make it happen. It's engrained in their culture, as real as a symbolic crucifix or the communion. Social reinforcement is also a powerful tool when you live in her shadow, I guess."

"Powerful? It's perpetual. Every goddamn day, my friend. Every day. If you believe something can happen, if you believe it with every ounce of your heart and soul, then it *can*. And the drug concoction she uses eases everything along."

"So that's the fear," Drake said. "What else?"

Kirk loosened up slightly now that Drake had demonstrated a little understanding. "Real issues," he said, looking around as he spoke. "Corruption, big time, at high levels. Marinette is making millions and happy to spread some of it around."

"High level?"

Kirk snorted. "Where else? There's no proof, but . . ." He shrugged. "City's riddled," he admitted. "Cops. Judges. Governor's office. Bankers. You name it—if they hold any kind of power, she has influence."

"And intimidation like—"

"Like Beelzebub, Baron Samedi and the Grim Reaper all rolled into one. She owns everything she touches."

Drake began to see the depth and breadth of the evil they were up against. "And her business dealings?"

Kirk relaxed a little more, tasked by a question he could

answer without fear. "A mix of vile and unspeakable. Her property's coastal, bordering on the Gulf of Mexico. Drugs are delivered from several unpleasant corners of the world. Guns too. She sells impartially—to the Mob, the cartels, gang lords, whoever. Doesn't matter to her."

"She sounds bloody awful," Drake said.

"Oh, it gets worse. Human trafficking." Kirk shuddered then, odd for a seasoned cop, but when he continued Drake understood why. "And body parts," he said in a hushed voice. "They dig up graves around the city, steal the bodies and chop them up for parts. Don't ask me what they do with them because I really don't want to know."

"I've seen some fucked up things in my time, but . . ."

"Yeah, tell me about it. And, man, I've *seen* things too. Real, indisputable things. Zombies. Supernatural shit. Weird as hell."

"Drug induced? She's some kind of voodoo queen, I'm told?"

"Hey, man, voodoo isn't bad anywhere except through the eyes of Hollywood. It's all sensationalized. When I came here, I saw how deeply entrenched it is in the local culture. I needed to understand it so I could understand a good many of the people. So, I learned. The word voodoo means *spirit* or *deity*. Legends say that God was deceived by a trickster named Legba. When he quit earth, he left Legba behind in the form of a rainbow. A rainbow is a bridge between Heaven and earth. To access the rainbow, which was thin, his followers chose the form of a snake. This fabulous snake spirit was known as *Li Grand Zombi* in New Orleans and later had its name changed to *Papa Lebas*. In voodoo, the belief is that God uses spirits to arbitrate His parishioners' lives, to interfere and mediate. Voodoo is a calling, a spiritual lifestyle. To understand it, *you have to know the people.* There is no easy way around that."

Drake could see that Kirk felt deeply about the subject. The man had certainly tried to understand the voodoo culture and maybe he had succeeded, but nothing prevented a monster like Marinette from trying to pervert it.

"I am sorry she's corrupting the traditions and way of life of a nation," he said. "And if anyone can take her down, we can. Believe that. We've taken down the worst of the worst. At the moment, we're on the back foot, but . . . with your help . . . we can reverse all that shit and remove this cancer from your city."

Kirk eyed him closely, weighing the words. "What do you need?" he said after a while.

"Movements. Any schedules you may know of. Plans of the area where she lives. Known snitches. Known corrupt officials. Everyone can be squeezed. These grave robbers could be useful since they're her only known employees working *outside* her boundary. What cemeteries do they hit? That okay?"

"Is that all?" Kirk managed a sarcastic smile.

"For now. Time is against us though, pal." The thought of Alicia as a zombie wasn't a pleasant one.

"Got it." Kirk turned and moved off. Karin had already given him Drake's contact details. The Yorkshireman had another thought and called out to Kirk's back.

"How powerful is this Marinette anyway? I mean spiritually. Is her faith real? Is it all trickery or does she have power?"

"Power," Kirk turned, squinting into the light, "is subjective. She is a *bokor,* or *caplata,* a voodoo black magic witch. Whatever power she holds derives from the minds and hearts of her followers and employees. She possesses both spiritual and material wealth. Marinette is very well versed in the traditions of voodoo, its ritual affluence. I would say her power holds no bounds."

Drake nodded, letting the man go. So far, his arrival in New Orleans hadn't progressed too well.

But something else was about to happen that immediately raised his own spirits.

Dahl and Kenzie were in town. It was time to meet up and organize a serious kind of old-school assault. If you couldn't finesse a big V8 around a corner, you kicked its arse out and smashed the throttle until it complied. At least, Drake did.

He couldn't imagine Marinette had ever come up against anything like the old SPEAR team. Maybe it was time for her to meet some traditional blood, guts and fury.

CHAPTER THIRTY THREE

Marinette saw everything.

She watched, either through the eyes of her servants on the streets, the whisper of information between officials, the CCTV system around her property, or cameras installed on every busy corner from the Mississippi to Lake Pontchartrain.

Seated now in her private bedroom, away from guards, servants, captives and disciples, she ignored the second call from her new lieutenant—Lott. This was her space, her time. He should know better than to disturb her. She wore a long, black dress covered with swooping designs embroidered in gold stitching, that swept the ground as she walked. She wore her charms and amulets too and a shrunken skull necklace around her throat. She gazed at the reflection in her vanity table mirror, searching for a nucleus, the core of who she really was.

I am so many different faces to so many different people, I have lost sight of the woman I want to be.

The phone rang again. Marinette closed her eyes. In truth, Lott wouldn't call without urgent reason, but plain truth never softened the blow of rude interruption.

The true face of dominion is owned by its dependents. Never to rest, never to sleep; there to serve. Ironic really...

"What is it?" she answered the call.

"They have more friends."

Marinette sat up. "Who? The cartel?"

"No. Alicia's people."

They had learned their names the night before when Marinette had asked a very special favor of the newcomers. That had been a good night; breaking newcomers into the fold was always exhilarating.

"How many?"

"Three. Two males, one female. The first male, British by his accent, pumped Detective Kirk for information. Our man on the parabolic couldn't catch everything due to the wind off the river but he heard enough. This British guy then waited for the other two."

Marinette pursed her lips. Detective Kirk, despite his betrayals—which one day he would pay heavily for—was a useful tool, attracting the attentions of would-be investigators, enemies and idiots seeking to interfere in her dealings. Her lackeys watched Kirk discreetly; Kirk led them to potential issues.

"Keep watching them," Marinette said. "I'll be out soon. I want to see how many more come before we act this time. I want to study, to see how professionals seek to penetrate our defenses. Just watch them, Lott."

"Yes, my queen."

Marinette threw the cellphone down on the vanity top. Technology didn't belong in her private chamber. It was a necessary evil. Technology ruined the setting, changed the ambience. There was no place for it in Marinette's quarters.

But with business dealings as widespread, capricious and colorful as hers, the exception was essential.

An hour later, she walked to the office. It was a large, low-slung building overshadowed by an extensive tree canopy to the east of her main hall. The walls were thick and fitted with jamming signals. The inside was manned twenty-four hours a day, all year round. When Marinette arrived, she sought out Lott.

"What do you have?"

"They are moving fast, my queen. Already, they have guns and other military equipment."

"Ours?"

Lott looked uncomfortable. "Possibly. Our men sell without reservation."

Marinette understood. "Yes, as ordered. I will never reprimand a man or woman for following orders. Only for stupidity and betrayal. What are they planning?"

"It's hard to say," Lott admitted. "They appear to argue a lot. The men mostly. Once, we saw the big one and the woman kissing when they thought the Englishman wasn't around. He caught them and applauded. It was an odd moment."

Marinette stared at a bank of monitors, looking from screen to screen. Collectively it was a view of the streets of New Orleans, the ones she owned. They included police stations, law courts, bars and restaurants. In addition to the monitors was an array of telephones, a call center. Her eyes and ears on the streets made constant reports and were paid for beneficial intelligence. This noisy operation was based in a far corner and screened off. Marinette's other source of information was more personal, the private whisperings between powerful men and women that usually came at the end of a long night.

"Where are the newcomers?" she asked.

"Local helicopter rental company," Lott said with a hint of speculation in his voice.

Marinette narrowed her eyes. "Ahh," she said. It had been tried before. Trespassers flew over her property to scope it out, find a viable entry point, and get eyes on her business enterprises. So far, it hadn't worked.

"They are ex-military," she said. "But we have military of our own. Lay your traps carefully, Lott. Lay your traps carefully."

It was more than a suggestion, more than a command. It was a loaded warning. Lott would know the price of failure all too well.

"Yes, my queen," he said, a satisfying tremor in his voice.

Drake clung on, knuckles bone white, as Dahl piloted the chopper.

"Ever think about a refresher course, mate?"

"Don't need it, mate."

"The trees are not supposed to act as windscreen wipers."

"Stop your whinging. Bloody Yorkshire fanny. You're flying with an expert."

An expert in bullshit, Drake almost said but then held his tongue as another tree loomed. Dahl needed all the quiet he could get. Concentration didn't come easy for the Mad Swede. Kenzie, in the other front seat, didn't seem fazed.

"Approaching Marinette's property now."

Drake looked out the window. He didn't have to look far to see into Black Snake Swamp, a twisting quagmire of trees, streams, marsh and narrow pathways. To him, it all looked the same. Those that could find their way safely through would be very few in number.

"Thank God for GPS," he said.

"We're closing in on the coordinates," Dahl said. "And you're welcome."

He eased back on the throttle. Drake welcomed the

decrease in speed, though had to admit the Swede was improving by the minute. Their meeting earlier, after many weeks apart, had been somewhat bittersweet. There was no hiding the manly mutual respect and affection they shared but, since neither were badly injured, maimed or close to death, there was no need for open displays.

"Ey up, mate," Dahl had said in greeting.

"Now then, knobhead," Drake had responded.

All was well. Now, as they entered Marinette's lair, Drake worried about Alicia and the others. What the hell had they gone and done now?

"You see anything?" Kenzie asked, a pair of field glasses pressed to her eyes.

Drake did. Blending well with the tree canopy he made out a series of single-story buildings, like small warehouses but with flat, sloping roofs. Clusters of trees and acres of field surrounded the well-hidden complex. Drake saw several small figures wandering around.

"With businesses so immoral, and knowing that she's managed to survive all these years, we have to assume she knows we just buzzed her ass," Kenzie said. "And she'll have some serious firepower."

"If we hit them hard, and free the others quickly, we're good," Dahl said. "We have the GPS, maps of the area, ways in and out. We have the firepower, the experience. Just need the right place to land."

Drake was pumped for it. Every second these crazies held on to his friends was a fresh lesson in agony. The chopper buzzed along, skimming the treetops and then, dead ahead, Drake saw the vast expanse of blue sparkling waters that was the Gulf of Mexico unfolding between horizons.

"No good options," he said.

Dahl jerked at the collective, banking the chopper out over the edge of the treeline, up toward the deep, indigo vault of the sky, and then circled back across the vibrant waters. Once they were hovering, viewing Marinette's domain from the Gulf side, a new choice opened up.

"Nice beach." Dahl pointed the chopper's nose in the direction of Marinette's buildings, perhaps a mile and a half distant. "Get ready."

Drake rolled his shoulders, then made sure his weapons were to hand. A small Glock was complimented by an M4 Carbine Commando with an M203 Grenade Launcher. He carried shock and smoke grenades in addition to Kevlar armor and an ACH, an Advanced Combat Helmet, itself made of Kevlar. A backpack full of spare magazines and grenades sat ready to throw on when the chopper touched down.

They were twenty feet above the beach when Kenzie spotted an incoming bird. It was an old Bell machine, battered and scratched. The body looked like it had been hand-painted black, and the engines strained even at low speed and low-level flying. Drake counted at least six passengers as it glided sideways toward them.

"Land this thing!" he shouted.

Dahl had been turning the chopper's front end around as if preparing for a game of chicken with the oncoming helicopter, but now descended fast toward a pebble-strewn beach. Drake saw black-clad men leaning out of the other chopper.

"Cover," he yelled.

They opened fire, bullets slamming through thin air, missing their bird entirely due to the wild oscillation of both crafts. Drake kept his head low, watching Dahl. A sudden dark vision loomed out of the right-hand window.

"Fuck me!" Dahl shouted.

Drake couldn't believe his eyes. The enemy chopper was attempting to ram them, its left side approaching theirs. Drake threw his body across the rear seats as the enemy loomed closer, too close, grizzled and determined faces set hard as stone. Dahl's warning shout was lost under a grinding, screeching crash of metal on metal as the helicopters came together. Glass shattered. Metal was crushed as sparks flew. Dahl compensated for the impact as their nose swung wildly. Their chopper's skids struck the ground and then bounced back up, the hard contact shocking through the frame with a jarring blow. Drake clung on. Kenzie's skull bounced off the window. Dahl lurched forward and then back, cursing.

"Bastards wanna play," Dahl growled. "Let's play."

Drake cringed as the Swede, instead of powering their craft onto the beach, forced it back into the air. Its rotors thudded, working hard, the engine growling. It lifted and then came around, its nose now pointed at the side of the attacking chopper.

"You're in *my* arena now," Dahl rumbled.

The other pilot tried to evade, but Dahl was too fast. He flew straight at and then *under* the other chopper, avoiding any calamitous rotor contact, and throwing the pilot's focus off. Even Drake was stunned. Their enemies were in disarray. By the time Dahl came up the other side both Drake and Kenzie were ready with their guns.

Bullets stung the air. Holes sprouted from the chopper's black body. Windows smashed, the remaining jagged shards splashed with blood. At least two enemies were hit. When the pilot recovered and started to bring their bird around, Dahl swooped theirs down to the ground.

The skids touched the small rocks and settled. The

engine died. Doors were flung open. Drake, Dahl and Kenzie leapt out with guns raised in time to let loose a salvo of lead at the underside of the descending helicopter.

The craft wavered but kept coming. Men leaned out of smashed windows, trying to return fire. One was jolted loose, tumbling about fifteen feet onto the beach, breaking his legs and losing his weapon. Drake fell to one knee, M4 across one shoulder, firing upward. Beyond the juddering chopper, the bruised night formed a fitting backdrop to the unfolding mayhem below.

Drake ducked as bullets flew past him, running for cover. The enemy chopper settled on the beach as its occupants scrambled through the far doors, using the hull of the craft to shield them . . . Or so they thought. Dahl took out at least one of them at the ankles by firing underneath the still-roaring bird.

Drake surveyed the treeline. "If we get in there, we'll have better shelter."

Dahl nodded. "I'll cover you."

Drake scanned for a way in and then set off at a sprint, staying low. Both Dahl and Kenzie switched to full-auto, making their enemies duck for cover, giving the Yorkshireman time to cover the distance. When Drake hit the treeline, he dropped and skidded to a stop, skimming under vegetation before turning back to the beach, weapon steadied.

"Home." He switched to comms.

"Kenzie, you next," Dahl said.

As Kenzie broke for the trees, Drake sought to cover her and keep their enemies pinned down. His bullets skimmed metal framework and kicked pebbles and sand up from the beach, each one judiciously aimed. When one man showed a little too much of a muscular shoulder, Drake perforated it.

Kenzie was close. Drake kept firing. He didn't see Kenzie's eyes or her facial reaction, didn't hear anything over the sound of the M4, but he did feel a man's heavy weight crash down onto his back with brute force, and then felt the sharp jab of a needle entering his neck. Kenzie opened fire, removing the weight from his back, but by then it was too late for Drake.

He saw Kenzie dive headlong as dozens of feet rushed past him from deep in the trees, saw many guards approaching her with weapons raised. Already, his vision was blurry. He couldn't lift his gun. Shouts pierced the burgeoning fog running rampant through his brain. Drake's last vision was of Kenzie lying on the beach, face-down, a dozen men pointing weapons at her, and of Dahl throwing his gun to the ground but standing strong, fists raised as a dozen more closed in.

And then there was nothing but the dark.

Marinette perched on the edge of her throne, a glass of wine in one hand, a wickedly sharp, jewel-encrusted dagger in the other. Her special black leather glove with the thin knives that curled over her fingers was resting on the floor beside her. Tonight, she wore a ceremonial robe that covered her entire body and a black, weather-beaten top hat. Her eyes were fixed on the doors to her main hall.

Soon, they opened. Lott and a dozen other guards dragged three figures into her presence. Five minutes later they had managed to revive the figures enough so that they could be made to kneel upright before her.

"Drake. Dahl. Kenzie," Marinette began with that tuneful cadence in her voice. "Ex-Special Forces soldiers. Decorated soldiers. Yes, I know everything about you. The only thing I don't know is why you are here."

She waited. All three captives were bleary-eyed and sagging but they understood her question well enough. The one called Drake was already scanning the hall for a means of escape. The one called Dahl had been counting guards ever since he woke up. The woman, Kenzie, was staring at Marinette's dagger with an interesting blend of yearning and lust.

"Some bastard stuck me with a needle," Drake muttered. "That's why."

Marinette felt the insolence, the detestation and confidence radiating from him, from all of them. These new arrivals, starting with Alicia, were upsetting the unqualified balance she ordained daily over Black Snake Swamp.

"Our lifeforces are on a converging path," she said. "Only chaos can come from that."

"Where are our friends?" Dahl asked.

"I can't confirm that your friends will want to join you," Marinette said slyly, "ever again. They have seen how good life can be in my servitude. The rapture. The ecstasy. The lack of inhibition. They work for me now."

"Stop it with the bollocks and bullshit, lady," Drake said. "We're not here to dance a fucking jig with you."

Marinette raised a hand, stopping Lott who had drawn a stiletto and was poised to drive it through the back of Drake's neck. Alicia and the others had already been coerced to do a job for her. Maybe Drake, Dahl and Kenzie could join them. Together, they were a formidable team.

At least, they *were*.

"I'll test you." Marinette looked at the men as if they were a major ingredient in her next meal. "Assess you. Measure you in every way. And don't think you'll escape my attentions." She switched her impenetrable gaze to

Kenzie. "And if you all show first-class crazy skills, I will let you worship me in all ways for the rest of your lives."

The drugs were ready. There would be another ritual tonight. Marinette wanted Alicia and her friends fully under her spell before offering them the dangerous appraisal. As her men prepared to administer the drug, Marinette raised a hand.

"You are mine now." She licked her lips lasciviously and held the gaze of all three captives. "And I will use you in the worst possible ways."

As she laughed, looking up to the rafters and roof, she thought that there, among the cobwebs, she finally saw gods and demons resting, the black and the white of voodoo tradition, the good and the most vile evil. She thought she saw damnation and salvation riding hand in hand—a perfect, twisted vision of intertwined sins.

But it might just have been the drugs in her system.

CHAPTER THIRTY FOUR

Mai Kitano had boarded a jet the day before and was close to the American coastline, fixing her seatbelt and stowing her laptop as the plane began its descent. Hours had swept by during her flight whilst she read email messages from Karin, explaining everything that had occurred in New Orleans to date.

And that included the disappearance of Drake, Dahl and Kenzie.

They were up against a terrible enemy. Speed was all important. But Mai, by nature, was restrained. Twenty hours on a plane wasn't long enough to think this through and come up with a feasible plan. If everyone from Alicia to Drake had succumbed, Mai—alone—would need to be different.

She had worked with them all long enough by now to know what their approaches would have been. Hers would be better.

Mai exited Louis Armstrong International Airport and sought a cab to take her the eleven miles to downtown New Orleans. She was dressed inconspicuously, wearing blue jeans, a light shell jacket, sneakers and dark sunglasses. Her black hair was hidden beneath a *Jesters* baseball cap. She carried only a small holdall, cabin baggage, with enough clothes and general supplies for a few days. The cab took her to a nondescript hotel where she planned to make base.

An hour later Mai was still ruminating. Instincts she was trying to suppress insisted she get moving. Her brain, her experience and the facts of the last few days warned her that only a perfect plan would yield any kind of success. She'd left Chika and Dai behind without explanation. Of course, they knew her by now and didn't question the sudden departure.

Mai sat in her room's only chair, hands on a desk, staring at a wall that had been painted beige about two decades ago, listening to the rumble of passing traffic outside the slightly ajar window, the noise of pedestrians and an airplane cut through the skies. She used hand sanitizer, opened a bottle of water, and drank half.

Mai was fully aware that her next decision carried a deadly weight. The responsibility it assumed was like a sickle hanging over her head.

Who will help us?

Not the US government. She had no contacts for any of the ghosted Special Forces teams. The Disavowed guys were only three-strong. What she needed was an army. Multiple attack points. Numerous distractions. Swarms of men. Give this Marinette and her band of goons so much to worry about they wouldn't have time to guard Drake and the others. The big questions were—who would help her and where to start with Marinette?

Mai had an idea for the second question. It was highly unsavory and probably sickening but that was why it might potentially work. As for the first question . . .

Fighting her misgivings, finally, she made a call.

"Hey, how are you? This is Mai Kitano."

"Well, hello to you, the Japanese bombshell that reminds me a little of Maggie Q, Chun Li and Karen Gillan all rolled into one hard-hitting, dynamite-hot package."

"I knew this was a mistake." Mai almost cut the call.

"Wait, no, wait. You know me. Playing to the stands. I'm thrilled that you thought to call me."

"Don't be. You're a last resort."

"Right, well, that's hard to hear. I'm guessing this is a professional call?"

Mai shook her head and took a deep breath. Connor Bryant was the flamboyant and ostentatious owner of the private security firm, Glacier, a man they'd recently saved from the inferno in Los Angeles, and a man who'd offered them all a job. He was spoiled, tasteless and challenging, but they'd later learned that this outer persona was false, the expectation of a façade he used as the face of a tough and exacting business. More importantly, he'd fought and taken damage alongside fellow soldiers in Afghanistan.

"I can't state enough how professional this is. We need your help."

Bryant stayed quiet as Mai relayed the facts. It took a considerable amount of time to relate as Bryant took notes, and when she'd finished there was a grave silence.

"What a clusterfuck," he breathed eventually. "What's your plan?"

"*This* is my plan. You can't sneak into Black Snake Swamp. You assault it."

"But I can't operate on US soil. I have a contract, usually for war zones."

"This wouldn't be an official operation."

"You mean pure, unattached mercenaries? And how would you pay them?"

"They can have the spoils of Marinette's property. She's been operating for over a decade. Drugs. Guns. People-trafficking. We get to shut all that down too. Even if the authorities learned something later, they'd turn a blind eye."

"Maybe. Don't forget some of those authorities are feathering their own nests. Bound to be some fallout. And if that blows back on me, I lose my company; shit, maybe even my freedom. This is not a light decision, Maggie."

"Please don't call me Maggie. I had a friend that used to call me that. He was murdered in London."

"Ah, sorry. There I go sticking my oversized weapon in the wrong place yet again. Sorry, that was my alter ego speaking. You've rattled me."

Mai gave him time to compose himself, chance to think, keeping a lid on her own anxieties. If Bryant turned her down, she had nowhere else to turn.

"You know," he said finally. "When soldiers sit at home drinking beer and watching daytime TV, they get itchy. Off the job, whether they're still serving or not, they get restless. They need their team mates to help them cope. I know. I've been there. And I'm guessing so have you. Maybe we could keep this under the radar, mostly thanks to Marinette's own proclivities for secrecy, isolation and need for privacy. I think that's the key."

"Black Snake swamp is big," Mai said. "I have recon photos. I have GPS. You could hold the Battle of the Bastards in there and nobody would know."

"Whoa, a nice *Game of Thrones* segue, which just makes me want you more. That bastard Luther hasn't returned, has he? Don't answer that. I have drones that could recce the place better than your photos anyway. It's mobilizing the men to Louisiana and convincing them that the spoils of our little war will be fruitful that will take time."

"We don't have time." Mai allowed a portion of the strain that was consuming her to show. "Every hour, every minute..."

"I'm sorry but I'm risking a lot here too. Precautions

must be taken. Do you have access to weapons?"

"I have people I can call." Mai was thinking of local agency drop boxes in particular—weapons caches hidden in busy cities in plain sight but out of knowledge of everyone except special operations men and women—and also of Aaron Trent and Special Agent Collins of the FBI, who would be happy to help with locations. "I'll handle the weapons."

"Then we're in business. I'll call you by nightfall."

"Make it sooner," Mai said and hung up, still staring at the time-worn painted wall, still forcing down the acid that threatened to rise in her chest, the horrible dark thoughts flitting through her brain.

Uncharted territory. The words hit her, meant in more ways than one. She might be walking to her own death and dragging Bryant and his men along with her, but it was a sacrifice she had to make.

CHAPTER THIRTY FIVE

With full night came the most immoral sins.

Marinette knew that giving the newcomers even a moment to recover, to rest, to think for themselves, would be a big mistake. They would not be tamed so easily.

"Bring them to the main hall." She stood in her chambers, staring out of a round window at endless swampland across which a stunning sunset was about to drape its splendor.

"Also, take all the Carbonellis to the Wetlands. Tonight, an example will be made."

"This is your task for the newcomers?" Lott asked in surprise.

"Isn't it perfect? Not only will they be forced to zombify Flavio Carbonelli, the son of Tomasso, head of the entire southern states Mob, but first I will explain to them exactly how I make it all happen."

"That will fuck with their heads," Lott said.

"You sound unsure. Speak freely. You have reservations?"

It was a rare candid moment between her and her staff. Very few knew Marinette's most intimate secrets but those that did sometimes made for good sounding boards. The things they knew didn't make them any more valuable.

"This Alicia, Drake and the rest are specialists. The best in their field. Would we not be better just dumping them in the Gulf, my queen?"

Marinette understood his concerns. She shared a tiny sliver of them. It was why the spiritual balance felt off kilter, the ambiance of her domain slightly misaligned. She pressed cold lips to the amulets around her wrist before answering.

"The symmetry needs a reset," she said. "We will first destroy their minds by forcing them to zombify Flavio Carbonelli, and then we will take control of their souls in the greatest voodoo ceremony there has ever been. Start making ready for that, Lott."

She breathed on the glass, drawing a ritualistic *veve* in the fog before pulling on leather trousers, a short halter top in black silk with gold-filigree designs, knee-high leather boots and topping it off with the ubiquitous battered top hat. She smeared white body paint across the lower half of her face and outlined her eyes and mouth in black. Finally, she drew a thick, brown mottled python from its lair and draped it around her neck.

Less than a minute later, she was reclined on her throne, boots removed, legs crossed, as Lott and his strongest guards pushed, poked and prodded Alicia, Drake and the others before her. She counted eight of them—Alicia, Drake, Hayden, Kinimaka, Cam, Shaw, Kenzie and Dahl. Quite a mix of strong, vital bodies. Marinette wanted to use all of them, and she would, but carnal diversions would have to wait.

At least for one night . . . The thought gave her goosebumps.

Lott and his men forced the newcomers to their knees, backs straight. Marinette saw in their eyes that her concoction had been administered and that they were under her thrall. But, more beautifully, she saw that they knew and recognized everything that was happening.

"You can't resist," she said lightly. "You see and feel everything as normal, but your minds and bodies are mine." She petted the python as it coiled around her shoulders, noting the sudden tension in Alicia's eyes and storing it away for later use. "I could make you love each other." She grinned. "Fight each other. Kill each other. Your brains will know it is wrong and fight back, but resistance is pointless. Make no mistake, I know who you are. I know what you can do. But you are mine now. And tonight, I will teach you how utterly cruel and ruthless I can be."

She leaned forward. "And I will make you all *love* it."

Searching their eyes, she saw resistance; she saw hatred; she saw suffering. It was the perfect balm to her troubles. The balance was being reset. "And now," she said. "A few truths that will further increase your misery."

Lott urged everyone out except two tall and muscular, dark-skinned men. They were shirtless, wearing only loincloths, and bore the scrapings of Marinette's glove on every inch of their exposed flesh. They never spoke; they lived only to do her bidding, and thus were perfect, impeccable guards for moments like this.

"So, a few truths." Marinette rose from her throne and padded down the raised dais, bare feet sliding through dust. She stopped a few feet from the kneeling line of captives, letting the snake uncoil and thrust a mottled head toward them. Yes, there was an unaccountable fear in Alicia's eyes, distaste in Dahl's and interest in Kenzie's. A good mix of reaction from her subjects.

"There are two principal drugs, both laced by certain elements of my own design. Tried and tested." She didn't embellish. "The first—*scopolamine*—has been called the most dangerous mind-control drug in the world. You are experiencing its effect right now. Known as 'the Devil's Breath' and used mostly by South American criminal organizations, it has been used on countless tourists to gain access to their bank accounts, personal records and more. A drug-soaked business card handed over, a sprinkling on a map, a blow in the face. It is versatile and acts within seconds. I use the syringe simply because I like to leave my mark in your flesh . . ." Marinette licked her lips and grinned.

"This is not voodoo," she went on. "It is security enhanced by fear; protection multiplied by beautiful, terrible myth and legend. Now, if you could speak, you would ask: *What is scopolamine?* It is obtained from Nightshade; it can take your memory and as you know, your will, depending on the dose and what other elements are added to the mix. It is a truth serum, a Columbian super-drug used to manipulate both the old and the young by ruthless dealers. And once it's in your system, you become like a child, forced to obey an adult."

Marinette swept along the line of kneeling supplicants. She motioned for her special glove, pulled the supple leather over her right hand and let the razor sharp, thin knives rest lightly on Alicia's upturned cheek. Despite the hatred in the woman's eyes there was no resistance from her body.

"This is power," Marinette said. "This is real control. And now that you understand me, my operation, and your place in it, I will show you the favor I would have you do for me."

She nodded at the tall guards and Lott, let them move into position before telling the newcomers to stand up and exit. There was no resistance. Their movement was lethargic, almost automated, but they went without protest, as expected. Marinette followed, leaving her snake behind, and once more donning her boots. It was a short walk to the Wetlands, through a thick cluster of trees and to the top of a short hill before dropping down the other side toward a gently folded field. These were the marshes, and they lined her property for miles to the south, leading almost all the way to the beach. The safe paths among them were few and well-guarded.

"You three would never have gotten this far," she said, meaning Drake, Dahl and Kenzie. "It would take an army hours to cross these marshes and there are no domestic armies willing to make sacrifices like that these days. No FBI. No SWAT. No secret agency acronym with enough resources. Nobody is coming to save you."

She saw figures ahead. Several regular guards carrying guns, machetes and wearing body armor were standing in a loose semi-circle around three suited young men. She knew the face of Flavio Carbonelli, had studied it not only in the Press but in surveillance photos on many occasions. The other two suits were his friends; nameless, unimportant individuals he chose to party with.

All three men were fully coherent, having been captured and then brought here just an hour ago. Flavio Carbonelli set angry, youthful eyes on her and spat a curse in pure Italian.

"Do you know who I am? The fucking trouble you are in, *brutto figlio di puttana bastardo!*"

Not having the slightest understanding, Marinette ignored the insult. "You are Flavio Carbonelli. The eunuch son of Tomasso Carbonelli, head of some runt criminal organization trying to strongarm their way into my territory."

"I am not a *eunuch!*" Flavio's voice climbed several notches.

"We shall see. Do you fear death, Flavio?"

A tongue flicked nervously across dry lips. "You should let me go. Send me back to my family. Otherwise—"

"Oh, I will." Marinette interrupted. "I have every intention of sending you back to your family, only . . . *changed*."

Flavio had little time to wonder what she meant by that. His friends watched in silence as Marinette waved two of her guards forward. One held out an earthenware bowl half-filled with a thick, black liquid. Marinette took it and dipped a finger.

"Good. Now—Flavio Carbonelli, meet the SPEAR team." She indicated Alicia and the other soldiers standing quietly to her side. "American Special Forces soldiers." She continued to name them all individually. "They hate weasels like you. And this is the deal . . ." She turned her attention to the SPEAR team.

"Two of you will force this drink down his throat. Three of you will dig his grave. And three of you will bury him alive."

Flavio screeched and tried to run. The guards slapped and kicked him until he was a slobbering ball at Marinette's feet. She touched him with the toe of her boot. "You will not die," she said. "Not in the accepted way."

"And what . . . what of us?" one of Flavio's friends asked in terror.

"You are my witnesses. You will report to the insignificant head of his family. You will tell him what you have seen. And you will make it clear that, unless he leaves Louisiana, I will subject his entire family to the same state of being as Flavio. Except for him. I will leave him to deal with what they become."

As her men forced Flavio to his knees, Marinette drew

the SPEAR team aside, addressing them quietly. "My last piece of what I'm hoping is trauma-inducing information will deal with zombies," she said plainly. "And zombification. Yes, the word is overused. Stylized, even. It has comical interpretations. Hollywood has done it to death, pun intended. But zombification is a part of the true voodoo religion. And my . . . *version*. I use a heavy dose of scopolamine mixed with *coup de poudre:* human remains and animal parts. The poison takes effect almost immediately, rendering the quarry immobile, and giving them an incredibly faint heartbeat. Breathing is reduced so that the victim appears dead. Whilst still in this death-like state, our man or woman, like you people, is very much aware of his surroundings, has normal thought processes, but can't express himself. Now, the ritual moves on. The apparently lifeless body is buried in a grave, given sufficient air for eight hours—though they do not know it— then dug up. The potion has done its job. The *caplata*— that is me—then administers a hallucinogenic concoction called *Powder Strike,* which keeps the zombie in a chaos of submissive confusion. Easy to control. To manipulate. To mind-fuck. After as many months as the *bokor* desires, they render their victims clinically insane. If they're lucky, they die. If not, the state will find and try to take care of them."

Marinette waited until the newcomers understood the full consequences of what she was saying. She wanted them to be aware of what they were about to do. She didn't tell them that the voodoo religion required a psychological aspect and a spiritual and cultural predisposition to work. The victims needed to pre-believe in their *caplata's* abilities. Belief was essential.

But that was where her hallucinogenic powders came in.

"Kinimaka and Hayden, force that shit down Flavio's throat. Cam, Shaw and Kenzie, dig the grave. Drake, Dahl and Alicia, you will bury him."

Their eyes bulging in fear, Flavio and his two friends watched as shovels were produced and a grave marked out. When metal started chopping at spongy earth, Kinimaka knelt beside Flavio, took firm hold of his throat and skull, and angled his head upward. Hayden took the half-full bowl of viscous liquid and approached.

"Please," Flavio choked. "Please, no . . ."

Kinimaka pinched Flavio's nose. Hayden waited for the mouth to open. Flavio struggled madly but the Hawaiian's grip was like iron shackles. When his mouth flew open for a quick gulp of air, Kinimaka squeezed the middle of his jaw.

Unable to close his mouth, Flavio let out a silent scream.

Hayden carefully poured the liquid into his mouth. Flavio choked and spit and fought, but at least half the concoction made its way down his throat. The other half went down his chin and shirt. Marinette's musical lilt put an end to the struggle.

"That is enough. He is ours now."

Almost immediately, Flavio stopped fighting. Marinette had known it would happen, but the abrupt change never ceased to please and stimulate her. It was the moment a vital, distinctive individual lost all free will and became her slave for life.

Flavio was allowed to slump to the ground. For long minutes, the only noise was made by Cam, Shaw and Kenzie digging a six-foot-deep, man-size hole in the ground. Four guards brought a coffin from among the trees, a rough timbered thing that was barely adequate and would allow soil to dribble though many holes, but that was the idea. The more trauma Flavio suffered, the harder his mind would be affected, and the better the hallucinogen would work.

When the gravediggers were finished, they stood back, panting, shovels in hand. The guards took them away. Finally, Drake, Dahl and Alicia paced over to Flavio's prone and seemingly lifeless body lying at his friends' feet.

Flavio's comrades regarded the three soldiers in horror.

"Surely you can't . . ." one of them said.

"They serve me," Marinette said. "Now strip him, bind his hands, and put him in the coffin. Then bury it in the grave."

She watched as the newcomers did her bidding, her thoughts already turning to the grand, excessive, ferocious ceremony she was planning for one of the coming nights. Flavio's coffin was nailed shut and then lowered into the ground. Shovelfuls of dirt were thrown over it until it was buried. The ground was patted flat, leveled out, a crude stick planted to mark the grave. It was hard to believe and almost impossible to know that a living, breathing person lay under that disturbed patch of earth.

With her slaves following, Marinette returned to her home.

CHAPTER THIRTY SIX

Mai Kitano met with Connor Bryant in the darkest parking lot on the outskirts of New Orleans just as a light sprinkling of raindrops fell from a gloomy, overcast sky. The night matched her mood. Bryant was as insensibly dumb as ever.

"Looking good, Kitano."

"Are we alone?"

"Umm, yes."

"Then cut the Casanova shit. Even with a rocket-launcher you're no lady-killer. Where are we?"

Bryant tried not to look hurt and Mai knew instinctively that he was struggling not to retort with a rocket launcher joke. Shadows played across her face as she regarded him with barely concealed tolerance.

"Thirty responded to the call. They're either bored, need the distraction, or happy with the spoils we're offering. I guess, potentially, this is a get-rich-quick mission. That's how I sold it anyway. So, yeah, we got thirty on the way. Should be here by the afternoon."

Bryant squinted up into the sky as if looking for the time.

"That's not bad," Mai admitted. "And gives us at least a day to prepare. I've spent some time asking questions, *discreetly,* since we know that's one way the others were tracked. I can be discreet, Bryant."

"Hmmm . . . weren't you the cosplay queen of Tokyo?"

"In a different life, yes. Now, I'm part of a close-knit family. And I will save them, no matter what the cost."

"What did you learn?" Bryant moved it on.

"Disappearances. Murders. Examples made. All attributed to Marinette. The cops can't or don't want to risk dealing with her. She's got everyone believing she's some voodoo witch and can see and hear everything that occurs in the city."

"A network of eyes and ears." Bryant nodded. "No doubt extending all the way up the food chain. But that doesn't help us save your friends."

"No, it doesn't. But there's more. I saw some of these watchers, Bryant. Followed some. They're human robots, emotionless, sluggish—"

"You're telling me they're zombies, aren't you? Oh shit, no fucking way—"

"Stop," Mai demanded. "No. I'm telling you that they've been drugged. Badly, often and thoroughly. Their appearance on the streets helps terrify the locals, the believers and, yes, the police. They report everything and see all."

Bryant didn't look convinced. "So what do we do?"

"Well, as you said, the streets of New Orleans are immaterial. We need access to Marinette's camp, to know her capabilities, her guard numbers, the amount of people on her property handling all those business dealings. It's a big enterprise. But . . . most of all . . . there's one key factor I don't want to overlook."

Bryant looked wary. "And what's that?"

"This drug. There's a very good chance Marinette's already dispensed it to Drake and the others. She'd want them pliable, easy to control. If that's been her go-to weapon of choice until now, it stands to reason that she'd stick with it. Alicia's been there for days. Drake less so, but Marinette would want them docile. Not chained in a room they could escape from, but drugged up to the eyeballs so that she doesn't have to worry."

"And you have a solution for that?"

"Maybe. The problem is, when you start asking questions you generally get the answers you want to hear."

Bryant looked lost for a moment but then recovered. "Ah, I see."

"They tell you the basics to move you along. The truth perhaps, but the bare minimum. For me, Marinette's mind control is the key to her kingdom."

"And the so-called zombies?"

"Yet another layer. But if we solve the mind control issue, we gain a significant and powerful advantage *inside* Marinette's lair when we attack, useful because that fight is gonna be brutal."

"We're gonna need it," Bryant agreed. "You got skills, Kitano, I'll give you that. You got me hooked. How do we solve the mind control issue?"

"By digging deeper. Certain people know a lot more than they're saying and these people *want* to talk. They want rid of Marinette and her evil ways. She's perverting an entire city and an entire culture. She's a scourge."

"So how do you find these people? Is the effort worth losing hours of precious time?"

"During questioning, one woman let something slip. I could tell by her body language that it was a mistake. She mentioned that when Marinette is done with these so-called voodoo soldiers—her name, not mine—she sends them back to their families as empty, lifeless shells. It's a horrific, unspeakable act designed to intimidate a population and destroy a household. After that, I pretended that I already *knew* about the families dealing with this and—finally—got a name."

"And what good is that? We're wasting time here."

Mai sighed. "Talking to this woman will give us a better understanding of what we're dealing with. Of these voodoo soldiers. Those wronged should start by fighting back. Maybe she has some insight. C'mon, Bryant, she's a short drive away."

Mai watched Bryant's face as he struggled with the decision. There was no doubt he had a certain boyish charm to his features, a sparkle in his eyes. She could see where he might gain the confidence to assume women found him attractive. What he didn't understand was that any woman could get anything out of him in five seconds and with one line.

"I'll make it worth your while, Connor."

Less than thirty seconds later, they were racing through several back streets with a satnav arrival time of eight minutes. It took only half that time for Bryant to realize she'd conned him.

"Damn I like you," were his only words, but Mai allowed a smile to flit across her face. Despite all his flaws and vices, Bryant was still an innocent in several exploitable ways.

"How much money you worth?" she asked.

"Last count twenty million," he said without any sign of boastfulness.

"I can't believe a woman hasn't swindled you yet."

That gave him something to consider for the next four minutes.

They pulled up to a curb, parked and approached a nondescript, squat house. It was in need of attention—everything from the gate to the garden and the window frames. The front door had once been bright blue, the drapes yellowed and fully drawn. The place screamed aloud the attitude of an owner that was done with the world outside.

"Let me do the talking," Mai said as they unhooked the gate.

Mai fought anxiety as she approached the door. A big part of her wanted to grab Bryant's mercenaries and start organizing an assault. It also told her that every lost minute put Drake and the others in deeper danger. That profound unease was balanced by her belief that Marinette held on to the majority of her team using some form of drug. Nothing else would work.

Clearing her mind, she knocked at the door.

"This is my son, Henri."

Mai breathed deeply, drawing in a lungful of fresh air to combat the distress she was feeling. This woman, Dominique, was crying freely, having taken Mai and Bryant at their words that they were here to help, and was now, perhaps foolishly, providing her son as undeniable proof of Marinette's depravity.

Mai had known from the moment she met her that Dominique didn't care about herself. She just wanted justice for her son.

"No change since he . . . returned?" she asked.

Dominique shook her head. Mai sat without moving, watching as the woman basically ordered her son around the room: to stop, to turn, to watch, to speak a sentence. To say there was no life left in Henri would be an understatement. He moved and obeyed with a lethargic submissiveness and lack of emotion that Mai found intensely disturbing.

"I've never seen anything like it," Bryant whispered

before turning to Dominique. "Sorry, I shouldn't have said that."

"It is okay. You are right. My son disappeared three years ago and never returned to me. This husk, this shell, this is not my son."

"But you think there's a chance?" Mai asked.

"I know there isn't," Dominique said. "Before Henri was stolen from me, I was a successful pharmacist. At first, I made many enquiries. Now, I know his state can never be reversed."

"And she did this to him? Marinette?"

Dominique showed a flash of anger for the first time. "Do not *speak* that name in my house! I will not have that evil here."

"We are trying to stop her. To bring a modicum of justice to all her victims," Mai said. "I am sorry if we upset you."

"No, it is okay." Dominique pressed the tips of her fingers to her temple. "I would have that witch pay for her sins. God help me, I would. The drug she administers before the burial ritual and the non-stop hallucinogens afterward are what destroys minds. The ritual, the show, the resurrection—it's all theater. The hallucinogens strip a personality away, layer by layer, day by day, until nothing remains."

"And this other drug she uses?"

"A weaker version. Basically, a concoction for mind control. Mostly scopolamine in small doses, it completely bends a person to another's will. At the same time, that person retains brain function so they know exactly what is happening but can do nothing about it."

"And big pharma knows about this?" Bryant asked, shocked.

"Oh, they know. But they market it as useful to offset

motion sickness and to treat nausea. Even Parkinson's. It's heavily dependent on the dosage."

"Is there a remedy? A way to reclaim your son?" Mai asked.

"Not now. Henri was returned only after he passed the point where he could condemn his abductor. Unfortunately, they are clever. But there *is* a way to quickly reverse the effects of the weaker drug, scopolamine."

"So, anyone under her influence, stuck full of this drug, would recover fast?"

"Yes, providing she hasn't introduced the *coup de poudre* mixture, which severely unbalances the system. That's the first step to . . ." Dominique couldn't finish. Mai was looking at Henri and didn't want to repeat the word either. They let it drop. Henri stood motionless in a corner, unmoving, staring into space.

"Is there anything that could break through?" Mai asked. "An emotion? An object? A memory?"

"The television," Dominique said. "We watch cartoons. Sometimes, he smiles but it is so painful. It's the smile I remember of a young boy, an infant, the same as it was years ago but unreachable now. I can never again talk to the man my boy became."

Mai teared up, feeling the woman's anguish like an anvil resting on her heart. It was raw and it deserved restitution.

"Thank you for your help." She stood and laid a hand on Dominique's arm. "I am so sorry for your son's and your torment. We will make them pay."

Dominique nodded. The lone, terrible truth was that whether Marinette lived or died in agony, her son would never be the same and they would live this way for the rest of their lives. Mai had visited just one of Marinette's victims. One out of a hundred . . . a thousand . . . all living through countless years of misery and torture.

Their reckoning was coming.

CHAPTER THIRTY SEVEN

Bryant was able to lean on the owner of a nationwide pharmaceutical chain, a man who'd once been a tragic kidnap and ransom victim until Bryant sent men in to rescue him. The op worked and the man vowed he would be forever in Bryant's debt. It would take several hours for the orders to filter down through the correct chains of command, but it was worth the wait for the antidote.

To help pass the time, Mai and Bryant returned to their hotel and changed. When Bryant asked Mai why he needed to dress in dark clothing her answer was both plain and cryptic.

"So you can blend into the shadows, dumbass."

Still affected by their afternoon with Dominique and Henri, they climbed into the car as long shadows unfolded across the city.

"Where are we going?" Bryant asked. "Shouldn't we brief the boys?"

"We'll brief them tomorrow."

"And now you're taking me to . . ." he drew the last word out.

"To pay our fucking respects," was all Mai would say for now.

Bryant drove, following her directions. He was quiet and obedient, which proved how deeply he'd been moved by Dominique's pain. Mai took them down several side streets before asking him to pull over.

"You can stay in the car if you want."

Bryant's face grew wary. "That doesn't sound good."

Then he saw a small sign directing them to a place three hundred yards ahead: *Lafayette Cemetery*.

"Oh no, you are gonna be the death of me, Mai Kitano."

"It's the only place where her cognizant criminal staff are sent outside her territory," Mai said. "We have the time whilst we're waiting for the scopolamine cure."

"You're thinking hard interrogation, aren't you?"

Mai didn't answer. Whatever happened, this would help Drake, and Marinette's victims, and would severely hinder the woman's allies. She paused with her hand on the door pull.

"Are you coming?"

"I'm proud that you would want me along."

"Wait." Mai looked at him, her face half-hidden in shadow. "You *did* serve, didn't you? That story's not CEO company bullshit, right?"

Bryant's teeth audibly ground together. "I served," he said shortly. "Now, you coming or not?"

He exited the car. Mai sensed a far larger story behind the brush off and followed. For now, she wouldn't pry. Focusing ahead, she reflected on what she knew about Lafayette Cemetery. One of the oldest in the city, it was an above-ground burial site, containing over a thousand family tombs and laid out in a cruciform pattern to allow for funeral processions. The architecture of the numerous tombs was prominent and singular, with no two mausoleums the same and mostly gray in appearance. However, failing light gave them a whole new perspective.

"A New Orleans cemetery in the dead of night," Bryant muttered. "What could possibly go wrong?"

"You sound like Alicia. And it's not the dead of night yet. So, shut up and try not to wake the dead."

Bryant gave her an askance stare. "Is that the *fun* Kitano at play?"

"You'll never see the fun Kitano. Pay attention."

"Such a shame." But Bryant fell silent as they approached the cemetery gates.

Mai paused to listen. As expected, the entire area was shrouded in silence. She checked their rear. All seemed clear. The wrought iron gates were below head-height at the center point and easy enough to climb over. Mai did so soundlessly, Bryant not so much.

Once inside, they studied the terrain. The stars and moon picked out random pieces of architecture and the stony path ahead. Mai had never seen so many mausoleums in one place, like tiny, sad houses stretching away into the night.

"Can't see a lot," Bryant whispered. "Where do we go?"

"They're grave robbers," Mai said. "And, according to the localized version of the *Picayune* newspaper only two people were buried here in the last two days. I'd say we start with them."

"When the hell did you do that research?"

"Google's on your phone now, Bryant. It's not a big deal."

"Oh, smart ass and—"

"If you value your fingers don't complete that sentence."

The man grinned but said nothing. Mai found herself wondering why a regular, everyday guy would create a business persona that was so crass and discourteous, but then reminded herself how successful he was. Maybe the key was to be memorable—the reasoning didn't matter.

"The first grave," she said, stopping. "Or rather, tomb, is up ahead and to the right."

They slipped off the path and took cover at the side of

an old mausoleum. Not close enough to discern any details, Mai spent five minutes leading them closer. Soon, they were opposite the tomb, shrouded in shadow.

Ten minutes later, Bryant sighed. "Looks like we're too late. Or you messed up."

Mai didn't answer. She led him to the second tomb. Just being among these old graves made the hairs on the back of her neck stand on end. There was a heavy, overwhelming silence, a sense of stillness. Surrounded by thousands of dead bodies, Mai's senses told her she was being watched. But that couldn't be that case—she was confident in her abilities to remain unseen.

Unless those watchers weren't among the living.

Mai suppressed a shudder. Bryant glanced at her, but she could see in the dark of his eyes that he was spooked too. Mai found herself watching the tomb doors, their roofs, for signs of movement. It was irrational, but then so was creeping around an above-ground cemetery in the dark watches of the night.

"Have you seen enough?" Bryant whispered. "'cause I'm starting to wish I brought a cross, an axe and a fucking shotgun."

Mai studied the second tomb, seeing no sign of graverobbers. She consoled herself with the thought that it had been a long shot. "This place," she said, "does not feel entirely *comfortable*. I haven't stopped shivering since we arrived."

Bryant licked his lips. Darkness crouched around them, crawling up and down and in between countless tombs. There was no breeze, no sound, not the slightest sense of being on this earth. There was only the cemetery and its gloomy procession of somber buildings.

"And the man foolish enough to spend his nights

robbing body parts here," Bryant shook his head. "I really don't wanna meet him."

"Quiet." Mai's sharp hearing picked up a sound. Seconds later, disheveled gray figures trudged out of the darkness.

Bryant stiffened, mouth opening. Mai clapped her hand over his lips, pressing hard and sinking to the ground.

Four men approached the tomb. They wore tattered clothing and had scarves wrapped around their heads and face, the frayed ends hanging down to their hips. They didn't speak. One man took her attention, appearing to be around seven feet tall, lanky, and with a drawn, skeletal face. He watched everything keenly, his gaze piercing even the deepest shadows. When it passed over her, Mai found herself wishing she could sink into the ground.

All four figures stopped outside the second tomb. Three waited, arms hanging listlessly. The tall man checked his surroundings once more. Finally satisfied, he waved at the other men.

"Arms, legs," he said in a voice that reminded Mai of rocks being scraped together. "Eyes. Ears. Internal organs. Make it quick."

"Cimetiére," one of the men groaned. "is this the last?"

"For tonight it is."

Mai felt unaccountably relieved. Hearing them speak proved they were living, breathing opponents. That . . . she could handle.

"Ready yourself," she told Bryant.

"Are you fucking kidding? Have you seen the size of that skeleton motherfucker?"

"Connor," she whispered angrily. "Are you a soldier?"

"Maybe . . ." he said warily, drawing the word out.

"Then follow me."

Mai studied their comings and goings for a few more minutes. Graverobbing, she guessed, was easier accomplished in an above-ground tomb. She saw the men take out crowbars, hammers and a big, leather rolled-up bag of what she assumed were surgeon's tools before gaining entry to the tomb's man-size door. Cimetiére watched them, grating orders only when he needed to. The men moved and worked languidly, but Mai now assumed that was due to fatigue rather than anything sinister. It was entirely possible they'd visited many gravesites tonight.

Before they could get fully started on their grisly task, Mai started creeping through the undergrowth that surrounded her. As she prepared to attack, Bryant grabbed her hand.

"Are you sure about this, Kitano?"

"The more detailed descriptions we have of Marinette's home and operations, the more men we'll keep alive, and the better chance of saving Drake and the others we'll have."

Bryant sighed. "I guess that makes sense. But the skeleton's yours."

"Fine," Mai snapped back, focusing. "Now, back me up."

CHAPTER THIRTY EIGHT

Mai aimed her gun at Cimetiére and waved Bryant past.

"Don't move."

The tall man clenched fists at the end of two long, emaciated arms. The cavities where his cheeks ought to have been drew even further into his mouth. Mai trod very carefully.

"That backpack? Lose it."

Cimetiére dropped a bulging sack to the floor. Mai's eyes drifted toward it as the top, not properly fastened, fell open. Disgust filled her stomach as a severed hand fell out, followed by several ears and a plastic bag full of teeth. Other items glistened in the darker innards, bones and flesh picked out by a stark moon.

This is so terrifyingly wrong.

Bryant was at the entrance to the tomb, calling those working inside to heel. They appeared slowly, filing out as languidly as they'd filed in, showing no interest and no fear of the newcomers and their guns.

"Together," Bryant said. "And lose the backpacks."

More gruesome trophies were revealed as Cimetiére's men let their bags fall to the ground. Mai clenched her teeth until they hurt.

"Are you people crazy?" Bryant began. "You're—"

"There's no point," Mai said. "You'll never get through to them. How about this? We set you free if you answer our questions."

Her words produced an interesting range of reaction. Cimetiére snarled angrily and, if she was being totally honest, his face and reaction chilled her to the bone. Of the other three men, one looked up hopefully, one shuffled his feet, and the last fell to his knees in fear.

"No, no, she won't kill me," he blubbered. "She will turn me. Suffer unto me the burial of the dead. Not that. *Never that.*"

Mai knew she could never conquer such cultural terror. But not only that—the threat was *real*. It didn't matter that the reality of what happened was different—a fact Marinette understood and used very well—it was people's root belief that counted.

"A few questions," she said. "Ten more minutes and you're free."

Cimetiére reacted violently, lashing out at Mai with those gaunt arms. Fists knocked her gun away, and then he leapt at her. The thin face was a terrifying vision, flying through the night, the mouth a drooling snarl. Mai stepped back, seeking the fallen Glock, but Cimetiére's body struck her with shocking strength, knocking her off her feet. She landed on her tailbone, the impact jarring every bone in her body. Mai groaned, but saw her opponent coming. She rolled fast, striking at his face with an elbow. She struck bone, but he didn't react. He didn't go for the gun either. His snarling, enraged focus was entirely on her—the woman who'd usurped his good night's work.

Bryant was covering the other three. Only one appeared threatening. Bryant was ready for his attack, side-stepping and burying his boot firmly into the man's side. Ribs broke and he went down in agony.

Mai grappled with Cimetiére, who was incredibly strong. His seven-foot skinny frame bore down on her, his skull-like face and fetid breath so close she had to close her eyes. On her back, she rolled and kicked him in the groin—once, twice, three times. It had no effect, not even a wince. He didn't feel any of her blows but returned them with bruising power.

As they fought and rolled, they came up close to the bag he'd dropped on the floor. Mai felt the bile rise as her right cheek brushed the severed hand and the sack shifted, depositing more body parts across the ground.

"My . . . work . . ." Cimetiére moaned.

He was genuinely distraught. They rolled across the hands and ears, a severed foot. More trophies spilled out. Internal organs sealed in transparent bags. And eyeballs . . . Mai turned away, stomach heaving.

Cimetiére took the chance to deliver three stunning blows. Mai felt the air rush out of her. Fists punished her stomach; she almost blacked out as he slammed her temple into a paving flag. For a moment, she couldn't move, depleted, confused, tormented.

Cimetiére's claw-like fingers scraped her cheeks as they attacked her eyeballs.

Mai felt a rush of adrenalin. She screamed. Then Bryant's gun went off, the bullet slamming into the ground next to Cimetiére's right knee, shards of stone perforating his flesh. This time he did flinch, drawing to the side. Mai lashed out and rolled away, grabbing her Glock as she rose to her knees.

"Stop!"

But Cimetiére was running, sprinting away as though the dead were well and truly chasing him. In seconds, the graverobbers' leader had vanished amid the longstanding mausoleums.

"Thanks, Bryant," Mai breathed.

"You're welcome," he whispered back.

She looked away from the spilled body parts, wanting to unsee that particular vision, and fixed her sights firmly on the two more amenable men standing before her.

"Your leader's gone. Scarpered like a coward, running to his mistress. That gives *you* guys an even better chance."

Bryant waved his gun. "He won't come looking for you for hours, maybe days," he said. "Leave town. Marinette's attracted the wrong kind of attention now. She'll be history before the week's out."

"Help us and walk away," Mai said.

The youngest, dressed in the most rancid rags, held her gaze with hopeful eyes. "Ask your questions," he said.

"Building layouts," she said. Having studied the mediocre satellite images they could get access to, they still couldn't accurately discern all the camouflaged buildings or their size. "And our friends—have you seen them?"

She described Alicia, Drake and Dahl, adding Kinimaka for good measure. The young man nodded.

"I've seen them. They're not doing so well."

Mai's heart plummeted. "How do you mean?"

"The hallucinogen. Marinette has them under her thrall. They do as she pleases, their systems never clear of the drug. It will scar them forever, take them to a place they may never return from. Today, after sunset, she plans the greatest ritual of all. She will consume them."

Conscious of time, the preparation required, and Cimetiére's absence, Mai didn't push the youth. She got a detailed drawing of the buildings, a supposedly unused path through the swamp, of guard numbers and how many mercenaries Marinette employed to look after her various businesses, and got the hell out of there. Bryant stayed by her side the entire time.

Back at their car, Mai paused before switching the engine on. "It has to be tonight," she said. "The attack."

"I heard and I agree."

"Good, then let's get started. And . . . Bryant . . ."

"Yes?"

"You should know that I can count the number of people I trust with my life on the fingers of two hands. Before you stopped Cimetiére tonight you rated low on that list. Low enough to warrant little faith. Now, I'll have some hope when I walk into Hell with you."

Bryant's eyes glowed wide in the half-dark. "Thanks," he said. "I think."

"We've never faced anything like we'll face tonight, Bryant. Get ready for it."

Mai started the car.

CHAPTER THIRTY NINE

When Mai, Bryant and his force of mercenaries set off they had no idea of the nightmares that were waiting for them in Black Snake Swamp, no idea of the scale of suffering they were walking into.

"Three more stragglers joined during the night," Bryant had told her with a smile that morning.

Mai had nodded appreciatively. Now, as they paused on the edge of Marinette's domain, she found herself wishing it had been more.

"You know your orders," she said through a comms system. "Never stray. We're in hostile territory now so be prepared. Our targets are two miles south of here, but it's gonna seem further on these paths."

They passed among dense trees, clad in military gear including bulletproof vests and helmets with night-vision goggles, but preferring to use the glow cast by a million stars for now. Bryant had long since deferred command to Mai, making it clear to all that this was her gig.

Mai trod carefully. The graverobbing youth had revealed details about this path that he didn't need to. Maybe he was being helpful, but as she'd told Bryant, the people Mai trusted on this earth were few. She led the way. The path was narrow, forcing them to walk in single file. Water from a recent rain shower dripped off every leaf and bough, splashing off her helmet and shoulders, filling the wider marshes with an unceasing trickle that sounded like a new rainfall. As they penetrated deeper into Marinette's territory without incident, Mai began to think that maybe the youth had been good to his word.

The trees thinned to be replaced by wide fields. Still the path wandered through them. Mai waved them on. They were halfway to their target. Bryant was just behind, staying close, having vowed to watch her back as honorably as any of her trusted friends. Mai was touched. There was no bravado to his promise, no tactless attempt at seduction. For now at least, Bryant was being genuine.

Darkness crouched over their heads and all around. The stars were a good source of illumination, but scudding clouds often switched that luminance off. Staying low, the well-armed interlopers crept ever closer to Marinette's vice-stained lair.

Mai whirled as a cry pierced the silence. At first, she was annoyed to see the mercs had fanned out behind her, walking two or three abreast and not on the path. Then she saw one of the men tottering on the edge of something wide and black in the ground, arms out, staying upright only because his partner was holding him back.

"What did I say?" Mai hissed, then ran over.

The soldier was pulled back. Mai arrived just as he landed unhappily on his ass; she grabbed his jacket and yanked him forward. "Didn't you hear me? I said stay on the fucking path." Her voice was a furious whisper and, a second later she let go. "Fucking dumb mercs," she hissed, walking up to Bryant's shoulder. "What is it?"

"A stake pit," the man said, quiet horror in his voice. "Six foot deep. The bottom's lined with sharpened sticks."

"I know what a stake pit is," Mai said shortly then hit her comms. "This is a warning," she told them all. "Stay focused and follow orders. This is no place to die, my friends."

They moved on in tight, concentrated silence. The fields were flat, bordered by trees about a mile to each side. Mai tried in vain to penetrate the darkness, wondering if there were any watchers out there. Yes, the merc had been foolish to wander off the path, but the presence of a trap proved that this dark byway was anything but secret.

They approached another treeline. Mai could hear a rushing stream ahead, one of many that twisted through the swamp. Black boughs and foliage blocked their path. The route had vanished under low-hanging branches but that was to be expected. Vegetation grew fast around here. Mai continued slowly, stopping at the treeline. She bent to look down under a thick branch.

Oh my God, what the fuck is that . . .

It was big, cruel and black, with terrible serrated teeth, and it had been positioned where a person would step over vegetation and into it as they tried to keep to the path.

"Stop," Mai said. "Everyone stop."

She saw another contraption to the right and then one further along to the left. She shone her flashlight ahead and saw four more scatted up the path.

"Mantraps," she said. "Real bone-breakers. Tread with care, boys."

Passing the cold, coiled steel sent a shiver through her. The mantraps looked evil and radiated a dreadful cruelty that gave her goosebumps. Inanimate they might be, but nothing could dilute the pure sense of evil they exuded.

Five minutes later, the path ahead was clear, wending once more between trees. Mai checked their position, which was good and put them only thirty minutes or so from their target. They paused for five minutes as the night deepened and water dripped. But then another noise made Mai look up. Faint for now, it was the distant beat of rhythmic drums.

"It's begun," she said.

"The ritual? Shit, we need to get a move on." Bryant rose from a crouched position, peering ahead.

Mai was already walking. Again, she heard something at her back, and turned just in time to see a merc walking out of the woods, zipping up his pants, abruptly enfolded in a large net that snapped his entire body upward. Other mercs stared in horror as the net smashed into higher boughs that had been sharpened into curved scimitars. The merc just stuck there, the net rustling around him. Blood seeped along its webbing and trickled thickly to the swamp floor.

Mai was sorry for the merc, but this wasn't the time to show compassion. "Anyone else wanna shake it?" she asked harshly. "No? Then follow me and stick to the path."

The youth hadn't mentioned any traps. But he *had* told her not to stray from the path. With doubt in her mind, Mai led the way onward. When the starlight was obscured briefly by a shadow, she looked up at the tree canopy, rattled and wondering where the next attack would come from.

A figure was crouched about twelve feet high among branches. He was dark and thin against faint illumination and he appeared to be holding something in his mouth.

Mai flung herself to the floor, shouting out a warning. Dull thuds filled the forest. Something small glanced off her jacket and another off her helmet. Some of the others weren't so lucky. Mai rolled, looking back. She saw a merc with his hands to his right cheek, pulling a long, thin dart from his face. Another tried to pluck one from his throat but already they were losing consciousness, staggering to the ground. Their eyes rolled up into their heads.

Mai didn't wait any longer, turning her suppressed M4

carbine on the trees. She opened fire, shredding leaves, branches and bodies alike. The other mercs followed suit, sending a thick wave of lead twelve to eighteen feet high and decimating everything that lived up there. Mai heard several bodies fall through branches before thudding heavily and lifelessly to the ground.

After a while, she paused, calling for a ceasefire. Her eyes sought movement above them for another long minute before she gave the all clear.

"They're dead," a voice spoke in her earbud. "Both of them poisoned by a fucking dart. What the hell is this place?"

Mai kept it together. "You want spoils," she said. "You have to earn them. Moving out now."

Stepping over lifeless bodies, they pressed ahead. The drumbeat grew louder, and a faint crimson flicker stained the horizon whenever the vegetation thinned out.

"They got a lot of fires burning," Bryant noted.

"Good," Mai said. "Should keep them occupied."

"You're hoping the dart-blowing lookouts didn't get chance to report?"

"Doesn't matter. We're committed now."

They were nearing Marinette's outlying buildings. Mai saw several low structures outlined against the shadows ahead even though they were still fifteen minutes from her main camp.

"What the hell are these places?" a soldier asked.

Mai dreaded to think.

CHAPTER FORTY

Mai crawled through vegetation, her stomach soaked, blinking rapidly to shed water droplets. In the end, she fixed her night-goggles over her eyes and waited until they adjusted.

"Stay absolutely still," she whispered. "And quiet."

Peering forward, she wondered if her eyes were playing tricks. Men wearing only loincloths were shunting other men and women into line with eight-foot-long, stone-tipped spears. They looked fit, with rippling muscles and healthy faces. In contrast, the people they pushed and shoved, staggered with dull lifelessness, their gait and body language screaming that all vitality had been drained out of them. It was the first time Mai had set eyes on the so-called zombies.

"God help them," she whispered.

"Some things you can never unsee," Bryant muttered and other soldiers agreed.

Mai distinctly remembered telling them all to remain silent, but this couldn't be helped. The vision before them was hellish. Tall men with spears herded the listless into three long lines, making them wait until all was ready. Before they moved off, more figures appeared, these naked and daubed in paint, their faces decorated to achieve a skeletal appearance. They carried clay pots and sticks, and proceeded to throw the powdery contents of the pots over the lined-up figures before shaking the sticks at them.

Powder flew in thick clouds, coating men and women everywhere from head to toe. They showed no emotion, but the new arrivals proceeded to dance and caper around them, chanting in low, guttural voices. Mai didn't know whether to wait it out or seek a way around the spectacle, but held fast for now. The soldiers waited in silence. Three broke away to watch their backs and flanks without being asked, reaffirming some of Mai's faith in them.

The exhibition grew even stranger and more dangerous. More paint-covered people appeared, carrying large sacks by the neck. Mai watched the sacks as they bulged and writhed, guessing what was inside.

Snakes were pulled out by their heads. Wild with anger, they hissed and struck, bodies thrashing in fury. Those holding them didn't react, but placed them around the shoulders of the so-called zombies, letting them curl and crush and squirm. Blood soaked the ground. Mai guessed that whatever venom the snakes had once possessed had been drawn out, but the bites would still be painful. Contradicting her thoughts, neither the snake-bringers nor the lifeless figures reacted.

"This is more than insane," Bryant whispered. "I feel like Lovecraft at the Mountains of Madness."

Mai was impressed but put a finger to her lips. Nothing in her past had prepared her for this vision of sheer Hell. The snakes hissed and bit and coiled. The naked figures pranced back and forth. The spear-holding guards jabbed where they pleased and the uncaring, indolent line of people took it all without a sound. Mai was glad when, finally, the procession moved off in the direction of the fires.

"Must be headed for the ritual," Mai said.

"Wait," a soldier said. "This *wasn't* the ritual? I mean, fuck me, how bad is *that* gonna be?"

"Just stay focused and kill anything that threatens you, us, or our targets," Mai said. "A clear, concentrated head will get you all through this."

Nobody answered. Mai didn't blame them. The unknown factors facing them were immeasurable, from spear-and-dart toting warriors to paid mercs with guns, and from zombie-like figures to the swamp queen, Marinette. Mai had no doubt she'd be a formidable opponent.

But nothing would stop her now. They decided to file after the slow-moving line, using it for cover, seeing no sign of any other guards. It took another twenty minutes to travel the short distance into Marinette's main camp.

From their vantage point amid a thick cluster of trees and foliage Mai, Bryant and the thirty remaining soldiers beheld the most depraved vision of purgatory they could ever imagine; their impending battleground, their final destination.

Marinette's ritual grounds seethed with horrors.

CHAPTER FORTY ONE

Torches set atop poles blazed from one end of the vast field to the other. Chanting filled the night. Four enormous bonfires raged, flames raging against the dark, black smoke billowing upward. Mai couldn't keep count of the number of people she could see, from guards to mercenaries with guns, to naked dancers, to the robotic walking dead, to the painted stick-wielders and spear-holders, to groups of men grasping machetes and others beating drums. The shadows being cast upon the far treeline bordered on madness: terrible stick-figures, elongated limbs reaching and swaying. Mai felt her grasp on reality falter.

"At least now we know how we got this far," Bryant said. "Everyone working for Marinette is here."

"The greatest ritual of all," she echoed the youth's description of yesterday. "I wonder what it is."

Hands gestured at the sky. Bodies swayed and knelt and rolled and danced. A ritualistic chant grew in volume. The bonfires blazed at four sides, forming a square with a wooden, raised platform in the center. It was to this platform that Mai now focused her attention.

"I think that's Marinette."

They were close enough to see a tall, black-haired woman wearing leather trousers and a black top hat. Her face had been painted to resemble a skull and she carried a long, ball-tipped cane and a sword. She stood watching her worshippers, her minions, her subordinates and slaves, a look of satisfaction on her face.

"Any sign of Drake and the others?" Bryant was squinting.

That was the problem. Mai couldn't see her friends anywhere. She swept the field twice with ever-increasing anxiety. *What if they're lying in a shallow grave, aware of their predicament, slowly turning into . . . into . . .*

A frenzied increase in activity brought her attention back to the ceremony. The turbulent, drug-and-violence-fueled atmosphere swept across the field, taking even Marinette's watching mercenaries under its merciless spell. They fired their weapons into the air, howling. The drumbeat intensified. Marinette thrust her arms toward the skies. Her followers copied, dozens and dozens jumping and chanting at the star-littered vault of the night, and then the robotic walking dead were forced to follow suit.

Mai was mesmerized. It was the sheer diversity of people, the whole assorted array caught under one banner. It was the unfiltered ferocity, the brutal adoration. They crawled along and kissed the earth; they squirmed to the edge of Marinette's platform and begged to lick her feet. They tested themselves by thrusting their hands into the raging pyres. They strapped each other to crosses that had been hammered into the ground to form an X-shape, and then whipped, stabbed and flayed each other.

"Split up," Mai said. "Half of you need to be on the other side of this field so that we can strike from two directions. Be careful and look out for captives along the way."

It was their best move. Imperative, under the circumstances. A two-pronged assault would work best and would also allow her soldiers to seek out Drake and the others. Mai was sure they'd be attending this ceremony, one way or the other. It was just a question of when Marinette chose to use them.

Forced to wait, Mai could only watch.

Guttural voices joined to form a rasping chorus; faces lifted upward. The drummers were in a frenzy; sweaty, painted faces running, giving the appearance that their flesh was melting in their fever. Marinette took center stage with her legs spread wide, her aggrandized, skeletal features upturned, and a thick-bodied python rolled languidly between her uplifted arms.

"Fuck me," Bryant whispered. "I wouldn't want that—"

He clammed up as Marinette transferred her sword to one hand, produced a small blade, then sliced the animal in half. Blood splashed her feet. She threw both halves to the crowd who fell on the pieces with rabid abandon.

With that sacrifice the whole area fell silent. The sudden overwhelming hush resounded in Mai's ears, confusing her senses. One of the mercs, named Trey Hayes, who'd led half her men to the other side of the field spoke up to say they'd arrived.

"Sit tight," Bryant said. "We don't know what the hell's going on here."

A sentence that grew increasingly relevant. Horror rose once more in Mai's chest as three heavy sacks were lifted onto the platform. The contents were carefully rooted through and select items removed. Mai saw two severed hands, one male and one female, laid down. These were complemented by ears and eyeballs and the husk of a heart. Marinette then also placed a bottle of black rum, a box of cigars, and a plate of food in their center.

"Weirdest Yuletide tradition I've ever seen," Bryant whispered.

Mai shushed him. This wasn't the time for stupid jokes, though the wisecrack did remind her of Alicia and Dahl. Maybe Drake would have said something about pork pies.

Mai forced the sentimentalism aside, unable to tear her gaze away from the unfolding spectacle of depravity.

Marinette rose and intoned a chant, legs spread, arms raised to the sky. Those close to her platform fell to their knees and chests in supplication, groveling. The drummers were blurs, streams of paint flying off their bodies. Sweat, desire and animalistic intensity saturated the air from soil to clouds. Mai could barely move.

Then her comms beeped. "This is Hayes. We got a situation here."

"What?" Mai focused with an effort.

"I sent some guys to check around. They found some rough huts about three hundred yards to the south. Seems a line of prisoners is being dragged between those huts and the ceremony."

"Prisoners?" Mai latched onto the word. "How are they different from the . . . robotic people we saw?" She couldn't bring herself to say the Z-word.

"They're in chains, the lot of them. Manacles around wrists and ankles and one long chain looped through the entire line that's being dragged by half a dozen big guys with guns. The prisoners look like I would after drinking three bottles of Tequila, but are still more responsive than the zombie dudes."

Clearly Hayes had no issue with the Z-word. Mai frowned. "In what way?"

Hayes grunted. "Seems like they're trying to resist, only . . . their bodies won't let them. It's weird and frankly quite painful to watch."

"Are our targets among them?"

"Not yet but there are at least fifty people here and they're pretty well huddled together."

"How far away are they?" Mai was wondering if they

could free Drake and the others before they reached the ceremony.

"You should be seeing them now."

Mai averted her gaze from the wild shenanigans between the four bonfires to watch as a long, sorrowful procession of prisoners emerged from the far treeline. The very sight of them was heartbreaking—men and women wearing torn clothing, their heads hanging, wrists bleeding under the heavy, steel manacles, trudging along at gunpoint. At first Mai saw no signs of resistance but then noticed one man raise his head and look to the skies as if sending out a silent scream.

"They're being forced against their wills," Bryant whispered. "And know exactly what's happening."

"Marinette's drug of choice," Mai said, watching the long line weave its way toward Marinette's platform. Desperately, she searched for any sign of her friends, sweeping night-vision goggles across the sad convoy, but the flare generated by the bonfires, the standing torches, and the sway of the group made it impossible to pick faces out.

"Shit, we're gonna have to get closer."

"Wait," Bryant said. "They're *coming* closer."

It was true in the fact that they were approaching Marinette who stood at the center of the field. Her body language and the ceremony now appeared to be reaching a crescendo, some final verse. Anticipation was a living, squirming monster in the air, heaving, writhing and inundating the field from end to end.

"Make ready," Bryant told his men. "And good fucking luck, boys."

There were heartfelt whispers of affirmation. Mai rolled her shoulders, lifted her semi-auto, and prepared herself.

Wait...

As the prisoners approached the platform they drifted further apart. The thick chain dragging them was thrown to the ground. Their guards parted, allowing more freedom of movement as they lined up at the base of the platform.

A familiar figure stepped into view...

Drake!

And then, close by, she saw Kinimaka's big frame and then Dahl's. Alicia and Kenzie. She saw Cam, Shaw and Hayden—all alive and under some kind of thrall. The sight sent a spear of hope through her heart.

"Make ready the antidote," she told Bryant. "This mission is now a red-hot motherfucking *go*."

CHAPTER FORTY TWO

Matt Drake fought the swampy purgatory controlling his mind with every fiber of his being. Nothing existed but battle and the movements his body was forced to make. Ordered out of the hut, they were clapped in irons and marched through trees and marshes. Pain filled him, crammed every particle of his awareness from head to toe: a raging internal fire. The agony promised to relent if he just gave up all control, and his mind. Lesser men would have succumbed, but Drake was made of harder, sterner stuff.

Nevertheless, he followed the herd.

They came out of the treeline and were confronted by a stunning spectacle. Towering bonfires that reminded him unnervingly of their last mission. Dancers moving with wild abandon. Drummers fueled by doses of crazy. Guards and mercenaries and zombies. It was the hellish vision he never thought he'd see. And there, at the center of it all, stood their narcissistic queen—Marinette.

Drake had to admire her. A complex enigma, she radiated sensual violence, deadly comfort and loving servitude all wrapped in one inhuman, piquant and wholly carnal package. There was no middle ground, only extremes and the promise of something far worse than death. His eyes focused on her as she stood above them on her wooden platform.

"*Ade due, Samedi! Ade due, Samedi! Secoise entienne mais pois de morte.*"

Eyes raised to the skies, she chanted. Smoke from the billowing bonfires swept by her. Flames outlined her. She was a goddess, a dream of madness. Drake couldn't move, could barely remember who he'd been before coming to this place. Those around him, their faces passing between full recognition and vague memory, also watched the rapture unfold.

"*Ade due, Samedi! Ade due, Samedi! Secoise entienne mais pois de morte. Ade due, Samedi!*"

Drake stood to the right of Marinette's platform, his head tilted sideways as he gazed up at her. Thus, he was in a good position to see a mini-explosion in the air. White smoke plumed up from the ground in impenetrable sheets for several seconds before drifting away. And then . . . as if appearing out of nowhere . . . there stood a voodoo god.

Marinette called his name: "*Baron Samedi! Loa of the Dead. You bless us with your company, aura and spirit. Loa of resurrection! You exalt us with your lifeforce. We stand at the crossroads between the worlds of the dead and the living. Honor us with your desires!*"

Despite his condition, Drake felt a deep-rooted, dark swell of fear. The living man standing before them was the embodiment of death. He wore a top hat to match Marinette's, a black tailcoat, dark glasses and cotton buds in his nostrils. His face was painted as a skull, and his hands covered in soil as if he'd recently dug through a grave. Without pause, he strode up to the wooden platform and faced Marinette.

"What you got for me, slave?"

Drake was aghast, wondering if his mistress would react badly. But she opened her arms and gestured at the offerings that lay before him—severed body parts, cigars and rum. Baron Samedi glanced over them, turned to

Marinette and used the belt of her leather pants to tug her toward him. He opened his mouth and waited for Marinette to cover it with her own.

Drake gazed on as sexual tension, violence and dark adoration filled the air. Standing at the spot where Samedi had appeared he now saw a short line of black men, all with machine guns. An honor guard, maybe. It reminded him that he, too, had been a soldier and that the metal tube sticking out of the ground at the guards' feet was nothing but a smoke delivery system, proving something . . . something he couldn't quite grasp. Reality drifted away, and he found himself wanting to be Samedi, wanting to serve Marinette in any way possible.

Alicia, by his side, fell to her knees and crawled up to the platform before resting her chin on the wood and staring upward in adulation. Drake saw something else crawling in the wake of Samedi—the biggest alligator he'd ever seen—and even the armed guards trembled as it shuffled past.

Marinette kissed Samedi until he pulled away. Then she carried on with the ceremony, exalting the fires, the night and the swamp. Her followers knelt and swayed in ecstasy and adulation, completely taken by the moment. Samedi picked up the rum, uncorked it and swigged heavily from the bottle before taking a moment to light a fat cigar. When the alligator stopped close to the platform, he gazed down at it with a twisted grin on his face.

Drake could tell he was waiting for something.

A moment later, Marinette ended her chant, sank to her knees and laughed wildly. Samedi produced a Taser and hit the gator with it. Its tail snapped sideways in fury and its dagger-lined mouth shot open. Incensed, it darted forward into the mass of kneeling supplicants.

Samedi laughed. Marinette held her reverent pose. Drake drifted back into lucidity long enough to understand this was the voodoo queen's way of showing that she could summon a god, that her power was all, and that she held their lives and deaths between her hands.

Marinette reached for two writhing sacks Drake hadn't previously noticed. She whispered something over them, maybe a prayer, opening them at the edge of her platform, the contents spilling over the backs of her kneeling, swaying congregation. Drake wanted to scream a warning as dozens of snakes swarmed onto and among them, but his body and brain didn't work in tandem anymore.

Instead, the horrors continued.

Samedi grinned, gestured and swigged rum. A man gave himself willingly to the gator, gnashed between deadly teeth and a devastating bite. Snakes slithered unchecked. Marinette stared into the bonfire flames, exquisite face shining and reflecting the blaze. The ceremony reached its peak.

Drake saw them coming.

Some old instinct focused his gaze upon them. Dahl was looking too, and Hayden. They spied a stream of men led by a familiar woman. Mai Kitano broke out of the undergrowth and attacked the ceremony.

Drake saw Marinette swivel around as though telepathic, eyes locking onto the attack. She issued an immediate order through a hidden comms system nestled deep in her ear. All around the field, her men started forward. Guards and mercenaries looked up to spot the danger.

Marinette's next act filled Drake with a terror the like of which he'd never felt before.

"Alicia . . . Drake . . . Dahl . . . Cam . . . Shaw . . ." The list went on until all his friends' names had been called out and they were staring at her, waiting for their orders.

"Turn now and fight. Tear each other. Rend each other. Kill the face that you most love. Kill . . . kill . . . KILL!"

Drake was consumed by a blinding hot fury.

CHAPTER FORTY THREE

Mai laid it all out for her men as they attacked.

"Hayes . . . take your men straight at those guards with machetes. Todman, switch right . . . hit the spear throwers with five men. Annis . . . subdue the worshippers at the front of the platform with two. Gross and Peaple . . . you got the drummers and the guards over that way. Bryant, you and I are taking Marinette and any other guards that get in our way."

"Copy that." Todman.

"Got it." Gross.

"Take care," Mai said. "And make no mistake. This is the fight of your lives. You think you've fought in Hell before? Well, nothing I've seen comes close to this. Stay sharp, watch your six, and fight for your teammate. See you all on the other side."

Running hard, she saw Hayes and his men stream out of the far trees. Bryant was at her side. Hayes captured the attention of the machete-wielding maniacs who shouted then attacked. The other leaders, Todman and Gross among them, were already close to a bunch of guards. The drummers were still beating their hides, and the grotesque dancers were capering back and forth; the mercenaries grinning and shouting among themselves. But, one by one, their attack was being noticed.

"Here we go," Bryant cried and started running.

They circumvented the milling, brain-challenged

automatons. Mai passed just feet from the gator's thrashing tail before hurdling a mottled brown snake. A zombie saw her and reached out, fingers grasping, but she was far too quick. The platform was ten feet away. Those guards in front of it saw the emerging attacking force and shouted a warning.

They raised their guns.

Mai opened fire, shredding a man at the middle and sending him hurtling backward. Bryant was at her side, backing her up, and took out another man who'd targeted her. Behind her a soldier tripped, rolling past the gator and into a herd of legs. Lethargic arms reached for him, but he was dragged clear by his friends. Mai killed two more guards on the run.

To her left, across the surface of the platform, she saw Drake and the others. Her attention was grabbed when she saw Drake throw a punch at Dahl and then Alicia dive for Drake's throat as Kinimaka grabbed Hayden. Above, Mai saw Marinette snarling and shouting orders. She heard, *"Tear, rend, kill,"* and pulled up short.

They're gonna slaughter each other.

Mai darted left, alone. There were too many guards, mercenaries and crazies around to draw any more of her men aside. The antidote was safely in her backpack, and she'd envisioned some discreet window in which to deliver it. Now . . . it had all turned terrifyingly *Lord of the Flies.*

Drake spun, elbowing Dahl in the side of the head before swinging a fist around. Dahl simply ducked his head, taking the blow on the skull and, by the grin on his face, enjoying it. Drake's knuckles stung.

Dahl hit him with a shoulder, forcing him backward.

Drake held on for a moment, accepting the ride, then planted his feet and threw Dahl to the right. The Swede staggered to one knee. Drake pounced onto his back, driving fists into the man's kidneys and spleen.

Focused, he saw a dark blur as Alicia flew at him and then a stunning impact. She crashed into his clavicle, driving him off Dahl. Drake shouted out in pain. Alicia struck left and right with punishing blows. Drake's head filled with pain. He brought both arms up for cover. She delivered a boot to the groin.

Drake sank to his knees in agony.

Alicia bore down on his neck, trying to crack it. He became aware once more of Dahl, who rose and sent three hammer blows into Alicia's midriff. Alicia folded. Drake rose fast, delivering an elbow strike to Dahl's cheekbone.

Inside, he knew it was all wrong. These were his friends . . . his greatest, most invaluable friends . . .

Stop . . . stop now . . .

Battling through the fire-torn shadows and under the evil gaze of Marinette and her god—Samedi—Drake caught glimpses of Kinimaka trying to crush the life out of Hayden; of Kenzie sneaking up on Dahl from behind; of Cam and Shaw locked in speedy, expert combat; and of Mai Kitano coming around the platform.

The sight cut through the haze. Mai . . . ?

But death and conflict surrounded him, an overbearing, ruthless barrier that he couldn't penetrate. His blood sang, the darkness inside him bloomed, and all he could think about was destruction. It was Marinette's desire, her command, her basest need. Though a part of him fought back, wanted to stop, the primary craving was for the annihilation of all those he held dear.

Dahl threw Alicia to the ground. Drake drove a boot at

the Swede's knee. Hayden used Kinimaka's own strength to raise her feet off the ground and drive her heels into his shins, which sent him crashing like a felled tree. Cam threw punches at Shaw, drawing blood each time he hit, but taking precise strikes to the eyes and neck and ears every time he missed—vicious, debilitating blows. The pair circled each other, looking for the perfect opening, a single mistake.

Kenzie shot up from the shadows, a deadly snake striking at Dahl's back. Unprepared, the Swede fell under her rain of blows, crashing face-first to the ground. When his blood flowed, Drake felt a terrible, devastating tightening of emotions inside—deep-seated fear for his friend followed by the horrendous need to worsen those wounds.

Then his vision was suddenly full of Alicia.

She snarled. She struck left and right. Drake staggered and hit back, forcing her into Kenzie. Somehow, the two women locked limbs and fell over. Dahl crawled clear. Blood surged through Drake's brain, his vision full of death and violence.

Marinette lauded over it all, her lips moving. Samedi smoked and drank at her side, whispering in her ear. Drake saw the flaming bonfires and heard the deep rhythmic pounding of the drums, saw worshippers and zombies on their knees. It was all as it should be; a tribute to the exalted, flawless voodoo queen.

Alicia and Kenzie were grasping and punching, fighting dirty on the floor. Drake saw Dahl sit up, shaking his big shaggy head for focus, the perfect height for Drake's boot. He pulled his foot back for a devastating strike. A black shadow flitted past him so quickly he thought it might have been a ghost, a shadow warrior . . .

. . . a ninja . . .

*

Mai saw only one risky option. There was no breaking this up. To get among her battling friends would only result in her own death. Nothing would work here except pure stealth. And once . . . in a life far, far removed, so long ago as to be a long-lost smoke and mirrors history . . . she had been trained by the last remaining ninja clan to be the best of the best.

Using shadow to her advantage, she grasped the pile of syringe-based antidotes she'd taken from her backpack and slipped in among the fighters. First, she glided around Drake, too fast for his drug-filled consciousness to take in, and stopped at his back. A quick jab of the syringe and the mixture should make its way through his system, alleviating the effects of the scopolamine. At least, Mai hoped it would. This was their only and last resort.

She dropped the syringe, darted to the left, and came up beside Kinimaka. The fact that her friends were focused on each other was a tremendous help. The big Hawaiian blinked but his eyes were fixated on Hayden . . . ironically. Mai flitted in close, jabbed, and withdrew in less than a second. She went low, spun, and then came up in front of a startled Hayden, sinking the needle into her thigh. Both fell to their knees as Mai slipped away.

Marinette was at the edge of the platform, shouting orders and waving at guards. Samedi was staring left and right, bellowing orders. Mai heard communications from her soldiers: Bryant, Peaple and Todman in combat; Hayes and Annis lining mercs up in their sights; Gross in a deadly hand-to-hand fight. They'd lost men. They'd killed men. It was blood-drenched, scorching chaos out there.

They needed the full SPEAR team.

And it was coming. Drake, Hayden and Kinimaka were open-mouthed in shock, taking it all in. Mai slipped past Cam to jab Shaw in the bicep, then turned and took a punch from Cam as he squared up to her.

Mai was shocked at the youth's speed. She knew he was fast, but nobody had matched up to her before. Nobody. She saw immediately why he'd been one of the Romanian gypsy world's best boxers. The blow stunned her. She gasped, weighed her options, then leapt at the kid, falling on top of him and hitting him with the syringe as they went down. Injecting his shoulder, she rolled and darted away.

Then she rose.

The team were mostly on their knees, shaking off the aftereffects, trying to come to terms with a new truth, shrugging their way out of a living hell and welcoming a return to reality.

Kind of, Mai thought. *Reality is pretty much Dante's Inferno right now.*

She'd left Alicia and Kenzie for last. The sight of Alicia crawling and tussling on the ground, beset by Kenzie, hair muddied, clothes ripped, flesh bloodied, was something she'd like to get on camera for later blackmail opportunities, but this was entirely the wrong time. She had four syringes left. She dropped heavily onto Alicia's back, knees digging into the blond's shoulder blades, and jabbed the needle in hard. Then she twisted to the right, simply sliding off a prone Alicia onto Kenzie, stabbing her in the arm.

Mai reared backward, checking her perimeters. Imminent danger deterred, she had to take the commander's analysis of the battlefield.

Bryant fought among the worshippers, who, at Marinette's command, had turned viciously on the attackers. Others including Hayes, Peaple and Todman were doing battle with the mercs. Illuminated in crimson, leaping flame, and framed by the blackest of black nights they struggled to survive, every second a nightmare.

The brain-dead ranks had spilled out over the field, wandering from skirmish to skirmish. The guards were attacking Mai's men with machetes, spears and knives. The bordering trees danced with flame and shadow, and the terrifying images of stickmen chased each other between horizons.

The drummers, in their rage and madness, hadn't stopped. They were banging the taut leather with one hand and holding battered AKs in the other, shooting infrequently. A python as thick as Mai's arm slithered across her boot.

Stunned, momentarily lost for words and correct choices, she stared.

Matt Drake touched her arm. "Ey up, so . . . where do you want us, love?" he asked.

CHAPTER FORTY FOUR

Drake stood ready, every limb fused with resolve. The truth was, his system had been depleted, the drugs warred inside him, the reality he now faced was a living nightmare, but the sheer relief he felt at being saved, at having his life handed back to him, at Mai and her team's suicidal, wholehearted assault, powered through every poisoned vein in his body. It cleared the fog from his brain. It brought the soldier in him to the fore.

Dahl was at his side, Alicia too. Their friends were ready to join the fray. Admittedly, they all looked worse for wear and the drug wasn't entirely done with them yet, but their wills were their own. And they remembered everything.

Everything.

From kneeling at Marinette's bare feet to kissing them. From forcing the brain-consuming drug down a man's throat to burying him alive. From the blows they'd given each other to the blind fury they'd felt.

Drake nodded at Dahl's bloodied face. "You okay? Sorry, mate."

"Yeah, you punch like a whippet. I guess, like me, that you were holding back on the power?"

Drake blinked. "You held back?"

"Of course, didn't you?"

"Umm, yeah, yeah, sure."

"Long time no see," the Swede went on nonchalantly. "Been up to much?"

"Bagged a serial killer. You?"

"Nice." Dahl nodded in appreciation. "Went to dinner with Bryant. Shagged Kenzie. Worshipped a voodoo witch queen. Nothing too much out of the ordinary."

"You ready to get back to work then?"

Dahl clenched his fists. "Damn fucking right I am."

To Drake's left Alicia stood patiently. "Ey up, love," he said, turning to her.

"Don't talk to me."

"You still upset we split for a while?"

"What do you think?"

"I think the way you kicked me in the balls says yes."

"Don't flatter yourself. I kick everyone in the balls that way."

Drake stared at her. "Are we good?"

"Don't give me puppy eyes, Drakey. We'll talk after we kick this Marinette bitch's ass back to Planet bloody Zombie."

Mai held up a hand. "We're taking out Marinette, Samedi and her guards," she said. "Look out for crocs and snakes. Are you ready?"

Alicia yelped. "*Snakes?* I forgot about the snakes!"

But they were already moving. The SPEAR team, as one, with Mai leading, Hayden and Kinimaka to her right, Drake, Dahl and Alicia to her left, Cam and Shaw two steps behind, ran for Marinette's platform. Kenzie was to the far right, skirting the platform, having noticed three knife-wielders fighting a single soldier and liking the look of the flashing blades. Drake jumped and rolled onto the platform with his friends, his family, ready to extract full retribution from those that confronted them.

Marinette stood resolute, flesh gleaming with sweat and reflected fire. She'd already pulled on her special glove, the leather gauntlet tipped with the wicked blades, and held a machete in her other hand. Samedi had smashed the empty rum bottle and stood with its jagged edges raised, sweat making his face paint run. Between his lips still hung the fat cigar.

Racing toward the platform were Marinette's mercenaries, the key fighters and leaders that looked after her various businesses. Hayes, Gross, Peaple and their men got in the way, slowing them down.

"Kneel," Marinette said, that lilt still in her voice. "Grovel, and I might let you see tomorrow. Do you want to worship my body?"

Drake felt the pull; the remnants of the drug and the depths to which he'd sunk the last few days influencing his decisions, and fought it. He closed his eyes, shook his head, staggered. Guards were climbing the platform. Worshippers too. Marinette and Samedi had called for them. How much time had he lost, fighting her hold on him, tearing her psychological claws from his skin?

Mai went up against Marinette. Samedi lunged at a faltering Dahl, the broken bottle slashing the Swede's skin. The pain cut through his indecision nicely though, making him snap back to reality. Drake saw it and slapped his own face—once, twice—until symmetry returned.

He was here to defeat Marinette, not idolize her.

A man came at him, machete brandished. Drake headbutted him to his knees then twisted his arm, forcing his machete into his own neck. A second man slashed with a knife which Drake captured and then used, coating the platform with gouts of blood.

Marinette's mercenaries were still closing, despite being slowed down.

To the left, Marinette was a surprise, matching Mai

blow for blow, the blade-tipped glove on her right hand a functional weapon. Drake saw Alicia kick a snake off the stage, launching it in the air like a football. He saw Hayden and Kinimaka bowl four guards off the edge of the platform. He saw Cam and Shaw fighting side-by-side, their fast, incapacitating blows sending guard after guard to their knees.

A man came at him from the right, features burnished by the bonfires' leaping flames, a curved sword held high. Drake flung his knife into the man's screaming mouth, silencing him permanently, and picked up the sword.

Gunfire resounded around the field. Mercenaries fought mercenaries, their orders and aspirations clashing, at least for today. The drummers were coming now too, AKs poised and ready. Drake clenched his fists as a surge of guards struck the platform.

Alicia darted to Mai's defense and, when Marinette struck the Japanese woman aside, filled the gap. The voodoo queen had guards and bodyguards coming, but was alone for now. Alicia wanted vengeance. She struck, then ducked, barely avoiding the swipe of Marinette's claw. She leapt high and came down with an elbow, felling the woman. But Marinette was powerful, holding her pose on one knee as Alicia drove down again. Mai then rushed in from the left, striking hard. Marinette slapped at Alicia, the tiny knives slashing four thin bloody lines across her thigh.

Alicia bellowed in pain and went down to one knee. "Watch out!" she cried. "Bitch is Freddie fucking Krueger!"

But the pain and the blood were warming her system up. Alicia embraced the pain.

Drake and Dahl saw that Mai's men were struggling throughout the field. The man they'd heard her call Hayes was alone, fighting enemies with machetes. The ones called

Todman and Annis were rushing to his aid. Drake and Dahl ran to join them.

The machete-wielders turned and stood their ground, meeting the onslaught. Drake grabbed his opponent's arm, held the weapon blade down, and struck hard with his free hand, smashing his foe's head to the left—once, twice, three times until he stumbled. Drake then wrenched the machete away and slit the man's throat.

Dahl picked one opponent up and threw him into two more, bowling them over before falling on top of them, descending like an avenging angel—an angel that spit blood and bellowed curses.

Mai's remaining soldiers were exchanging gunfire with some of Marinette's mercs, positioned behind bonfires and rectangular stone objects that looked like altars. The drummers had attacked them from behind, killing many in cold blood, but the remaining soldiers had overcome that obstacle and were pinning their enemy down.

Bullets strafed the top part of the field, skimming men and slashing through the trees, bombarding the terrifying stick figures that danced through fire and shadow. One worshipper with crazy eyes tried to attack the soldiers *through* the bonfire, dying horribly in the flames. Another snatched up a blazing log and ran at them, screaming in pain as he came. The soldiers took care of him, but looked rattled, losing focus.

Hayden fell off the platform, landing on her shoulder. A moment later, Kinimaka thudded to her side, big shoes planted safely to the left of her head. He fought off three worshippers and reached down, lifting an unconscious man and holding him in front of Hayden and himself as a guard fired at them. Bullets ripped into the man, making him spasm and twitch in front of Kinimaka; an almost completely effective shield, apart from one bullet which was a through-and-through, and passed less than an inch to the right of Kinimaka's skull.

To their right, Kenzie had appropriated two swords. She fought alongside a soldier called Peaple, skirting the furious, thrashing gator and trying to avoid zombies, decimating the ranks of Marinette's spear-throwers. Kenzie chopped the head of a spear off as it came at her face, felt the splintered end pass her by, then thrust her sword through her attacker's stomach. She whirled, sword a spinning blur above her head, and chopped partly through one man's arm and another's thigh before coming to a stop on one knee. Peaple used his Glock, firing bullets at point-blank range.

"I got a spare!" he cried. "Catch!"

"Don't bother," Kenzie cried back. "I got my best choice right here."

A man ran onto the point of her sword.

Marinette spun on the platform, kicking Alicia in the stomach and sending her tumbling off its edge. She hit the marshy ground with a thud, air blasting out of her. For several seconds, stars and black skies filled her vision. She couldn't breathe. But, as she heaved, the hurt eased, and her lungs gained a little air.

God help me, this is one rough night.

She sat up, wracked with pain but now able to see clearly. A choice presented itself—return to Mai's side or help on the battlefield. She took a moment to assess the fight. It was as she turned that a claw-like hand settled on her shoulder.

"What the fu—"

More hands joined it. White, lifeless faces filled her field of vision, gazing down at her. She was underneath them, surrounded. They reached for her, shuffled all around her, blocking out the light, her ability to see, and all hope. They tugged at her clothes, pinched her skin, clawed at her body. She saw no hope in their gazes, no recognition of what they were doing. They were mindless, shambling figures, existing only for the pleasure of one atrocious mistress.

Together, relentless, they fell upon her.

CHAPTER FORTY FIVE

Alicia had to fight. She couldn't hurt her mindless attackers, but she could force them aside. She kicked out and tripped them up. She used judo to throw them aside and into each other. She made space, searching for a way out. It took time, and those seconds cost her. A deep scratch along the wrist. A twisted finger. Her bones ground together as numerous grips tightened. Her air was cut off as hands grabbed her throat.

All the ground she'd gained was lost.

Alicia collapsed. She saw filth-coated knees, shins and ankles. They trampled her, tried to crush her into the very earth. Spots danced before her eyes. White faces loomed and then, almost too close to focus, she saw teeth closing in on her face.

And then a savior, a ray of light. A figure barged through the crowd, knocking the senseless mass aside. It reached down a hand and found her arm, pulling hard.

"You okay?"

Alicia breathed deeply. The spots receded. Her vision cleared. The man who'd saved her, pulled her ass out of certain death, was Connor Bryant.

"Yeah," she gasped. "Thanks Bryant. One of those fuckers tried to *bite* me."

"It's all right." Bryant nodded. "You can thank me later."

She recalled his proclivities and went with it. "Name your vice."

"Umm, okay then." He grabbed her and pulled her away from the already returning zombies. Alicia now had a few seconds to assess the battle.

"I'm at a fucking loss . . ." Alicia said. "Talk about extreme . . ."

Bullets slashed from bonfire to bonfire. Worshippers attacked without thought for their own safety. Those that remained of the drummers fought out in the open, still chanting, still dripping paint. Marinette's guards were accosting those near the platform, turning the tide of battle.

Mai's soldiers had been hit hard—Alicia counted only about fifteen left alive. A bonfire had been smashed apart, the grass and undergrowth around it catching fire, rivulets of flame running across the ground like lava.

The gator hissed at her back. Alicia whirled and stepped away, dodging to the side as it attacked. The open mouth passed her by, the tail smacking her legs. Bryant stood his ground, putting three bullets into it.

"Why do they always focus on me?" Alicia wondered.

But then a cry split the air, a keening howl. It was Samedi, atop the platform, having witnessed the death of the beast he'd brought to the ceremony. He leapt like an athlete, hit the ground running, and came straight at them, flying across the ground with his broken rum bottle held high and his well-chewed cigar hanging loosely from the side of his mouth. The skeletal face was snarling, terrifying, the coattails flapping in his wake like a cape, the top hat tilted at a precarious angle. This was the *god* that Marinette had summoned, the man appearing out of fog, the final proof of her exquisite magnificence to keep her followers engaged.

Alicia didn't see a god; she saw a complicit,

manipulative criminal. She waited patiently for his onslaught, dodged the bottle, and put out an eye with a stiffened finger-jab. She broke his jaw and then his larynx, let him slump to the ground choking to death. Standing over him, she looked up at the platform.

"They can handle her."

She and Bryant spun away. Hayes and Todman were under pressure from guards. Alicia ran in to back them up, accepting a spare gun from Todman.

Mai struck again and again at Marinette. The other woman didn't falter and didn't back down. Somehow, somewhere, she'd had considerable training. The blade-gauntlet was an issue too. Already, she'd swiped Mai twice with it, drawing blood both times.

Marinette dove in fast, striking low and then high. Mai span away, returning with a sidekick. Marinette caught it and heaved, pulling Mai off balance before throwing her aside. Mai landed, rolled and came up in a defensive pose just as Marinette struck.

The two women clashed hard, bones juddering. Sweat flew off Marinette's shining limbs onto Mai. The same sweat made her arms and upper body slick. Corded muscles strained along her biceps as she forced Mai backward. One of her bodyguards, a guy she called Lott, managed to climb up from where Mai had put him down minutes ago.

"Get her!" Marinette cried.

Lott lunged. Mai had her hands full with Marinette and took a blow to the face that wrenched her neck. Lott drew back his arm again, but Cam attacked him, punch after punch breaking ribs and pounding into the sternum. Lott went down as Roppolo had before him, a victim of Cam's boxing prowess, clutching a broken body.

Mai circled Marinette, ignoring the body parts she stepped on, the human detritus laid down earlier for Samedi's faux summoning. Marinette blocked her first attack and darted away. Mai landed two blows with her second attack. Marinette staggered.

Sensing victory, Mai leapt once more. Marinette dropped to the floor, swung her legs, and sent Mai sprawling. Her bladed glove raked Mai's back, shredding clothes and a bit of skin. Mai rolled and kicked her back.

"This is madness!" Mai shouted. "How can you not see?"

"Madness is relative," Marinette said. "My followers believe that I am a queen."

"You rob them of their minds!"

"Only some." Marinette smiled. "And all of them—*every single one*—can be revived."

Mai paused on the verge of an attack, stunned. "They . . . what?"

"It's another torture, another torment I like to burden them with. Resurrection is such a pure magnificent agony for them, and then the additional distress of my greatest revelation—that I have a restorative mixture they will never be able to explain to anyone—is the sweetest of jewels to my eyes, the deepest rapture."

Mai stood unmoving. This woman had concocted some recipe, some mixture, that returned people from their zombie-like state, *which she explained to them only after they could no longer communicate.* There was a *cure*. This changed everything. They couldn't kill Marinette now; they needed her very much alive.

Mai sensed Cam at her side. Shaw was finishing up to the far right of the platform. Kenzie was approaching like a storm, eyes fixed on Marinette, black hair framing her face, the bonfire raging at her back and two swords held down by her side.

Peaple and Todman were fighting back to back with Drake and Dahl, thinning out the machete-wielders. Annis and Gross were alongside Alicia and Kinimaka, smashing through the ranks of mercenaries. Hayes had gone down, but had regained his feet, head bleeding, and was being helped by Hayden. Five other soldiers remained of the force she'd brought with her.

Marinette also surveyed the battlefield. The odds had turned against her. Out of her main mercenaries, the ones that enforced and led her businesses, most were dead. Her leaders—The Baron and Mage—were even now backing away, running for the treeline. Marinette cursed them, praying that their flesh would rot from their bones. The mindless were milling and shambling around as they always did. Her worshippers, her true followers, were the only ones left fighting.

And it wasn't going well for them.

Marinette saw a way out, but it would have to be done fast and it would have to be done now. There was time . . . barely. She used her comms system to summon one last ace in the hole.

Mai shot forward with an attack. Marinette deflected it, slipping to the side, and swung her gauntlet at Cam, narrowly missing his face. She kept turning. Mai felt momentarily flummoxed as she watched the voodoo queen jump off the platform to the ground and run toward the farthest, fiery blaze.

Where does she think she can go?

Marinette hurdled streams of flowing fire, dead bodies, and evaded the reaching, scraping hands of voodoo soldiers. Alicia saw the run, shouted for Drake and Dahl and the others, and gave chase.

Marinette was sprinting straight at the tight battling knot of her remaining few dozen worshippers.

Drake ran. Mai leapt off the platform and gave chase with Cam and Shaw at her side. Kenzie growled as Marinette flew by. And in the next moment Mai saw a true horror emerging from the far treeline.

It ran at them, over seven feet tall and skeletal thin, a naked figure of corded muscle, body paint and filed-off teeth. It carried two whirling machetes. Its face was made to look like a skull, and it screamed at the top of its voice, a rasping, nerve-shredding abrasion like nails down a chalkboard. Even the remaining soldiers stopped and stared, forgetting that their guns could stop it.

Mai already knew that it was deadly.

Cimetiére had been waiting for Marinette's signal.

The distraction worked. Marinette darted among her followers as Cimetiére cleaved Gross aside, separating the flesh from his right cheek. He smashed another soldier away, vaulted a third and charged at Drake and Dahl. Gross rose in his wake, undeterred by the wound, and charged toward Cimetiere, but the Yorkshireman and the Swede were ready.

They stood their ground. Cimetiére slashed left and right with his machetes, slicing the air between them. Drake and Dahl awaited their chance. Alicia approached from one side, and now Kenzie from the other.

Hayden and Kinimaka ran up to Mai. "Where did the voodoo witch go?"

Mai pointed. "Joined her fans. Are you guys okay?"

"Okay? No," Hayden said quietly. "We were forced to do some horrible things that we now have to live with. And we were forced to watch each other do stuff too."

Mai felt the trauma spilling off them in waves. "I had a little experience of that from my time with the Tsugarai clan. Believe and remember that that none of it was your fault. You couldn't help yourselves. It hurts, yes, but being of sound mind you would never have allowed it to happen."

Her words helped, she saw, but offered only marginal comfort for now. She couldn't wait any longer. Marinette was among her followers, a fact that didn't bode well, and they were rising, over twenty strong, in a dense mass, linking arms, unarmed but undeterred.

"Leave this place," one screamed.

"Your men are dead. Your guards are dead. Your mercs have all run away. Your businesses are terminated. This is the end for you, Marinette, and you should stop cowering behind your flock." Mai's severe tones passed through the crowd.

Most of the others came to stand with Mai, in front of the interlinked people and the blazing bonfire; the team she'd saved, the friends she'd regained. Surrounding the clearing, the shadows were now empty of errant life, flickering, laced by dying, smoldering fire, as though Marinette's evil gods had deserted her.

Nearby, Cimetiére leapt at Drake, kneeing him in the chest. Drake grabbed the man's legs and hurled him to the side, sending him sprawling face first. Dahl then crashed onto him, but Cimetiére flailed, rolled and struck back. A machete batted the Swede aside, flat side first, almost breaking his eye socket. Cimetiére rose like a demon shooting up from Hell. Alicia stepped in and kicked him solidly in the groin.

"See," she told Drake. "I treat 'em all the same."

But Cimetiére only glared, unmoved by the attack. Alicia gawped. The giant swept a machete down at her face. Alicia staggered back into Drake, tangling them both. Cimetiére leapt forward, snarling. The descending machete was silver and dripping blood and couldn't be avoided. Drake could only find the time to raise a hand over Alicia's face, knowing it would be struck hard by the vicious blade, that the flesh and bone it hit would be cleaved in two . . .

A resounding clang made him jump. The machete's powerful descent had been arrested by a sword. Kenzie's sword. She had somehow managed to slip the weapon in between Drake and Cimetiére and stopped the disfiguring attack.

Cimetiére howled. He turned on Kenzie. Machetes swung and crossed in the air, swiping incessantly as Kenzie backed up, wielding her own weapons in defense. Cimetiére's strength was boundless, his fury limitless. He forced her further and further back, never relenting. But he wasn't adept; he didn't possess Kenzie's skills with a sword. One overreaching swing gave her chance to slide the point of her weapon through his armpit and out the other side. An instant later her second sword chopped down on his wrist, severing it. Cimetiére glared at the offending limb as if he wanted to crush it.

Kenzie didn't relent, recognizing the insanity raging before her. Men like Cimetiére could take bullets and keep coming. She planted one sword though his neck and the other through his heart and then watched as he collapsed forward, the hilt of the second sword thrusting into the ground and holding him upright.

"Marinette?" Alicia said.

They all turned. Mai was approaching the crowd of worshippers, backed by her remaining soldiers and the rest of the SPEAR team. Two shots in the air parted the crowd, but it still pressed dangerously close as Mai started through.

Drake and the others ran to her side.

Together, a wedge, inseparable, they watched each

other's backs as they forged a path through Marinette's silent followers. It took time and effort; more than a few faces were battered along the way, more than one reluctant figure thrown into another. Drake followed Mai, pushing left and right, alert for weapons. He saw a metal tube plunging toward him, caught it and jabbed it back at its wielder's face. Their wedge was compressed from both sides.

As they neared the center, Mai was struck across the face by a heavy plank of wood. Drake caught her as she fell sideways, then passed her back along the line. She was woozy and needed a few minutes to clear her head. Drake made the man who'd attacked her wish he'd missed.

Finally, they came to the center of Marinette's followers. Drake felt the air leave his body and stopped in stunned amazement. There were no words, no phrases to describe what he saw.

Marinette lay on her side, on the ground, unmoving.

Her own followers killed her to save her from the law. The ultimate act of adoration. In a way, they'd sacrificed her to save her. It was simple and shocking, as fucked up and insane as everything else that happened in this godforsaken hellhole they called Black Snake Swamp. He bent down and put a finger to her neck, checking for a pulse.

There was none.

"Dead," he said. "The witch is dead."

CHAPTER FORTY SIX

Drake walked away from the crowd.

"Can you call the cavalry?" he asked some of the soldiers. "The cops?"

"It's a dead zone, sir. No signal."

"Damn right it's a fucking dead zone. And my name's Drake, not sir. You guys helped save my life, an act I'll never forget."

They nodded solemnly, scouring the battlefield for their fallen comrades. Drake glanced from the dejected worshippers to the lifeless corpses, the still-wandering, zombie-like figures and his teammates. Far from a time to take stock and rest, this was a time of action.

"They must have vehicles," Drake said. "And cellphones, maybe a cell tower that's been temporarily taken offline. Marinette ran a business from here."

"We should head back to the main buildings," Mai said, coming around.

Drake shuddered at the thought. "I guess . . ."

They gathered, Bryant and his men, Mai and the SPEAR team. Not wanting to leave anyone behind they decided that the worst of the threat was over, the danger lessened, and that strength in numbers was the best way forward.

"I can't believe we're all back together again," Alicia said as they walked.

They'd appropriated weapons from dead mercenaries and Drake held his at the ready. "I did come to rescue you," he said.

"And you fucked that up too."

"No chance of a kiss then, love?"

"Sure, there's a gator and a few snakes back there would enjoy that."

Hayden was walking with Kinimaka, Cam and Shaw. "Do you remember anything?" their unofficial team leader asked.

"Everything," Shaw said with a shudder. "And I'd rather die than succumb to mind control ever again."

Kinimaka nodded in agreement. "It seems an age since we were with Trent and the boys in LA."

Drake looked over at his comment. "You met up with Trent? The disavowed guys?"

"Yeah, we'll tell you all about it later. We saved Trent from some Russian Madam's revenge attack."

"Shit, and I thought my serial killer gig was impressive." He nodded at Alicia. "What did you do?"

"Got pissed, tried to shag a soldier, got pissed, kissed a soldier, got—"

"I get the gist of it."

"Oh, and then we had a barfight. Good times."

"To be fair," Drake said. "We came closest to rescuing you. If Dahl hadn't smashed his chopper . . ."

"Stop with the euphemisms."

"Ah, that's not a euphemism. We crashed down on the beach."

"Three of you?" Alicia shook her head. Hayden and Kinimaka hung theirs. "I think we all underestimated Marinette," he said. "And overestimated our own skills whilst apart. Together, we're the best. Separate—we're just as fallible as the next guy."

Drake could see the truth of it. If they'd come at Marinette as Team SPEAR from the beginning maybe they would not have had to bear witness to the worst of humanity. As it was . . .

"We did some dark things in there," he said, glancing among the trees and marshes they passed. "Things that will haunt me forever." He allowed his words to tail off, still aware of the faint stupor in his head. "And I wish that I could say the effects had completely worn off."

Alicia regarded him with speculative eyes. "Let's see, shall we? Drake . . . kick Mai."

"Hey, I just helped *save* your asses," Mai complained. "You should be kissing mine."

"All right. Drake, *kiss—*"

The conversation faltered as they came to the main building where Marinette had drugged and revealed her power over them. There was no happiness here, no sense of relief. As soldiers, they took comfort and respite in banter. It helped them through the darkest of times and didn't mean that they didn't respect the sacrifices of the fallen, of those that had risked and lost everything to save them. It honored them; cherished them. It reminded the survivors that they still lived and why.

"Let's find those phones and get the hell out of here," Drake said.

On that, they all agreed.

CHAPTER FORTY SEVEN

They didn't want to sleep until it was done, and then they couldn't sleep. Hours passed, most of the next day. The authorities quizzed them, and pushed them, but at the end of it all they'd unraveled one of the worst, darkest drugs, weapons and people trafficking organizations in America, and who wouldn't want to at least appear to be happy about that? With Marinette dead, those that had hung on to her coattails and prospered, lived in the hope that they would be spared scrutinization.

Drake didn't hear anything about what had transpired after they left the swamp. He was happy when he walked out of the police station into the bright, warm light of day and saw his friends waiting for him.

"Ah, that's bloody great," was all he said. They knew how he felt.

Alicia took them to Bourbon Street, the scene of the initial crime, but found the quietest place around. The only thing she wanted was to talk to her friends. When they sank down in comfy seats, surrounded by ambient noise and subdued light, Drake felt a tiredness deep in his being that threatened to take him right then, right there.

"I admit," he said aloud. "I won't last long."

"We should reconvene when we're rested," Hayden admitted. "But I wasn't sure . . . am not sure what happens next."

Drake downed an entire mug of coffee and called for another. "How did it feel for you? Being apart."

"Awful," Alicia said.

"Lonely," Dahl said.

"Acceptable," Kinimaka said. "As long as I believed it was short term."

"Bryant wants to give us a job," Dahl told them. "No restrictions."

"I like him," Mai said. "The guy came through when most needed."

"He saved my ass," Alicia said.

"And let's not forget," Kenzie put in. "What we said after we beat the Devil and the Blood King. Something's not right with this president."

Hayden and Kinimaka voiced their agreement. Drake recalled the worry. And the longer they left it the worse it would be. "Our enemies might have forgotten we were ghosted by now," he said. "But I doubt it. And that's the main reason we separated to start with."

"And why we had to save Trent's ass," Hayden admitted. "The Russians only found him because he returned back home when the Strike Force initiative folded."

The knowledge confirmed Drake's fears. "It's too early to stay together," he said. "Trent dropped his guard. Returned to old ways. Stayed with Silk and Radford. A discontinuation is necessary for us."

"For how long?" Mai asked.

"Months," Drake said. "I think we should split up again."

Alicia turned away. Mai sighed and sat back.

Dahl raised a hand. "We don't *all* have to split up," he said. "We make our own decisions. If anyone wants to ride with Kenzie and me, they're welcome."

"Dangerous," Drake said.

"Are you meaning ride in a general way?" Alicia asked. "Or . . ."

"Whichever," Dahl said with a grin.

"Damn, I'm sold. Where we going?"

"Well, *not* to New Orleans, that's for sure. Never again."

"Something has happened to my family," Cam said. "In Romania. We do not keep in touch—ever—but occasionally visit pre-made chat rooms to check for major problems. Mostly because that problem might affect us personally, not because we have feelings for each other. Anyhow, when I checked earlier, wondering if our relations with Marinette might have alerted anyone to my whereabouts, a new message had been uploaded—the first in years. It read: *The Carnival has ended.*"

"What does that mean?" Alicia asked. "I thought you didn't care about your family."

"I don't. But their issues, failings and dealings could put a target on me. A target worse than our current situation. And the phrase *the Carnival has ended* is basically a three-minute warning of impending apocalypse."

Alicia gawped. "A what?"

"Family apocalypse," Cam qualified. "But it is worrying."

Dahl nodded at Cam and Alicia, and then Kenzie. Finally, he included Shaw. "Are you sticking around us? I wouldn't blame you if you wanted to leave."

"I'm staying," Shaw said. "Despite Marinette, this is the first time in years I felt like I belonged to a real family."

Dahl smiled. Hayden and Kinimaka sat back. Hayden spoke up quietly. "Mano and I will head off for a little while, maybe meet you later. We still have things to do."

Dahl nodded, accepting without question. Which left Mai. The Japanese woman, their savior, sent out a sad smile.

"I understand all of your decisions," she said. "I do. But

Connor Bryant deserves more than just the brush off for putting his life and his company on the line. He really does. And I won't so easily walk away from that obligation. I will stay and work for him."

Drake was surprised. "I do feel grateful to him, but that doesn't mean we should jump on his payroll."

"Somebody in this team has to stay watchful," Mai said. "On the front line. Do you remember Zuki? The Japanese princess that pitched samurai against ninja and Tsugarai in the search for the Four Sacred Treasures? Rumors are she's bargaining her way out of lockup. You can't ignore that kind of threat."

"The new president made ignorance our only option."

"Maybe, or maybe there's another way."

With little else to say, and a wave of tiredness surging over him, Drake made his way to his bedroom and struggled to slump into a deep, dream-ridden sleep. Maybe tomorrow he would feel differently about the separation, but the cold truth of the matter was that he was right, and they all knew it. Hayden had agreed with him. And they were talking months apart, not years. The separation was almost over, the isolation at their backs. When they met again, they could begin to heal, to unify, to make new headway in a changed world.

Whatever came next it would be different, but they would be ready for it. And despite everything they had suffered at the hands of Marinette, in the end they had proved their worth and love for each other a hundred times over. Alicia would understand in time; Drake was sure of it. And if she didn't, he would be devastated, but he would be replete with the knowledge that he'd protected the woman he loved.

Wasn't that more important?

Drifting away, safe and alone, Drake was sure of it.

CHAPTER FORTY EIGHT

The body was dead to the touch, lifeless. It had no discernible pulse. The skin was cold, the eyes closed, the heart stilled. To all but the closest inspection and the fully initiated, this appeared to be the case.

Marinette was dead, praise Damballah.

Drake had seen her body, felt for her pulse. He hadn't known of any recipe or mixture able to revive the almost-dead. Mai, who did know, had been practically comatose, and by the time she revived and learned that Marinette was dead, hadn't thought to question Drake's word or ask how.

So when they buried Marinette, they buried her alive.

There were people on her property who knew that the voodoo soldiers could be revived. Cimetiére knew. And her business lieutenants—The Baron and Mage—would ensure the survivors were brought together and fully prepared for the ceremony to bring their witch queen back from the dead.

Black Snake Swamp waited in everlasting darkness, as patiently as the slow-beating heart of a reanimated corpse, for her most terrible and triumphant return.

THE END

DAVID LEADBEATER

Please read on for more information of the Matt Drake and Relic Hunters world.

I hope you enjoyed this book, the first in a different direction. It was immense fun to write, to explore the characters in different, challenging situations, but there's no doubt this team will always find its way back to each other. They are family for life. I'm completing this story still in lockdown—June 5th 2020—and staying hopeful for positive future change. The next release will be Relic Hunters 5—*The Rocks of Albion*—in October and then early 2021 will bring Drake 27!

Until then, stay safe, take care and happy reading!

AUTHOR'S NOTE:

I ran a special competition through my newsletter and Facebook for five lucky readers to take part in this book's final battle. With over 1000 entries the competition was stiff, but the following people were picked out to join Drake, Alicia and co in the action-packed finale.

Trey Hayes
Rick Gross
Craig Peaple
Jackie Annis
Colette Todman

Join me on Facebook or subscribe to my very infrequent newsletter through my website (www.davidleadbeater.com) for the chance to join Drake and the team in the next book!

If you enjoyed this book, please leave a review!

Other Books by David Leadbeater:

The Matt Drake Series
A constantly evolving, action-packed romp based in the escapist action-adventure genre:

The Bones of Odin (Matt Drake #1)
The Blood King Conspiracy (Matt Drake #2)
The Gates of Hell (Matt Drake 3)
The Tomb of the Gods (Matt Drake #4)
Brothers in Arms (Matt Drake #5)
The Swords of Babylon (Matt Drake #6)
Blood Vengeance (Matt Drake #7)
Last Man Standing (Matt Drake #8)
The Plagues of Pandora (Matt Drake #9)
The Lost Kingdom (Matt Drake #10)
The Ghost Ships of Arizona (Matt Drake #11)
The Last Bazaar (Matt Drake #12)
The Edge of Armageddon (Matt Drake #13)
The Treasures of Saint Germain (Matt Drake #14)
Inca Kings (Matt Drake #15)
The Four Corners of the Earth (Matt Drake #16)
The Seven Seals of Egypt (Matt Drake #17)
Weapons of the Gods (Matt Drake #18)
The Blood King Legacy (Matt Drake #19)
Devil's Island (Matt Drake #20)
The Fabergé Heist (Matt Drake #21)
Four Sacred Treasures (Matt Drake #22)
The Sea Rats (Matt Drake #23)
Blood King Takedown (Matt Drake #24)
Devil's Junction (Matt Drake #25)

The Alicia Myles Series
Aztec Gold (Alicia Myles #1)
Crusader's Gold (Alicia Myles #2)
Caribbean Gold (Alicia Myles #3)
Chasing Gold (Alicia Myles #4)
Galleon's Gold (Alicia Myles #5)

The Torsten Dahl Thriller Series
Stand Your Ground (Dahl Thriller #1)

The Relic Hunters Series
The Relic Hunters (Relic Hunters #1)
The Atlantis Cipher (Relic Hunters #2)
The Amber Secret (Relic Hunters #3)
The Hostage Diamond (Relic Hunters #4)

The Rogue Series
Rogue (Book One)

The Disavowed Series:
The Razor's Edge (Disavowed #1)
In Harm's Way (Disavowed #2)
Threat Level: Red (Disavowed #3)

The Chosen Few Series
Chosen (The Chosen Trilogy #1)
Guardians (The Chosen Trilogy #2)
Heroes (The Chosen Trilogy #3)

DAVID LEADBEATER

Short Stories
Walking with Ghosts (A short story)
A Whispering of Ghosts (A short story)

All genuine comments are very welcome at:

davidleadbeater2011@hotmail.co.uk

Twitter: @dleadbeater2011

Visit David's website for the latest news and information:
davidleadbeater.com

Printed in Great Britain
by Amazon